"Maggie, *d...*"

Peter knew she had become aware of his arousal, the undeniable change in his body. "You've been lying here against me, all warm and soft. You feel wonderful. But I'm not going to start making demands."

She drew back, slowly raising her eyes to his. Her lips were parted, red and moist, the most desirable thing he'd ever seen. Miraculously, she didn't pull away. Instead, she reached up to touch his face, her fingertips delicate and curious.

There were a thousand reasons he had to stop this, but before he could think of one of them, her mouth moved against his in a caress so sweet it tore a groan straight out of his soul.

"Baby, stop!" He turned his head aside. "On top of everything else, you don't need this."

She stopped, looked at him with not-so-innocent eyes and slowly shook her head. "You're so wrong. I think this is exactly what I need...."

Dear Reader:

Dreams, like flowers, can be fragile, but once they are pressed gently between the pages of a book, their colors and textures can be savored again and again.

This month, six wonderful authors—Ginna Gray, Lisa Jackson, Mary Kirk, Victoria Pade, Mary Curtis and Patricia Coughlin—bring you their versions of "the stuff that dreams are made of"... gently pressed between the covers of six Silhouette **Special Edition** novels.

Writer and dedicated dreamer Patricia Coughlin believes that "when you open a Silhouette **Special Edition**, you want to meet strong, compelling characters and be swept up in their unique adventure. You want to be touched emotionally, feel your heart race and ultimately be left with a sense of fulfillment. So do I," she confesses, "and I'm thrilled to share my dreams with you in the pages of a **Special Edition**."

For bedtime reading—anytime reading—our authors and editors hope you'll choose Silhouette **Special Edition**. These romantic novels are designed to bring you sweet dreams you can savor again and again, night after night, month after month. And the morning after, why not drop us a line? We always welcome your comments.

Sincerely,

Leslie Kazanjian,
Senior Editor

MARY KIRK
Phoenix Rising

Silhouette Special Edition

Published by Silhouette Books New York

America's Publisher of Contemporary Romance

To the owner-operator
of the grape-purple conventional
Kenworth Aerodyne VIT that on August 14, 1987,
between 1:00 and 2:00 p.m.,
was parked in the McDonald's lot,
Glacier Hills rest stop,
Ohio State Turnpike eastbound.
I'd have given a lot for a ride in that truck.

SILHOUETTE BOOKS
300 East 42nd St., New York, N.Y. 10017

ISBN: 0-373-09524-4

First Silhouette Books printing May 1989

Printed in the U.S.A.

Books by Mary Kirk

Silhouette Desire

In Your Wildest Dreams #387

Silhouette Special Edition

Promises #462
Phoenix Rising #524

coauthored as Mary Alice Kirk

MARY KIRK,

born and raised in Baltimore, Maryland, labels herself "a true daughter of the working class." She studied piano for thirteen years and holds a degree in American studies and history; however, it was when she began penning fiction that her creative energies found their focus.

Mary says she writes novels to reflect her "profound respect for the capacity of the human spirit to survive and flourish. As a writer, I also feel very much a part of the ongoing dialogue among women who are questioning what it is they want in life and love, and I strive to present the most hopeful visions this dialogue offers."

She is married to a biology and horticulture teacher with whom she shares the pleasure of raising their two sons.

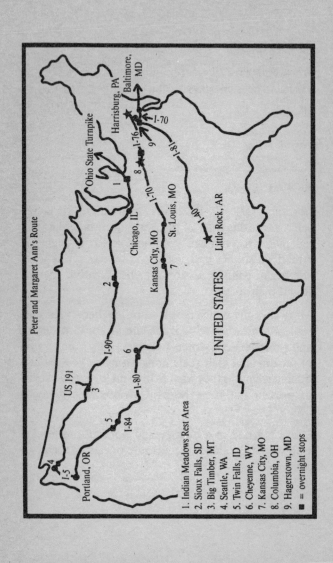

Peter and Margaret Ann's Route

Ohio State Turnpike
Harrisburg, PA
Baltimore, MD
I-70
I-76
9
8
I-70
I-81
Chicago, IL
St. Louis, MO
I-40
Kansas City, MO
Little Rock, AR
1
2
US 191
I-90
6
3
5
I-80
I-84
4
I-5
Portland, OR

UNITED STATES

1. Indian Meadows Rest Area
2. Sioux Falls, SD
3. Big Timber, MT
4. Seattle, WA
5. Twin Falls, ID
6. Cheyenne, WY
7. Kansas City, MO
8. Columbia, OH
9. Hagerstown, MD
■ = overnight stops

phoenix...

A mythical bird of great beauty fabled to live hundreds of years in the wilderness, to be consumed by fire on a funeral pyre, and to rise from its ashes in the freshness of youth: often an emblem of immortality or of reborn idealism or hope.

Chapter One

INDIAN MEADOW REST AREA NEXT RIGHT.

The blue-and-white sign came into view along the shoulder of the road, and Peter Lericos switched on his blinker. His black eighteen-wheeler barreled onto the exit ramp, chrome flashing in the overhead lights. Slowing gradually, the leviathan rumbled into the nearly empty parking lot, its engine subsiding to a rough purr as Peter guided the vehicle toward the low brick building that housed a Hardee's restaurant and other travelers' facilities. He turned into the area designated for truck parking, where, with a blast of air brakes announcing its arrival, the rig came to a halt.

Peter cut the engine, and was instantly struck by a shocking silence. Quickly though, noises from the highway rushed to fill the vacuum; a diesel rig accelerated in a grinding strain, a horn blared. Cars sped along, headlights on in deference to the coming darkness. The cars were lost, though, amid the rows of trucks that rolled between the white lines on the asphalt like pinballs out of a chute—all shiny steel and blazing lights. A hot Sunday night in July, and it was rush hour on the Ohio State Turnpike.

Peter opened the door of his Kenworth tractor, then let his arm fall loosely to his side. He had to will the muscles in his neck and shoulders to relax, allowing his head to fall back against the headrest. His fingers felt as though they were permanently curled to the shape of the steering wheel, where they'd been glued for most of the past fourteen hours. His body still buzzed with the vibrations of the truck. His right foot was cramped inside its running shoe, and his eyes burned from too little sleep and too much caffeine; the lids felt gritty as he let them drift closed. Finally he raised a hand to rub his face, his long fingers ruffling his full beard before combing the shaggy black hair off his forehead.

Getting clear of New York City traffic had taken longer than usual, and the storm in the Pennsylvania mountains had slowed him down, but neither had kept him from covering the miles he had set out to log that day. Logging miles was the goal on the independent trucker's road to financial success. Yet as Peter swung his legs around to jump out of the cab, he wondered if he would ever learn to take those miles as they came and stop when he'd had enough.

Standing beside his truck, he stretched his body forward and from side to side, trying to work out some of the kinks. Then, straightening, he glanced at his watch. Eight o'clock and not quite dark. Vacationers who hadn't yet reached their day's destination still constituted the majority of people making use of the rest facilities—an elderly man walking his dog, two travel-weary children tussling over first use of the water fountain. The families would move on, though, and the trucks would come. Soon the place would be lined with tractor-trailer rigs, their drivers stealing a few hours' sleep. It wasn't a great stop, hardly picturesque—not much was in northwestern Ohio—but Peter found the sleeper compartment in his Kenworth more comfortable than most motel rooms, and where the rig was parked didn't matter.

At the moment, the only thing that did matter was getting some sleep. He sensed, however, that it was going to be one of those nights when, tired or not, sleep would be hard to come by. Nighttime was always the worst. When darkness fell, memories tugged at him. They were growing dimmer with time, the rage and despair they evoked wearing thin as reality sank in: he was as free as he wished to be, his life his own. Sooner or later, Peter hoped, his subconscious would get the message. Until it did, though, he was grudgingly resigned to the fact that sometimes at night it took a while before he was able to lie down and close his eyes.

Walking helped. It had become a bedtime ritual, along with recording his day's mileage and expenses. Thus, Peter took a circuitous route to the men's room, trudging from one end of the fenced-in rest area to the other. As he walked, he watched the big rigs pulling in.

Tractor-trailers fascinated him. So did the culture that surrounded them. It was a unique phenomenon in American society, and he hadn't been part of it for long that he couldn't appreciate it from an outsider's point of view. Mostly trucking was hard work, plain and simple. It was lonely and monotonous and physically draining. but in the year he'd been hauling—six months with Paul Flatt and the past six on his own—he had learned that the movies popularizing the truckers' way of life had captured something essentially true: the image of the trucker and his rig, alone on the highway, free of any ties that bound him to a place or another person. The modern-day cowboy, from his boots to his Stetson. His open range was the interstate highway system. His six-gun was his union card. And the unwritten code he and his fellow truckers shared was held inviolate: take care of your rig, stay clear of police, and love your woman—if you were lucky enough to have one.

Peter didn't think of himself as a trucker. Not really. Not yet, anyway. But the life-style offered him what he needed; it wasn't necessary that he find it deeply satisfying.

After making a full reconnaissance of the lot, he toured the interior of the brick building, where the smell of fried chicken from the Hardee's made him realize he was hungry. He had eaten enough restaurant food for one day, though, so after washing up he returned to his rig, heated a can of beef stew on the hot plate and carried his meal to a picnic table on the grass beside the parking lot.

A light breeze was blowing from the west, where the last rays of sun were turning the summer sky a deep lavender. As he sat enjoying his meal and the midwestern evening, Peter continued his casual observation of the area's growing population.

Casual became more alert when he noted a small figure walking down the ramp from the interstate. A hitchhiker, judging from the backpack. A woman. She was slight and, in the deepening twilight, easily could have passed for an adolescent boy in her dark T-shirt and faded jeans. The way she walked gave her away, but if it hadn't, the mass of dark hair that tumbled free as she pulled off her floppy-brimmed hat would have.

The woman ignored the restaurant and walked across the lot to slump onto the bench of a vacant picnic table a short distance from Peter's. He watched as she propped her elbow on the table and let her head fall forward to rest on her hand. An instant later she ran her fingers through her hair, heaved a tired sigh and pulled a sandwich out of her pack.

Peter frowned. Hitchhiking was bad news in his book. It disregarded the realities of life, too often with tragic results. For a woman, it seemed an especially stupid thing to do, and he had little patience for stupidity.

With a grunt of self-derision, Peter acknowledged how old he was getting to be. Time had passed, and easygoing attitudes had fled along with it. Fifteen, twenty years ago he would have invited the woman to join him, and they'd have exchanged road stories while they ate. Later, maybe, he would have pulled out his guitar, and they'd have had a couple of beers together. Then, well, probably she would have gone her own way, both of them satisfied that they'd spent a pleasant evening. Or maybe, if the mood had been right, she would have stayed with him. But that was then, and this was now. And so here he sat, eating his stew and passing critical judgments, while the woman chewed a squashed sandwich and cast wary glances at her surroundings.

There wasn't much point in being bitter over the passage of time. The gray hairs in his beard and on his scalp, few though they might be, were damning physical evidence of a foregone conclusion: an accounting of his lifetime credits and debits would show him heavily in the red. But he could not balance the columns overnight. It would take years to make up for all he had lost. And if he wanted to feel bitter about something, there were more important things than the loss of his reckless youth or a solid black beard.

After he had cleaned up from his late supper, it was fully dark and Peter was dead tired, but he still wasn't ready to shut himself inside the tractor. Doggedly he began another tour of the rest area. He had been walking about fifteen minutes and had wandered to the far end of the lawn, where a high chain-link fence separated it from a dirt road and a cow pasture. He was near a stand of maples, about to head toward his truck, when the sound of a woman's voice stopped him.

His head jerked around, and his eyes strained to see through the darkness under the trees. It was the hitchhiker. She was at the other end of the lawn, exchanging unpleasantries with a man who must, Peter reasoned, belong to the battered old pickup parked at the curb, its door open and its engine running. Peter couldn't hear the words the two were speaking, but it appeared from her gestures that the woman was trying to persuade the man to leave.

There was no one else around. Only a scream would have drawn anyone's attention, and by then it might have been too late. When he saw the man reach for the woman, Peter started toward them. It was one thing to think, *I told you so*. It was something else again to let the woman suffer the consequences of her own foolishness when he was around to prevent it.

She was backing away from the man, shaking her head insistently. Peter caught the tail end of her heated commentary as he approached.

"—don't want a ride. Just go away!"

She didn't sound frightened. Only angry.

The man grabbed her again, and she seemed to whirl away. Peter broke into a run but was brought up short when, in the next instant, amazingly, the guy was lying flat on his back. The woman was crouched, her arms outstretched, prepared for another attack.

So much, Peter thought, for chivalry. He stopped several yards away to see what would happen next, though by now he was more curious than concerned.

The man stood up slowly, and in that way people have of disbelieving the obvious, tried again to approach the woman.

"Mister, what's it going to take to make you understand?" she said, her voice low and shaking with anger.

"Honey, you're the one who don't understand," the man whined. "I don't know why you're getting all upset. I only want to have a little talk."

"'Talk,' my foot," she snorted. "You take your filthy hands and your filthy mouth and get away from me."

Having ascertained that the lady was in control of the situation, Peter let his mouth twitch into a dry smile. She was all feisty belligerence, and he couldn't help but admire her. At an inch or so over five feet tall and about an ounce over a hundred pounds, she was facing down this full-size creep without a scrap of fear in her stance or her tone. She was simply outraged.

The creep wasn't interested in her attitude, though, for he lunged at her once more.

Things happened fast. Peter started forward. He heard a quickly drawn breath, a grunt, then a sharp cry as a large body crumpled onto the dirt.

The man swore crudely, rolling to his side as he struggled to his feet. "You—you broke my arm! Why I ought to—"

"What you ought to do is get out of here." Peter halted a few feet away, acknowledging the woman's startled glance with a nod before turning back to her would-be attacker. "Or maybe," he added, "you'd like her to break your other arm, too."

"Butt out, mister," the man growled.

Peter growled back. "The only butt getting out is yours. Move it. Right now. Unless you want to find yourself making friends with the police."

The man looked from Peter to the woman. With a disgusted snort and a pained groan, he strode across the grass to his pickup, holding his injured limb close to his body. Peter watched until he had banged the door closed, yanked the transmission into gear and screeched out of the parking lot, spraying loose gravel behind him.

Then Peter turned to the woman. She stood perfectly still. "Are you all right?" he asked.

"Fine," came the short reply.

"If you want to come sit in my truck in case he—"

"I could have gotten rid of him myself."

Peter stared at her, thinking that, yes, fifteen years had been a long, long time.

Finally, with a sigh and a sardonic smile, he said, "You're welcome." And feeling very old and very tired, he went back to his rig.

As night rolled in, the rest area was jammed with trucks; by midnight, the sultry darkness was filled with diesel fumes and the rumbling sound of engines idling.

Away from the parking lot, across the lawn, Margaret Ann Miller sat with her back against a tree, concealed in the shadows. She had studied the place thoroughly before deciding that maybe it would be safe to sleep for a couple of hours. She would have felt safer if she could have dug a hole and crawled into it or climbed one of the trees and hidden in the leaves, but, given her limitations, this would have to do.

Unfortunately, even the minimal illusion of safety was soon shattered when a car pulled to a stop at the curb ahead of her and its headlights blasted her tree-shrouded cocoon. Beyond the glare the unmistakable silhouette of a bubble on top of the car made Margaret Ann's heart jump to her throat. Her reaction, which had grown all too familiar in the past twenty-four hours, was instant. Her palms got sweaty, her insides quivered and her breathing became erratic.

She looked around quickly for a place to hide. Even as she thought about trying to fade farther into the trees, the car door opened and a uniformed figure got out and started walking toward her. Margaret Ann shrank back against the tree trunk, willing herself not to panic. Her backpack with her wallet in it was behind a tree several yards away, and there was no other way this Ohio police officer could identify her. Was there?

Then he was standing in front of her.

"Good evening, ma'am. I'm Officer Monroe, Ohio state police. You need some help?"

"No." Her reply was a hoarse whisper.

"You're all right?"

"Fine. Thank you."

"My partner and I saw you sitting over here and thought maybe you were hurt." He paused. "You know, it's against the law to sleep here."

"I'm not sleeping," Margaret Ann pointed out.

"Well, just what are you doing?" Monroe inquired. When Margaret Ann hesitated, he spoke again, this time not so politely. "Look, ma'am, if you'd like to come with me, I'll escort you to a motel off the next exit. You can't stay here. We've got vagrancy laws."

With an inspiration born of terror, she laughed. "My husband wouldn't appreciate that, sir."

Monroe looked around. "And where is he?"

"Oh, he's aslee—uh, resting."

"Really?" His tone was disbelieving. "Which truck?"

Margaret Ann glanced toward the rows of trucks she'd watched form during the past two hours and waved in the direction of the rig parked at the head of the first row. "That one," she said.

"The black Kenworth?"

"Mmm."

"Why aren't you in there with him?"

She shrugged, her stomach churning as she elaborated on the tale. "We, uh, had an argument. I took a walk."

After a brief silence the trooper said, "This isn't a safe place to be walking in the middle of the night. Don't you think it's time you went back and made up?"

"Sure." She shrugged again. "Sure, I'll do that. And, uh, thanks for your concern."

"No problem. I'll walk you to your truck."

"Oh, that's okay. I can find my way back."

"Go right ahead. I'll wait to see you get there safely."

Margaret Ann stared up at the state trooper, the wild fluttering in her stomach solidifying into a cold tight knot. He was calling her bluff. And she was going to have to call his. The stakes in this game were too high for her to give up now.

Rising to her feet, grateful for the darkness that hid her trembling, she stuck her hands in her jeans pockets and began to saunter toward the lot. Monroe followed, and when they reached the curb, he stopped to watch as she continued toward the rig to which she had so blithely claimed allegiance. The closer she got, the louder her heart pounded and the faster her thoughts raced. What was she doing, playing chicken with a cop? She couldn't actually climb into the truck! Could she?

A glance over her shoulder told her she might have to. The trooper was still watching.

Margaret Ann stopped alongside the rig and looked up. She felt like David facing Goliath. Forget the long shiny trailer. The tractor alone was enormous, from the over-size sleeper box, with its angled roofline and vista window, to the blunt-nosed front end that seemed to go on forever. It was midnight black all over, but for the shiny steel gas tanks, exhaust stacks and grillwork. Nothing gaudy or show-offish about it; this monster meant business. Margaret Ann's short but intensive exposure to trucking, the result of waitressing in her aunt's truck-stop restaurant, told her the Kenworth was a top-of-the-line model. And since companies rarely provided such expensive rigs for their drivers, she had no doubt that the man driving it also owned it. This was confirmed by the red lettering on the door that read simply, *P. A. Lericos*, followed by a string of digits that constituted an operating license number.

Lericos. The name was vaguely familiar. Could she have met this trucker at Aunt Dorothy's? Maybe. But she hadn't recognized the man she had seen climb into the tractor—the one to whom she'd been so rude earlier. At the moment Margaret Ann didn't know whether that was something to be grateful for or to cry over.

Still, it gave her an idea—not a great one, but if worse came to worst, it might work. She could keep her all-important anonymity and, she hoped, buy enough time inside the truck to convince the cop to go away.

The risk was a big one. She was shaking like a leaf when she took hold of the metal bar to pull herself up onto the lower step of the cab, and she didn't know where she would find the nerve to go through with this. But one last look over her shoulder at the still-attentive state trooper made it clear she didn't have a choice. That was the trouble with breaking the law. Once you took the first step, the only choice left was to keep going.

Peter froze at the sound of the cab door opening. He was sitting on the side of his bed, naked but for a pair of dark briefs, the T-shirt he had just removed still in his hand. The leather curtain separating the sleeper from the cab was down, and at the muffled sound of movement, followed by the click of the cab door shutting, he tossed the T-shirt aside and curled his fingers around the edge of the curtain. Cautiously he moved to the edge of the bunk and, when no further noise reached him, jerked the curtain aside.

The next instant he was face-to-face with the most frightened human being he had ever seen.

She was sitting sideways in the passenger seat, one hand braced on the console. Her other hand was clenched in a fist, knuckles pressed to her mouth. He recognized her immediately as the hitchhiker he had tried to help. Beyond surface appearances, though, nothing about the woman whose eyes were locked with his was the same.

Her eyes! For one breath-stealing moment, Peter saw the truth reflected in those sapphire pools. He had seen fear before—more than his share of it—but not like this. This was terror. Stark bleeding terror. An elemental thing that made his flesh grow cold.

In a flash the woman's eyes swept over his bare skin and minimally covered loins, then snapped back to meet his gaze. And the fear was gone. Vanished, as though it had never been. Peter drew a sharp breath and watched as, slowly, like a flower opening under time-lapse photography, her countenance changed. The fist fell away from her mouth, her lips relaxed into a tentative smile, and she blinked once, almost lazily.

The transformation was complete, and Peter was aware that he was witnessing something truly astounding. He was in awe that anyone could so thoroughly disguise an emotion as powerful as the one she had revealed only a split second before. He did not, however, doubt the cause of the act. There was only one thing that could motivate a person to such lengths: the lady was desperate.

"Hi, Charlie. Hope I didn't wake you up."

Peter's gaze didn't waver at her casual greeting. She was good; her voice wasn't even quavering. He knew this performance must be costing her plenty, but what was its purpose?

There were not a lot of options. He chose the most logical one and calculated a response. Rolling the curtain upward and securing its snaps, he assumed a careless pose and spoke in a quiet drawl. "Well, well. If it isn't Wonder Woman. And it appears she's friendly, after all."

The woman's expression as she gave her wild mane of shoulder-length hair a toss was a beguiling mix of embarrassment and pouting. "Now, don't get nasty on me. I know I was rude before, and I'm sorry."

"Gee, that's nice."

She chose to ignore the sarcasm in his tone and, Peter noted, she did a better job of that than she was doing of ignoring his state of near nudity. From the way her eyes kept drifting downward, then skittering back to his face, either she was more uncomfortable about it than he was...or she was wondering how to capitalize on the situation. At her next words, he was fairly certain it was the latter.

Looking around the dimly lighted interior of the cab, she said brightly, "You've got a great rig here, Charlie. It is yours, isn't it?"

"Mine and the bank's."

She made an appreciative sound. "It's a real eye-catcher. Can't remember the last time I saw anything this big or, uh, fancy."

"Golly, thanks," Peter returned. Then, with a snap of his fingers, he said, "Don't tell me. You hoped I'd give you a personal tour and, shall we say, introduce you to the amenities."

He ended on a note of blatant sexual innuendo, expecting her to smile coyly in return. She didn't. Although her tone remained flippant, there was a guilessness about it as she said, "Sure. I was a little curious."

"Curious, huh?" He knew where this was heading. "Let's see, how does the rest of this line go? You've always wondered how they fit a bed inside one of these boxes and had to know if the stories about truckers' hedonistic tastes were true." His eyes raked over her, then fell pointedly to the bed. "Well, here it is, babe. No black satin, but I'll bet you could overlook something like that, couldn't you?"

His meaning could not have been more obvious if he had told her to strip and lie down. Peter saw the shock register on her face and knew immediately that he had guessed wrong; she was not trying to make some quick cash selling sexual favors. What stunned him, though, was that he could see she was considering it, anyway. For an instant her facade cracked, and he glimpsed once again the terror that was driving her. Her eyes widened, flashed to the sheets turned back over the blue cotton spread, then returned to lock with his. She swallowed hard, and he was certain she was about to offer him a dearly paid sacrifice in the form of her body. He had to admit, he'd had offers that were far less tempting.

But Peter understood desperation. Even desperation this shocking was not beyond his experience, and he had no intention of either exploiting it or being exploited by it.

He shook his head. "Sorry, babe. I'm not interested. A man can't be too careful these days, and I try hard to protect my virtue. Now, if you don't mind, I'd like to get some sleep." With a nod toward the door, he indicated it was time for her to leave.

A look of intense relief flashed in her eyes, but it was followed quickly by confusion. Then—he could almost see her marshaling her forces—she tried a new and surprising angle.

"Well, Charlie, I guess you really don't remember me. I've gotta say, though—" she sighed "—you were a whole lot nicer a few years back when we met at that other truck stop."

Peter's eyebrows arched. "We've met, have we?"

The woman shrugged. "I didn't realize it before—when that guy was bothering me, I mean. It was dark under those trees. But just now, when I was walking by, I noticed the name on the side of your truck and realized I knew you." She laughed. "I thought I ought to say a proper hello."

"Refresh my memory," Peter snapped. He had to admire the look of injured pride she gave him—an artful lowering of her gaze and a crestfallen tilt of the lips.

"I'm sorry," she muttered. "It was a long time ago, I know, but—"

"Where?"

"You really don't remember?"

"Where was it?"

"Well, that's the thing. I moved around a lot for a while. I'm not sure if it was Philadelphia . . . or maybe Baltimore."

Baltimore. Peter's eyes narrowed, and he searched his memory hard, trying to match her pretty face—the blue eyes and wide mouth, the upturned nose sprinkled with freckles—with one he had known. He couldn't. But maybe... Damn, maybe he *had* met her.

Then reason set in. She had said it was a long time ago. Any more than three years and it could be true that his path had crossed hers in the second city she'd named. Not, however, in a truck stop. He didn't know what she was up to, but he had to admit she had gotten to him. The word *Baltimore* could still put a funny feeling in the pit of his belly.

Peter bought a few seconds' recovery time by picking up his discarded T-shirt, shoving his arms through the sleeves and stretching it over his head. As he flipped the hair out of his eyes, he happened to glance out the small vent window that was propped open at the foot of the bed. And something caught his attention.

A state police car. Two troopers standing at the curb talking. Intuition told him that the presence of those officers in the lot and the woman's presence in his truck were connected. One of the troopers kept looking his way. Had she had a run-in with them?

He didn't know, but suddenly he didn't care. He had never been good at playing games, and he was tired of living in a world where they were necessary. He yanked the T-shirt down and turned back to the woman.

"Come on, lady, let's cut the crap. I don't know you, you don't know me, and I got the impression before that you'd just as soon keep it that way."

She drew back at his harsh tone. "Hey, Charlie, don't turn bully on me. Maybe I just wanted to say I was sorry. Maybe I was nervous before and said something stupid, when I should have said thank you."

"So why not say thank you and be done with it? Why the story about meeting me in a truck stop?"

"I thought I had," she replied sullenly. "Like I said, I did recognize the name on your truck."

"You've seen Lericos painted on the side of a truck before?"

"Yes. At least, I think it was on a truck. Anyway, I've seen it. And I did work at a few truck stops, so it could have been on your truck."

It could have been, but it probably wasn't. Peter didn't care one way or the other whether she placed him in her memory; on the other hand, he was not inclined to offer her any hints.

"Look," he sighed. "Let's have it. What do you want from me?"

The woman drew a shaky breath, and, dropping her gaze from his, she lifted one shoulder in a tentative gesture. "I was sitting out there and...and an old blue pickup drove in, and I thought it was that guy who...well, you remember. I, uh, got scared." She glanced at him. "You did say I could sit in your truck in case he came back. Didn't you?"

Yes, he had said that, but she was no more scared of that jerk than a cat was of a mouse. The state troopers, now, that was another story.

It didn't matter. Peter understood he was being asked to give her refuge. For some reason she couldn't say it outright, but she'd been willing to go to great lengths—perhaps even sleep with him—in order to stay inside his truck.

He was aware that appearances meant nothing about how dangerous a person might be. A big mean-looking thug might inspire fear, but this little imp with the pretty face could be more dangerous. She could be planning to rob and murder him in his sleep.

But she wasn't planning anything of the sort. He needed nothing more than his instincts, which were fine-tuned to spotting criminals of all shapes and varieties, to know that.

Deliberately he leaned forward and looked out the window at the police car. He glanced from it to her and back again, making it clear that he knew the score. She never blinked or flinched or in any way acknowledged his gesture, but he caught a brief glimpse of something in her eyes that tore at him. The plea was more effective because she tried to hide it, yet it couldn't have been plainer than if she had actually said "please."

"All right," he told her. "You can stay. But I meant what I said. I'm not interested in any quick sex. Switch places with me, and I'll sleep up front."

When he started to move forward, she jumped. "Oh, no! I don't want to—"

He stopped short, their gazes meeting at a distance of a few inches.

She drew a ragged breath. "I'll—I'll sit here. It's okay. Go on and . . . and go to sleep, if you want."

Peter studied her a moment longer. Then, with a dry laugh, he agreed. "You want to sleep sitting up, that's fine with me."

He turned off the two swivel lights above the bed and unsnapped one corner of the curtain so that it half-covered the opening. Reaching for his jeans, he put them on before lying down. In the event that he had to do some fast moving in the middle of the night, he wanted to be prepared.

There was a chance he was being a fool. He knew that. He also knew that his money and credit cards were where she couldn't get them and that her martial arts skills would not hold up against the tricks he'd had the misfortune of learning the hard way. It was also regrettable but true that the slightest noise would wake him.

Somehow, though, he knew that Wonder Woman meant him no harm. It didn't bother him that he was probably helping her avoid a vagrancy charge. She looked as if she had enough problems as it was. Before he drifted off to sleep, Peter decided that, in the morning, he would ask her where she was going. If she was heading northwest, she might as well ride with him.

For a full minute, Margaret Ann stared at the half-closed curtain. Then slowly it began to sink in. Impossible though it seemed, her ploy had worked.

An almost inaudible whimper escaped her, and she clutched the seat with shaking hands, turning slowly to face front. There she sat, slumped in a quaking heap, her eyes squeezed closed, every muscle in her body having turned to water. It was several minutes before she had the power either to move or to reason. One thought dominated all others: she was safe, at least for this one night. She was sitting inside this wonderful truck while its owner, astonishingly enough, was lying in a bed less than four feet away, presumably falling asleep.

Margaret Ann shuddered, reliving the moment when she'd realized what he thought she wanted from him. She had expected his next question to be how much she charged. For a moment, when it had looked as if sleeping with him was the only way to keep from getting caught, she'd thought she would have to play out the scene. Thank heavens she would never know if she could have gone through with it. It appalled her that she had reached such a point in her life. Not that sex had ever been pleasurable or loving, much less the sacred experience she had been raised to think it should be. But nothing could be worse than the last experience she had been forced to endure, and somehow that had made the notion of having sex with a stranger at least remotely bearable.

Margaret Ann opened her eyes and glanced over her shoulder into the darkness of the sleeper compartment. She frowned at the sight of the long masculine legs now covered by blue denim. He hadn't wanted to sleep with her, and she was grateful for that. But if he had, and she hadn't been able to finagle her way out of it without getting evicted from the truck, she would have survived. He wouldn't have hurt her. Somehow she knew that.

A flush of warmth crept into her cheeks at the vivid mental image of Mr. P. A. Lericos's virile body. His name sounded Greek, and he had the olive-toned skin and the dark hair to go with it—and there had been plenty of both on display. He hadn't shown even a hint of embarrassment, sitting there so casually, dressed in almost nothing. But then, she admitted, he had little to be embarrassed about.

He was probably only a shade over average height, but the broad shoulders and the muscled chest and thighs made him seem bigger. His silver-etched silky black hair was long enough to fall over his heavy arched eyebrows and to hit the collar of his shirt, had he been wearing one; with the full beard concealing much of his face, the effect was very sensual. The beard hid his expression, though, and for that reason she wasn't sure she liked it. His high, sharp cheekbones and thin, hard-looking mouth were striking. And his eyes, well...his eyes were incredible. Sparkling amber gold and ringed with the thickest, blackest lashes she'd ever seen. A shiver raced along her spine as she remembered the way he had stared at her.

Why had he decided to let her stay? He had seen the police. He had made it clear he knew what she was up to.

Deciding it was better not to speculate too closely, Margaret Ann reasoned that Mr. P. A. Lericos was, after all, a truck driver. That certainly didn't mean he would go out of his way to break the law, but if he thought she was trying to avoid something as innocuous as a vagrancy charge—which, she knew, was how it appeared—it didn't seem so strange that he would choose to aid the cause.

Relaxing a little, Margaret Ann shifted more comfortably in her seat and began to look around. It really was a great truck. The burgundy plush seats and matching carpet were hardly worn. The cream-colored leather that covered nearly everything else still had a trace of that telltale new-car smell. There was an elaborate radio and tape deck built in overhead beside the CB radio. And on the floor between the seats was a case full of cassettes.

A clipboard sitting on top of the console caught her eye, and, indulging her curiosity, she picked it up to leaf through the papers attached to it. The top page was something called a Bill of Lading, and, though most of it made no sense to her, the destination was clear: Seattle, Washington. As she turned a page, it amused her to discover that her obliging trucker was also remarkably conscientious. He kept careful track of his expenses, logging even the smallest items in neatly labeled columns.

What really amazed her, however, was the next sheet of paper, whereupon he had gone so far as to project each day's exact mileage. He had made notations about rest stops and restaurants at precisely calculated intervals, including the one they were in. Beside each stop was an estimated arrival time. He had driven that day from New York City, where, the Bill of Lading helpfully told her, "587 ctns. lds. drs." had been loaded into his trailer. It appeared he planned to spend tomorrow night near Sioux Falls, South Dakota. Looking at the sheet, Margaret Ann had the feeling he could probably pull into a stop within thirty seconds of the time he expected to get there.

As she stared at the neat masculine handwriting, a wild idea began to form in her mind. It probably wouldn't work. Then again, the gamble she had taken yesterday didn't have much chance of success, either. Success depended solely upon her resourcefulness and nerve. There was no safe harbor. She was running. Running until even *he*, with his horrible but influential friends and every political favor called in, couldn't find her. At that moment, Seattle seemed about as far as a person could go.

So what if it was a crazy idea? The whole world was crazy right now. And nobody was around to disapprove as she grabbed a pen, located a well-worn map and began scribbling on a piece of paper torn from the clipboard. One thing she knew for sure. In the middle of the most frightening sequence of events of her life, a man, a complete stranger, had offered her a measure of peace. She didn't trust it, knew it wouldn't last if she was forced to explain herself. Still, it didn't seem crazy to take whatever refuge she could beg, borrow—or steal.

Chapter Two

When Peter awoke at five-thirty Monday morning, he was alone. Wonder Woman was gone. He supposed it was a good sign that she could have left without his hearing her; he must be sleeping better. Oddly enough, though, he was disappointed. He had been looking forward to sparring with her again and maybe having her company for the day. The long hours on the highway were tedious. Talking to other truckers over the CB helped, but that got old after a while.

Still, he admitted, it was probably better this way. He had spent most of his adult life perfecting the art of culling facts from fiction. Wonder Woman would have continued telling tall tales, but it wouldn't have been long before he'd have known her real story. And he had a feeling it was a story he didn't want to know.

The lady had trouble written all over her. And trouble was something he did not need. In the past he had thrived on it, and it appeared he still had a penchant for attracting it. But things—and people—could change. Life was full of choices, and one didn't *have* to do the thing that common sense argued against doing, even if it did appear more interesting, more challenging, more satisfying.

Wonder Woman had affected him powerfully, more so than anyone had in a long time. Considering how easily he had offered to help her, it seemed likely he would be tempted to go on offering. Which meant getting involved with someone in a way he knew he should avoid. So it was a good thing, he concluded, that she had removed herself and both physical and emotional temptation she presented from his path.

Peter slid behind the wheel and reached for his dark glasses. As he rolled the Kenworth down the entrance ramp onto the interstate, he made a determined effort to force last night's incident from his mind. He was not able, however, to erase the memory of those compelling blue eyes—eyes that knew fear and anger but that he sensed could also sparkle with humor and delight. Eyes that had reminded him of his own pain and vulnerability. Eyes that reminded him of what it meant to feel fully, intensely alive.

It had been a long time.

Margaret Ann's feet hurt. So did her head and just about every other part of her. She hated heat and humidity, and the fact that it wasn't nearly as hot and humid in Illinois as it had been in Baltimore did not make the sweat dripping down her face any less uncomfortable.

Air conditioning, on the other hand, made an enormous difference. She sighed in relief as she opened the glass door of the rest-stop restaurant and felt the cold blast hit her. The lobby was packed with travelers who had stopped for lunch, and she dodged through the crowd to the rest rooms. A few minutes later she headed for the bank of telephones on one of the lobby walls.

Grabbing a phone near the back, she placed a collect call from "Sally" and held her breath while the operator verified the charges with her friend Jane Dubrowsky. Sally was the code name they had chosen, and Margaret Ann heard the nervousness in Jane's voice as she accepted the call.

When the operator left the line, Margaret Ann's breath rushed out along with the question that had been pounding in her head for the past thirty-six hours. "Jane, it's me. How's Jimmy?"

"He's fine," her friend answered, then hurried on. "Oh, Margaret Ann, I've been so worried! Why haven't you called?"

"I'm sorry. I didn't get a chance yesterday."

"Where are you?"

"I can't tell you that—and you know why." Margaret Ann smiled. "You're a wonderful friend, Janey, but you're a terrible liar."

Jane sighed. "Yeah, I know. It's the fear of burning in hell. I can still see Sister Marie St. Anthony expounding upon the virtues of truth and the heinous sin of lying."

"I'm trying very hard right now not to think about Sister Marie St. Anthony and sins and burning in hell."

"Margaret Ann, stop it. You can't honestly think you're the one committing the sin here. Dear Lord, every time I look at poor little Jimmy, I— Well, I just can't believe anybody would blame you for anything!"

They could—and would, Margaret Ann thought bitterly. And if Jane had known the entire story, her friend might blame her, too—if for nothing else, for her stupidity.

"How's his arm?" she asked.

"Broken but mending," Jane informed her. "I did it just as we planned. Took him to the emergency room across town and gave them Mark's name. They never questioned it."

"Is the break bad?"

"No, thank heaven. The doctor said it will heal fine. He'll have a cast for about six weeks."

"Oh, Janey," Margaret Ann whispered. "I can't stop thinking about him. I'm so worried something will happen and...and he'll find him. And if he finds him, he'd find *you*, and—"

"You can stop worrying right now. This is the middle of nowhere, remember? No one's going to find us. And Jimmy's fine. He's having a great time with Mark. The barn cat had kittens yesterday, and the two of them spent the day badgering me with questions about exactly how that had happened. So be warned. Your son is now well-informed—about cats, at least. I left it to you to translate things into human terms. Actually, I don't think I did a half-bad job of it, if I do say so myself. You owe me one."

"I owe you for a lot of things," Margaret Ann said quietly.

"Nonsense," Jane returned.

"You could get in a lot of trouble for helping me."

"Let somebody try to stop me! I'll tell them what kind of shape Jimmy was in when you brought him here. Listen, Margaret Ann, I know you think you're handling this the right way, but really, I can't believe it wouldn't be okay to march yourself into the police station with a good lawyer and tell them what happened."

"Then what?" Margaret Ann shot back. "Hear them tell me I'm lying, that I'm not fit to be a mother and that my son is better off where he was, without me? Uh-uh.

Forget it. I lived through that scene once. I'm not risking Jimmy's welfare ever again.''

"But, Margaret Ann—"

"Besides, I haven't got the money for a decent lawyer. I'd get stuck, like I did the last time, with some new law-school graduate who hasn't got the first notion about how to stand up to *his* lawyers and their bag of dirty tricks. It'd be over before it started."

Jane's response was unequivocal. "It's not fair."

"Fair?" Margaret Ann laughed harshly. "Fair is something we teach our kids. But we aren't doing them any favors, because sooner or later they're going to find out that life *isn't* fair. It's like teaching them to believe in Santa Clause, then expecting them to thank us when they find out we lied."

When Jane spoke, her voice quavered. "Oh, Margaret Ann, you make me want to cry. You used to be so open and full of fun and . . . and *happy*. How did a nice girl like you get herself into such a god-awful mess?"

Margaret Ann's voice was as wobbly as her friend's. "I don't know how it happened, Janey. I can't tell how much is my fault and how much is, well, call it circumstance. It's so complicated. And if I ever get out of it, I'll probably spend the next ten years recovering."

"You'll get out of it," Jane insisted. "You always knew how to come back fighting."

Margaret Ann didn't say how little fight she had left in her or how terrified she was that, this time, no matter how hard she fought, she would lose. It was crucial to keep thinking positively. If she let herself consider the consequences of losing, she'd go crazy.

"Is Jimmy there?" she asked. "Can I talk to him?"

"Of course. He and Mark are in the other room, building Legos. I'll get him."

Margaret Ann listened as Jane called Jimmy. When he picked up the phone and said "Mommy?" she could no more have prevented the tears from streaming down her cheeks than she could have stopped the sun from shining. His voice held all the hope and excitement and adoration that leaped within her own heart when she thought of him. But it was the note of hesitation, the frightened uncertainty, that tore at her until she thought she would fold up and die from the pain.

She pressed a hand to her forehead and took several steadying breaths before she tried to speak. "Hi, sweetheart. How are you?"

"Fine. Mark and me, we built this giant space station. And we're going to build another one, but we might run out of Legos. Did Aunt Jane tell you the cat had babies? Five of them. And Mark and me, we got to watch her feed them."

Through her tears, Margaret Ann smiled. "That sounds like fun. You and Mark are getting to be friends, huh?"

"Yeah. When are you coming? You said you'd only be gone a little while."

"I said I didn't know how long I'd be gone," she corrected carefully. "And I still don't know. It might be a few weeks. We'll have to see."

"But I want you to come back now."

"Oh, sweetheart, I'll be there as soon as I can. I promise. Jane said you've got a terrific white cast. Is it okay? Does your arm hurt?"

"Not anymore," Jimmy replied reluctantly, not wanting to be diverted. "Mark signed his name on my cast, and so did Aunt Jane. And I'm drawing skeletons all over it."

Margaret Ann chuckled. "Well, save me a spot to sign."

"Okay. Will you bring me something?"

"Oh, I think I can manage that. Now let me talk to Aunt Jane again."

"But I don't want you to go yet."

"Jimmy, I have to. I'll call again as soon as I can. Okay?"

"Mommy, please—"

"I love you, sweetheart. I love you very, very much."

There was a long pause before a tiny voice murmured, "I love you, too."

Margaret Ann knew he was crying when he handed the receiver over to his surrogate aunt.

"Jane? Lord, I'm sorry. I've left you with another problem to take care of. I shouldn't have called."

"Margaret Ann Miller, that's the dumbest thing you've said yet. He needed to talk to you."

"I needed to talk to him, too, but it tears me apart every time I hear his voice. What must he think of all this? I keep wondering if he'll ever get over it."

"A little boy should never have to live through what this child's lived through. But he'll be all right. You'll see. Kids are amazing. You just get back here and spend some time with him, and he'll bounce back."

"I hope so. And if you really think it helps, I'll try to call again tomorrow. I can't promise, but I'll try."

"Do what you can. And Margaret Ann . . . ?"

"Hmm?"

"Be careful."

Margaret Ann drew a ragged breath. "I'll be as careful as I can be and still do what has to be done. It's the only way Jimmy and I will ever be safe. Believe me, Jane. He won't give up."

Margaret Ann clung to the receiver long after she had hung up, and she stood with her eyes closed, her head pressed against the back of her hands, willing herself not to cry anymore. Turning to leave, she wiped a hand across her cheeks, picked up her pack and walked out into the noonday sun.

Inside the building, one shoulder leaning against the wall six feet away from the telephone Margaret Ann had been using, Peter stood staring after her.

Thank God, he's here.

Margaret Ann offered up the silent prayer as she trudged across the crowded night-lit parking lot toward the familiar black Kenworth. It was comforting to know that some people in the world were totally predictable. Charlie—she couldn't think of him as Peter, though she had seen his name on the manifest sheets the night before—had planned to drive 696 miles today. If only it hadn't taken her so long to hitchhike the same distance.

It was one in the morning, and Margaret Ann was exhausted as she stopped beside the Kenworth and stared at the door handle. Drawing a deep breath, she reached for it, putting what concentration she had left into opening the door as silently as possible. Tonight she did not want Charlie to catch her; she didn't think she could withstand the confrontation that was sure to ensue. All she wanted was to sleep.

Dawn was breaking on the horizon when Peter awoke with a start, certain he had heard the cab door closing. He never slept with the curtain closed—used it only for undressing until the lights were out—so it was immediately obvious no one else was in the tractor. It didn't take him more than a few seconds to glance out both side windows and to look in the mirrors at the long trailer. He saw no one from any angle. A quick check of the cab told him nothing was missing, and he knew he ought to count himself lucky that he had not been robbed—or worse.

It wasn't rational, much less safe, but he could not fall asleep with the doors locked. Not yet. He had been warned it might take a while for all the residual effects of his two-year-long nightmare to wear off; he was making progress, but sleeping was one area in which the feelings could still control him.

At noon, Peter ran into Paul Flatt at a rest stop near Rapid City, South Dakota. He had first met the road-hardened trucker when each had been at the lowest point in his life. When it had come time for them to put the pieces back together, Paul had taught him how to drive an eighteen-wheeler and started him on his new career; in return, Peter had researched the locations and hours for every Alcoholics Anonymous meeting Paul could attend while they were on the road. Now Paul was a walking advertisement for AA nationwide, and Peter was trucking on his own, but he still valued the months they had spent together in Paul's rig. The older man had lived through some bad times with him and was one of the only people on earth who had any notion of exactly how bad they had been.

They saw each other infrequently these days, and after they had eaten, Paul announced he was ready to inspect the new rig his protégé had purchased since their paths had last crossed.

"I told you, didn't I?" Paul teased as the two men walked across the parking lot. "When you bought my old bucket of bolts, I said you wouldn't drive it six months before you'd go buy yourself a new goodied-up set of doubles. Happened to me that way. Happens to every professional sooner or later. Yes, indeed, you're in it now, up to your teeth."

"That's the truth." Peter chuckled. "Whenever I make a payment, I feel like I'm working off the national debt."

As they approached the Kenworth, Paul offered Peter a sidelong look from under a graying brow, then let out a low whistle. Grinning, Peter followed as the wiry man with the bowed legs took the long walk around the sixty-foot-plus rig. When they reached the driver's door, Paul's gaze lingered for a moment on the shiny chrome that gilded the black tractor, until, finally, he let out an appreciative sigh.

Tilting his balding head thoughtfully, he asked, "Don't you ever wish you were back there, wearing a suit and making use of those fancy degrees you've got?"

Peter met the older man's faded blue gaze. "You know the answer, Paul. I'll probably always miss it. But those suits and degrees didn't buy me loyalty or justice. And they never bought me happiness, either."

"Yeah," Paul returned, his tone mildly skeptical. "I know you said that a year ago, but you've had a while to think on it. And I just wonder if it isn't time you gave yourself another shot at doing what you like doing best."

Peter's denial was tinged with a bitterness that he wished weren't there—and a longing that he feared would never go away. "I can't go back, Paul."

"What about your family?"

"I keep in touch with my parents and my brother and sister. They know I'll come if they need me. But that's the only reason I'd go back."

Paul studied him a moment longer. Then, with a resigned shake of his head, he got down to business. "Well, let's take a look at this witch of a rig you bought. She's a beauty, all right. But black! Why it's downright lecherous looking. If I didn't know you better, old buddy, I'd say you were finally thinking about taking up with the ladies in a serious way."

Peter laughed as he watched Paul climb in to have a look-see. Still smiling, he strode around to the passenger side and reached for the door.

He stopped with it half-open. Hanging from the metal catch on the inside of the door frame were several long brown hairs. He knew they hadn't been there last night, because he had opened and closed the door several times, and they were too obvious to miss.

He knew, now, what had awakened him this morning: Wonder Woman. She had paid him another visit last night.

The news bothered him considerably. He had thought about her almost constantly since overhearing her phone conversation the day before. He remembered the anxiety in her voice when she had talked to the woman, Jane, who he guessed was a friend. He remembered the tears running down her cheeks when she had talked to Jimmy, who he was certain was her son. He remembered the tenderness of her expression, the gentle smiles that came through her tears. Most of all, he remembered how she had sounded as she reassured the child that she loved him and would be with him as soon as she could, all the while her hands were trembling and her face was contorted with anguish.

Peter recognized courage when he saw it. He also recognized that something was critically wrong here.

She was running from the police; no doubt about it, and it wasn't a mere vagrancy charge she was afraid of facing. She had said Jane could get in trouble because of her. And she made an impassioned speech about not being able to afford a decent lawyer, and about how she wouldn't trust one anyway, because she wasn't going to risk Jimmy's welfare *ever again*. Yes, those had been her words.

How bad was it? What had she done? Or was it something she was about to do? What would happen to her if she was caught? How old was Jimmy? And what was the business about a broken arm?

There were lots of questions he couldn't answer, and Peter had promised himself that, since he would not be seeing her again, he would do well to forget the whole thing. As he fingered those few strands of brown hair, though, it became clear that forgetting was not a possibility. If she thought she could go on using him as her port in the storm... Well, as foolish as it undoubtedly was, he'd probably let her. But he damned well wanted to know which way the storm was blowing.

Chapter Three

If her heart had been pounding any harder, Margaret Ann was certain it would have burst. Like the fugitive she was, she lay flattened on the wet ground behind the bushes that bordered the mountainside rest area as she searched the parking lot. There was no sign of a police car, but the sight of the black tractor and its towering trailer, parked in the last line of trucks toward the back of the lot, brought a moan of relief. Struggling to her feet with her pack hooked over one shoulder, she made her way furtively toward it.

It had been a close call, and she didn't ever want to repeat the experience. If only the idiot she had been riding with hadn't been a speed demon. If only he'd had the sense to figure out why all the trucks on the road had slowed down. But he had whizzed along doing almost eighty, and the state trooper had, of course, nabbed him.

The trooper had been sharp. He had looked at her long and hard, and his questions had been far too pointed for

Margaret Ann's comfort. Was she Mrs. Speedy? No? Well, he hoped she wouldn't let this little incident prejudice her view of the great state of Montana. She wasn't from around here, right? No, he didn't think so. Back East, wasn't it? New York, maybe? No, farther south. Washington, D.C. or . . . maybe Baltimore?

Margaret Ann hadn't hung around to find out if he was merely being friendly. It was far more likely that the trail she was deliberately leaving had grown too hot, allowing the long arm of the law to stretch across the continent and find her. She had waited until the trooper went back to his car to write out the ticket, until she was certain he wasn't watching, then she had taken off.

For the past five hours she had traveled on foot in the pitch-black night, certain that at any moment she would be overtaken by police with dogs and megaphones blasting at her to give herself up. As if her rampant paranoia weren't enough, the thunderheads that had been hanging in the sky all evening had let loose a walloping torrent of lightning and rain. The terrain had been rocky and slippery, and she had fallen a couple of times. If she hadn't been so terrified of getting caught, she would have quit running and looked for a place to hide. But in her mindless desperation, she had clung to the idea that, if she could only find Charlie and his beautiful truck, she would be safe. It didn't make a bit of sense, but she absolutely couldn't help herself.

She didn't even try to be quiet as she pulled open the door and tossed her backpack onto the passenger seat. Hauling herself in after it, she paused briefly at the sight of Peter sitting on the bed against the padded back wall of the sleeper. Her first thought as she met his gaze was that tonight, at least, he'd had the decency to keep his pants on.

Peter raised one dark eyebrow, cast a pointed glance at the backpack and gave her a slow smile. "Well, Wonder Woman, it's about time. I'd about given up on you."

Margaret Ann let out the breath she'd been holding and closed the door behind her. "Don't bug me, Charlie. I can't take it tonight."

"My name's not Charlie."

"Mine's not Wonder Woman, either, but we'll both be better off if we let it go at that."

"I don't doubt it. But, you see, I've got this thing about names. Everybody's got one. It's kind of nice and orderly, don't you think? Makes keeping track of people so much easier."

"Call me whatever you like," she grumbled, struggling onto the seat. "I don't care. And I'll get out of your truck and go away if you want. But first—" she slumped in utter weariness and let her eyes drift closed "—first I've got to sit for a minute. Just give me a minute. That's all."

After a brief silence, she heard a shuffling sound. When Peter spoke, his voice came from directly beside her.

"Mother of God," he breathed. "Look at you."

With difficulty Margaret Ann opened her eyes and let her head roll toward him. Braced on one knee between the seats, he reached up and pulled the floppy felt hat from her head. Her hair, as it tumbled to her shoulders, was possibly the only thing about her that wasn't wet or mud stained.

Peter's bright gaze registered shock, which slowly darkened to anger as he looked her over from head to toe. She sensed the anger was not directed at her, however, when he shook his head slowly and said, "No offense, babe, but you're not a pretty sight. Looks like you hitched yourself to the back of a truck and let it drag you the last two hundred miles.'' With the tip of one finger, he touched a scrape on her cheek.

Startled by the gentleness in both his voice and his touch, Margaret Ann jerked away. ''Yeah, well, I promise not to bleed on your carpet, okay?''

''Screw the carpet.''

Her eyes widened at his growled comment. Then, before she could protest, his hands were on her. He was strong. His biceps bulged as he lifted her, and her fingers couldn't budge the hands spanning her ribs. As he hauled her against his bare chest, her nostrils flared at the scent of him. He smelled musky and warm and faintly of sweat. He smelled like a man, and for one panicked instant, she almost screamed.

The panic didn't have a chance to take hold, though. He pulled her into the sleeper compartment, set her on the side of the bed and promptly released her.

Feeling like a rag doll, she gulped for air, then looked down helplessly at the clean white sheets. ''I can't sit here. I'm filthy.''

''Soap and water,'' he replied, crouching in front of her to remove her running shoes. ''That's the answer to the dirt problem. And I'll bet you wish all the answers were that easy.''

Margaret Ann started to bristle but instead flinched. ''Ouch! Oh, stop, don't touch them!''

She tried to draw her bare foot away, but his fingers, wrapped around her ankle, held it firmly as he looked at the blisters. Margaret Ann saw his thin, sensual lips press together in a grim line. When he lifted his gaze to meet hers, his eyes were like fire, searing through her. She held his gaze, and the message that passed between them was as clear as any spoken words.

Please, don't ask me anything.

I won't.

I can't trust you. I can't.

I know. Just let me give you what you need right now.

A tiny sigh escaped her, and she closed her eyes as he removed her other shoe. It took a while; the laces were wet and muddy. As she sat there submissively, the effects of the adrenaline that had been pumping through her began to wear off. She was so incredibly tired. In the past three days she'd had less than a night's worth of sleep. She couldn't remember the last full meal she had eaten. Her muscles quivered and her head was spinning. When she opened her eyes, everything inside the confined, dimly lighted space seemed distorted. Burgundy blended with cream. Cloth blurred into leather. Textures smoothed out into one flat plane.

It struck her as both terrifying and funny that she was actually on the verge of passing out. Maybe, she mused, it would be the best thing to do. He wouldn't throw her out unconscious, would he? She stared, glassy eyed, as Peter ran warm water into the tiny sink tucked beside the closet.

Setting a bar of soap and a washcloth on the narrow built-in shelf at the foot of the bed, he told her, "You go ahead and wash, then we'll see about some antiseptic for those blisters." He moved to the front and started to close the curtain behind him but stopped, studying her closely. "Can you handle this by yourself?"

Margaret Ann simply went on staring at him. His question had registered in her brain, but she was, quite suddenly, incapable of speaking. Or moving.

And somehow he knew it. Squatting in front of her once more, he reached for the hem of her T-shirt. Startled, Margaret Ann drew a sharp breath and tried with fumbling fingers to accomplish the task herself. Her futile attempts to lift her arms high enough to pull the shirt over her head reduced her to tears, however, and with a muttered oath, he tugged the shirt off and went to work on the zipper of her jeans.

"Don't tell me later how I didn't give you a chance to preserve your modesty. But then—" he shot her a quick look "—a lady who invites herself into a stranger's bedroom can't be too worried about a little thing like that, can she?"

Modesty was the furthest thing from Margaret Ann's mind. Well, maybe not the absolute furthest. She felt her face grow warm when he yanked off her muddy jeans, and she tried to cover her breasts when he removed her bra, failing because her arms were too heavy to hold up. About all she could do was whimper with relief when she realized he did not intend to divest her of her underpants, as well.

She didn't dare look at his face. It was bad enough staring at the hairy chest, the wide shoulders, the narrow hips and corded thighs, at the juncture of which a denim-covered bulge drew her gaze.

His body was terrifying to her simply because it was powerful and male. If she looked at his face and found even a hint of sexual interest in his expression, she was sure she would become hysterical. For in her unnerved state, she was in no shape to make distinctions between the man kneeling at her feet and the one who had caused her so much pain and grief.

When Peter's fingers threaded through her hair, Margaret Ann jumped, but his callused hand held her head in place, and he began washing her face and neck. It was impossible, then, not to meet his gaze, but her vision was cloudy and she had to keep blinking to focus. Dimly, she wished he didn't wear a beard, because it made it hard to tell what he was thinking. But even so, as she searched his features, especially those amber-prismed eyes, she felt the last bit of resistance drain out of her. The sexual interest she had been afraid of finding wasn't there. His expression held nothing more threatening than compassion and concern. And she was utterly powerless to refuse what he was offering.

She thought he asked if she was hungry. When she didn't answer, he mumbled something about how food would probably only make her sick, anyway. The next thing she knew she was lying on the bed—she didn't know whether he had lain her down or if she had fallen—and there were black spots and tiny dots of light flashing in front of her eyes. She smelled soap, felt something wet and cool moving over her legs.

An instant later, she knew only blessed, mindless darkness.

What was he going to do with her?

The question was paramount in Peter's mind as he sat on the side of the bunk, staring down at the small form sleeping there. She was out cold, lying on her side, one arm under her head, the other tucked close to her body. He had pulled the sheet over her and now watched the gentle rise and fall of her shoulder as she breathed.

She was quite pretty in an elfin sort of way. He liked her wide, expressive mouth. And he liked the freckles that dusted her nose and cheeks. Her skin was a translucent peach, and her hair, curling around her shoulders in an untamed mass, was a medium brown—a little unkempt at the moment, but pleasing. Her shape was lovely. Not a model's, to be sure—she was too petite for that—but sensual, womanly, with rounded hips and small, supple breasts.

A carnal image of those pink-tipped breasts made his pulse quicken and his loins grow tight. It had been a long while since he had felt anything but a passing and strictly physical interest in a woman, and the strength of his re-action to this waif astounded him. It also scared him. She made him feel things with an intensity he didn't want to feel, need things he was trying not to need. She was the embodiment of temptation, and he didn't know if he could resist the pull.

He was certain of one thing, however. He knew where she was from, or at least where she had grown up. Squelching his pointless erotic fantasies, Peter smiled crookedly. There wasn't another accent in the world like that of a native Baltimorean, particularly an east Balti-morean. Wonder Woman had rid herself of most of it, but in her exhausted state tonight, a few words had given her away.

Language experts and sociologists had been fascinated by the peculiar pronunciation for years: *warsh* for wash, *warder* for water, *ul* for oil, *aegs* for eggs. If asked where he had been raised, a true native would proudly pro-nounce "Ah'm fr'm Ballm'r, home 'a d'Or'ulls."

The fact that Wonder Woman did not always speak in this manner meant she'd had the opportunity to hear other speech patterns. College would have given her that, or even moving to the other side of town. Her tutored speech sounded natural, but under stress she slipped into the old ingrained way.

In search of answers and without a twinge of guilt, Pe-ter reached for her backpack and rummaged through the few articles of clothing until he found a wallet. He flipped it open, grunting softly when he discovered that either she had removed her driver's license or didn't have one. She had not, however, removed a tiny folded ID card stuffed deep inside the inner pocket.

Margaret Ann Miller. Yes, that seemed right. A nice German girl—probably Catholic, too. Her birthday was in November, and she was twenty-five—older than she looked and younger than she seemed. She had an apartment near Johns Hopkins University's Homewood campus—not the east side of town, but that neither proved nor discredited his origin-of-accent theory. There was no one listed to contact in case of emergency.

Thumbing through the wad of bills he found in another pocket, Peter was surprised she was carrying so much. More than seven hundred dollars. But there was nothing else—no picture, no credit cards—that might have told him something about her. And he had to know.

The desire he felt to help this frightened woman wasn't logical, yet he understood it. She had touched him in a way that was deeply personal, in a place inside himself that was, he was discovering, still raw enough to bleed. He knew almost nothing about her, yet he felt as though he knew her intimately.

She was behaving as though she were a criminal, but she wasn't one. He knew about criminals. He knew how they looked and talked, and he had listened to enough of them to know how they thought and felt. He knew more about criminals than nearly anything else—more, certainly, than he had ever wanted to learn. And he knew beyond a shadow of a doubt that Margaret Ann Miller was not now, nor ever would be, one of them.

He had witnessed her fear and desperation. He had seen her look of abject misery when she had tried to undress, only to find she could not. He'd heard her whimpers of exhaustion as he had bathed her scraped and bruised body. Again he felt anger at the thought that there was someone, somewhere, who ought to pay for every tear that had run down her face. No, she wasn't a criminal. She was a lovely strong-spirited woman who was fighting to the limits of her strength and courage for something she believed to be vital to her own, and her son's, survival. And she was very, very frightened.

It had been all he could do not to fold her in his arms and tell her everything would be all right, and he would have, except that she would have tried either to run away or to deck him. Besides, he wasn't sure everything *would* be all right. What was it she had said to the woman, Jane? *"I'll be as careful as I can be and still do what has to be done. It's the only way Jimmy and I will ever be safe. Believe me, Jane. He won't give up."*

Who was *he*? And what wouldn't he give up doing that threatened her and her son? And, more to the point, what was she planning to do to stop him?

Peter knew something else about Margaret Ann: she wasn't going to offer him accurate information. There was another way he might get it, though. It was a long shot, but at least whatever he learned would be the truth.

Shoving the wallet back into the knapsack, Peter turned out the lights, closed the sleeper curtain and climbed out of the truck. Locking both doors, he walked between the rows of parked tractor-trailers toward the small brick building that housed the noncommercial rest area's bath facilities. On the outside wall was a phone, and as he picked up the receiver, he glanced at his watch, grimacing when he saw it was three o'clock—five o'clock back East. His brother would not appreciate this.

The phone rang six times before a groggy male voice answered. "'Lo?"

"Nick, it's me." Peter waited a few seconds, listening to the muffled sounds and grumbles of a man roused from a deep sleep.

"Peter? 'S going on? Something wrong?"

"No, nothing's wrong. I'm sorry to wake you up." He hesitated, carefully choosing his words. "I, uh, need some information."

Nicholas's reply was quiet but fairly alert. "You're sure you're okay?"

"I'm fine. Really. But I've got this urgent need to catch up on the local news."

There was a long pause.

"The news. You mean, like, how are Mom and Dad and the rest of us?"

"No," Peter said slowly. "I mean the news, as in the *Morning Sun* and channels 13, 2 and 11 at six o'clock."

"And you say this is urgent."

"Right."

"Are you drunk?"

"I swear, I'm cold sober."

"You called me at five in the morning to—"

"Nick, I really need your help."

"Why?"

"Never mind why," Peter muttered. "Trust me. Please."

Another interminable silence ensued. If Nick demanded to know what was behind this bizarre request, Peter knew he'd have to hang up. Given who his brother was, given who he himself had been, he could not tell Nick anything without landing Margaret Ann exactly where she didn't want to be. He had counted on his brother's indestructible faith in him to carry them through this conversation, but maybe that wouldn't be enough. Maybe...

"The Orioles lost yesterday."

Peter closed his eyes and began breathing again. Then, smiling, he replied, "You can forget the sports and weather. Truckers talk baseball to death over the CB, and I lived in Baltimore long enough to know that, right now, the air conditioners are working overtime."

"I don't suppose you want to hear the arts and entertainment tidbits, either," Nick grumbled.

"Some other time."

"For God's sake, Peter—" He cut himself off, then sighed in resignation. "Okay. How far back are we talking here?"

"A couple of weeks. The headlines will do."

"Headlines. Well, we picked up Len Vincent last week."

It wasn't what Peter wanted to hear, but it was good news. "So, Vinny finally slipped up," he said. "Are you going to be able to make the charges stick this time?"

"Lord, I hope so. He's already wrangled himself out of a couple of them on technicalities. The boys handling the arrest got impatient and jumped the gun."

"That's too bad. What else is happening?"

Nicholas's tone was mildly disgusted. "All the headaches Vinny has given me, you *could* be a little more sympathetic. No. Wait. I get the picture. Let's see. There was a robbery at a savings and loan on Calvert Street, day before yesterday. A teller was injured. They've arrested one suspect but are still looking for a second one."

"Hmm."

"The residents of Woodland won their battle to keep Tighe Developers from tearing up the Langston estate for an in-town shopping mall."

"That's nice."

"More?"

"If you don't mind."

"You know, you've got a helluva nerve playing hard to please."

"Humor me, will you?"

"You want to be humored? All right, here's one for you. Your old friend Larry Silver is in the hospital."

Peter snorted at the mention of the name. Silver was a real-estate broker who, for the past five years, had been a member of the Baltimore City Council; he was outgoing and quick-witted, and people loved him. Personally, Peter had always felt Silver was a slick operator without a sincere bone in his body. No evidence of his involvement in any illegal activities had ever surfaced, but it wouldn't have surprised Peter to discover Silver was as corrupt a city official as Baltimore had ever seen—which, unfortunately, as everyone knew, was saying a lot.

Peter's tone was sarcastic as he responded to the news his brother had delivered. "Gee, I'm really sorry to hear the poor guy's feeling bad. I don't suppose it's serious."

"If what he says is true," Nick replied, "it could have been fatal. He claims his ex-wife tried to murder him."

Stunned, Peter was temporarily distracted from his goal. "Murder? Now, this is getting interesting."

Nick chuckled softly. "Yeah, and it gets better. Seems she threatened him with a gun, beat him up—karate and the whole bit. Broke some ribs, shattered a knee. I don't know what else. Can you believe it? I don't like the guy any more than you do, but let's be honest. He's no wimp. Either he's stretching the truth, or the lady is really something else."

"I hope she gets off easy," Peter muttered. "Having to live with Silver ought to buy her a plea of temporary insanity."

"I doubt it. He's pressing charges for assault with intent to murder and battery. And there's a third charge for kidnapping. She took off with their six-year-old son. Silver has custody of the boy.''

The boy. All at once the pieces fell into place, and a sick feeling of dread came over Peter. He thought about the woman sleeping in his truck, and it seemed impossible: Margaret Ann Miller married to Larry Silver? Then he remembered newspaper articles—society-page happenings and the like—where the names Larry and Marge Silver had appeared together. He remembered watching Margaret Ann flatten a man more than twice her size. Most of all, he remembered the fear and desperation on her face, later the same night, when the state troopers had been parked nearby. And suddenly it didn't seem impossible at all.

It took everything he had to keep his voice casual. ''You said she was his *ex*-wife?''

''They were divorced, I guess, a little less than a year ago,'' Nick replied, ''and it was one of the nastiest cases I've ever seen. The paper and TV news carried a blow-by-blow. He smeared her to hell and back again.''

''Why?''

''To keep the kid, apparently.''

''Bull. If Silver's the devoted-father type, I'll *walk* my next payload to the West Coast.''

Nick's comment was dry. ''You'd think he invented the role, to hear him talk. He's been making these heartfelt pleas during news interviews for her to bring little Jimmy back to him. But so far, there hasn't been anything about her responding. Nobody's seen her or knows where—''

Nick broke off, and a long, charged silence elapsed before he finished slowly. ''...where she is. Hey, Peter. About this, uh, private news briefing we're having. The one you don't want to explain. You haven't, by any chance—''

"Look," Peter cut in. "I've got to go. And I've kept you up long enough."

"Peter, if you've seen—"

Don't ask. Please, don't ask.

Aloud, Peter said calmly, "Nick, listen. It's almost three-thirty in the morning here. I've had a rough day, couldn't sleep and felt like hearing your voice. It's happened before, remember? So I called and we talked about impersonal things—nothing that means anything to either of us. That's it. Now go back to sleep."

Peter knew there were 1001 questions Nick wanted to ask. He heard anger and impatience in his brother's voice as he started half a dozen times to speak, only to cut himself off. Finally, he bit out a short statement that managed to convey all the questions.

"Do me one favor. Don't borrow trouble. You've had enough of your own."

"Yeah," Peter returned quietly. "I seem to recall one or two minor incidents."

"You might also recall that Silver would love to see you fry. For good, this time."

Peter's eyes narrowed. The professional dislike he had always felt toward Larry Silver had suddenly become a personal intense loathing. "Believe me, Nick," he said, "the feeling is mutual. But don't worry. If I find out I've got more than I can handle, I'll share it with you."

Nick's reply was more than a little irritated. "Thanks. That's real reassuring."

By the time Peter returned to his truck, he had decided what to do. He grabbed Margaret Ann's backpack and the clothes he had taken off her and stowed them in the outside luggage compartment. Then he made himself a cup of strong coffee and drank it while the diesel engine warmed up. When he was ready to roll, he zipped the safety net that would protect his sleeping passenger and closed both the slanted vista window curtain and the one covering the doorway to the cab, assuring that no light would leak into the sleeper compartment. At 4:00 a.m. the big truck rolled onto the interstate. And Peter settled in for what he knew would be the longest, hardest haul of his short trucking career.

Chapter Four

She'd been had. Margaret Ann realized it the instant she awoke. The truck was in motion; the muted drone of a diesel engine rumbled in her ears. Her effort to bolt out of bed was aborted by a mesh screen, which did not, however, hide the fact that her backpack was missing or that the dirty clothes she'd had on last night were nowhere in sight. Even her shoes were gone. She was all but naked, caged in the back of a moving tractor-trailer, headed to who knows where.

Her insides trembled as she struggled with the zipper on the safety net and fought her way off the bunk, wincing when her sore feet touched the carpet. She was panic-stricken. That wasn't anything new, but coming as suddenly as it did, like a comet ripping through her dreams, made it harder to get under control.

And control it she must, or she'd disintegrate. The best way she knew to defend herself—rather, the only way she could still manage—was to attack first. Defiance was the most effective weapon she possessed against the overwhelming fear inside her. Thus, preparing for battle, she dragged the sheet with her to wrap around her body, then reached for the divider curtain, tearing it off in a blast of popping snaps.

The sunshine pouring through the cab windows was blinding. With one hand up to shade her eyes and the other clutching the ends of the sheet behind her back, Margaret Ann ducked her head through the doorway and glared at her abductor.

"All right, Charlie. What do you think you're doing?"

He glanced over his shoulder, took in her appearance over the top of the his mirrored sunglasses and turned back to the road. "Well, good afternoon to you, too, Wonder Woman. Nice day we're having, isn't it? Just look at that view! These mountains always get to me."

Margaret Ann's voice was brittle. "Don't be cute. I asked what you're doing!"

One bronzed shoulder, bared by a sleeveless T-shirt, rose in a careless shrug. "Last time I looked, I was driving this rig."

"Yeah, but why am I still in it?"

"You were asleep."

"Why didn't you wake me up?"

"You needed the rest."

"What I *need* is to get out of here!"

"That wasn't the tune you were singing last night."

Margaret Ann bit off another retort, knowing this terrible fear that she was trapped made no sense. She had accepted the man's help the night before. He had shown her nothing but gentle concern. And as fanatical as he was about his schedule, it wasn't surprising he had taken off that morning at the appointed hour. Still, something inside her clung to the belief that, right now, trusting him, trusting *anyone*, was the last thing she should do. The worst mistake of her life had been trusting the wrong man. For all she knew, she could be on her way to a police station.

When the panic threatened to swamp her, Margaret Ann again fought to curb it. Leaning against the padded doorway to keep her balance, she pressed her fingers to the bridge of her nose and tried to speak in a normal tone.

"Where are my things?"

He hesitated a split second. "In the luggage compartment."

She looked around at the various shelves and closets. "All right. I give. Where is it?"

"Under your feet. The door's on the outside of the tractor."

"Outside! Well, darn it, stop this thing!"

"No."

Margaret Ann blinked. "What do you mean, 'no'? I want my stuff!"

"Why?"

"Why do you think? So I can get dressed and get out of here."

"And go where?"

"That's none of your business."

"It would have been my business tonight when you showed up in Idaho."

Margaret Ann blanched but couldn't reply. He knew that *she* knew where he intended to stop that night and that she intended to be there.

"Your things are safe," Peter went on. "The luggage compartment is locked, and if anyone tried to open it without a key, there'd be enough alarms blasting to wake the dead. Before I unlock it, though, we're going to have a talk.''

''I've got nothing to say to you. I just want my stuff.''

''But *I've* got something to say. And you're going to listen. Then, if you still want to leave, we'll see about getting your things.''

''We'll see about it right now!'' she insisted.

Slowly, deliberately, he reached up and removed his dark glasses. Just as deliberately, he turned, and for a moment his gaze locked with hers.

''No, *Margaret Ann*, we won't.''

He knew her name. But how? With her heart pounding, Margaret Ann tried to read the answer in his eyes. They were startlingly beautiful eyes, the very palest shade of brown faceted with gold, but they told her nothing. Yet, at the same time, she had the sense that they were capable of seeing everything she sought to hide.

Seemingly satisfied with her reaction, Peter replaced his shades. Shifting his attention to the road once more, he said, ''Why don't you find something to put on, fix yourself something to eat, then come have a seat.''

Of all the arrogant, audacious... A dozen different names she could call him came to mind, but before she got a chance to say any of them, Peter cleared his throat.

''I'd put that curtain back up, too, if I were you. Unless you want to cause an accident. The guy in that truck beside us is more interested in your attributes than he is in his driving.''

Confused, Margaret Ann frowned.

''Your sheet is slipping,'' Peter explained with a hint of amusement.

Snatching the sheet higher, she cast a mortified glance out the window to see the driver of the green tractor rig on their left giving her a thumbs-up sign in his side-view mirror.

She gasped, then hastily tacked the curtain back in place just as her admirer sent his greetings with a friendly blast of his air horn. But it was the sound of Peter's low chuckle that burned her ears as she hunched uncomfortably inside the sheet and fumed.

The fuming didn't last long, though, as she once more faced the predicament she was in. Wilting onto the bunk, Margaret Ann realized she might as well do as Peter had suggested—get dressed and find something to eat. What choice did she have?

Right on cue, he called, "There's a pair of cutoffs and a pile of T-shirts in the locker under the bed. Look around and you'll find running water, electricity and the bathroom. Help yourself to whatever's in the fridge and on the shelf under it. And while you're at it, fix me something, too, will you? I didn't stop for lunch."

Margaret Ann stared at the curtain, her jaw hanging open in disbelief. Then her eyes narrowed and, with mutters of outrage, she flung the sheet to the bed and started rooting for the clothes.

The T-shirts were miles too big. She picked out a bright blue one that covered the ragged hem of the cutoffs, which proved nearly tight enough in the hips to be uncomfortable. When she turned to the compact refrigerator, tucked neatly on a shelf over the closet, her pride fought a brief battle with her growling stomach. Pride lost. She was starving. Besides, after last night, how could she have any pride left? Peter Lericos, she was ashamed to recall, had seen about all there was to see of her, in more ways than one.

How much did he know, and how had he found out? Those questions occupied her thoughts as she made and ate a peanut butter and jelly sandwich. She'd have to be careful. If he knew only her name and nothing else, she didn't want to give herself away out of panic.

Wondering how much Peter knew about her led Margaret Ann to thinking about how little she knew about him. What sort of truck driver was he, anyway, with his cranberry juice in the fridge, the Bach organ music blaring away in the tape deck, and a copy of *The Sot-Weed Factor* on the enclosed bookshelf over the head of the bed? John Barth was hardly light reading, but there he was, along with Tom Wolfe, E. E. Cummings and a rare host of others. There wasn't a paperback Western in sight. Everything that *was* in sight was meticulously in its place. Margaret Ann had no idea how the average trucker kept his home away from home, but she doubted most were this fastidious.

But then, she already knew that Peter Lericos was neither an average trucker nor an average human being. Few people would have done for her what he had done. But why had he done it?

It was always smart to assume the worst; that was one of the lessons the past seven years had taught her. She wasn't suspicious by nature and hated what having to be did to her. She hated feeling isolated, cut off from the others who might have been friends. But this was hardly the time to be tossing caution to the wind and trusting blindly that a man she didn't know at all was on her side, only because he had given her a place to sleep. And yet...

And yet there was something about this man—something in his eyes that looked like wisdom, an awareness of things beyond her own experience, something that made her want to trust him. And that scared her.

It shamed her, too. He had taken her in and given her his bed. In return, she had been rude. Her guilt, as well as her ingrained good manners, made her remember his request for something to eat. But she didn't have to trust him with the story of her life in order to fix him a sandwich, did she?

No, but her tone was still grudging and wary as she called, "I'm making peanut butter and jelly."

"Is that my only choice?"

"Jelly and peanut butter."

"Oh. Well, then make it peanut butter and jelly."

A reluctant smile tugged at her lips. "You like it on bread, right?"

"Wrong. But I don't like it on anything else, either, so..."

The smile got the better of her. "Why buy it if you don't like it?"

"I don't know, but somehow, until I added a jar of peanut butter to it, the cupboard looked bare. I guess a house just isn't home with peanut butter."

"That's weird, Charlie."

"Probably. But since I have to buy the stuff, I figure I have to eat it."

"That's even weirder. And these eight jars of jelly are the weirdest thing yet."

"Naw, you've got to have them. Can't eat breakfast or midnight snacks without jelly."

"I hate to ask. Which one goes with peanut butter?"

"Nothing goes with peanut butter, but right now I'd eat it with pickle relish."

"Are you telling me to hurry up?"

"You're catching on."

"I suppose you want something to drink, too."

"Milk. Can't swallow peanut butter without it."

"Charlie, are you going to complain your way through this sandwich, because if you are, I—"

"Just get the damned thing up here, will you?"

"Yes, *sir!*"

"All *right!*"

There was something close to a grin on Margaret Ann's face as she finished making the sandwich, then stuck a straw into a carton of cold milk.

The grin disappeared, though, as her gaze fell upon the bed, where she had slept. The pillowcase, with its telltale stain of dye, had to go—unless she wanted her meager disguise to be in ruins. She searched until she found clean sheets, stripped the bed and remade it. Then, turning the stained pillowcase inside out and wrapping it in the sheets, she stuffed the bundle into a laundry bag she found. With luck, the dye would come out in Peter's wash without his being any the wiser.

With a peanut butter and jelly sandwich on a paper plate in one hand, a carton of milk in the other, and her trumped-up surly attitude in place Margaret Ann maneuvered her way to the front of the cab. The plate slid to a stop on the flat part of the console where she dumped it. The milk came dangerously close to sloshing onto the carpet before she wiggled the square carton into the round cup holder. She herself dropped into the passenger seat, gingerly planting her bare feet on the console in front of her and crossed her arms in a classic pose of unwillingness to communicate.

Peter took note of her posture, then lifted his glasses briefly to eye his sandwich. "Mint jelly, huh?"

"You don't like it—tough. I'm not making another one."

"I don't want another one. I like mint jelly." He reached to turn off the tape deck, picked up the sandwich and took a bite. "In fact, I love mint jelly. But how did you know?"

"A lucky guess."

"Out of seven other choices, any one of which would have suited most people better? Come on."

Margaret Ann considered. "Mint jelly is cool. Cool, like sophisticated, not like cold. It's not stuffy, like caviar or liver pâté, but not syrupy or boring, either, like grape jelly or strawberry jam. Mint jelly gets away with being jelly, but it isn't, really. It's a surprise. Something different, something that looks like but isn't quite what it's expected to be. Satisfied?"

He took another bite. "You think I'm cool, but not cold."

"Can we get on with—"

"And I'm not stuffy, syrupy or boring."

"What is this? I feel like I should be looking at ink blots."

"And I look like—but am not quite—what I'm expected to be."

"I swear, Charlie, if you don't cut it out, I'm going to scream."

"No, you're not." He exchanged the sandwich for the milk, took a couple of swallows and set the carton down. When he spoke again, his tone was quiet and sober. "Margaret Ann, if you were going to scream, you'd have done it by now. This conversation isn't about jelly. It's about how good you are at judging a person and a situation. I was worried about that." He laughed. "But not anymore."

He had done it to her again—left her staring and speechless. But then, as she thought about it, he had sounded a little shaken himself. How close to home had she hit with her careless assessment?

There were more important questions, though.

"Why would you be worried about me?" she asked. "I'm not your problem. At least, I wouldn't be if you'd stop and let me out. And if you don't want me in your truck tonight—''

"You must be dying to know how I found out your name."

The statement stopped her dead in her tracks. How did he do it? Throw a person for a loop and make them land just where he wanted them?

"You're obviously dying to tell me," she muttered through clenched teeth.

"When you emptied your wallet, you forgot one ID."

That news brought a small measure of relief, but her tone didn't reflect it. "So you know my name. So what? I know yours, too. That doesn't mean you've got the right—''

"I also know your address and that you're running from the police. But the most important thing I know, is that you're going to get caught if you keep doing things the way you've been doing them."

"I—I don't know what you're talking about. I'm not—''

"Margaret Ann." He cut her short on a note of reproach. "You sound like the nun I had in second grade. Once I asked her if nuns and priests were allowed to like each other, because I'd seen Father Mulligan with his arm around her. And I couldn't think of another reason a nun and a priest ought to be in a clinch. She told me she'd fallen and he was helping her up. Six months later she left the convent, he left the priesthood, and they got married. She tried to make me think that what I knew to be true wasn't. And for a while, when I was seven, it worked. But I guarantee you, at thirty-eight, there's not a chance it's going to work again. We both know the score. Let's not insult each other by pretending otherwise.''

With her eyes glued on the road ahead, Margaret Ann swallowed hard. She tried to think of something to say that would convince him things weren't as he had so accurately guessed, but she couldn't. Her thoughts were too scattered; she couldn't fabricate another lie fast enough. The crazy part was, she realized, she wanted to tell Peter Lericos the truth. The desire to do so was growing with frightening speed. But it wasn't only her own life she was gambling with here; it was also her son's. She could ill afford to give in to an irrational impulse. Besides, it was only a fantasy; she would never be able to tell anyone what had really happened—not all of it.

Nevertheless Peter had forced her into a corner from which there appeared to be no escape. In a whisper, she asked, "What do you want from me?"

"I don't want anything from you," he returned. "I want to give you something. Something that might make the difference in your getting out of this mess you're in."

She cast a puzzled look in his direction.

Peter caught the look and read it correctly. "A safe place to stay," he said simply. "You're exhausted. Even if you could get your shoes on, you'd never be able to walk. And given the condition you were in last night, I'd say it's a good bet you had a close call with the police. If they're looking for you, the last place you ought to be is thumbing rides on the interstate."

Margaret Ann chewed on her bottom lip. It was true, last night's fiasco had not been part of her plan; it meant the police now had a current description of her. And that meant Peter was right: the interstate was no longer safe. But what place was?

"Why are you doing this?" she asked. "You don't know me. I haven't done anything but make you lose sleep."

Peter guided the rig around a wide curve, waiting until the road straightened out before asking, "What will happen if the police catch you?"

When he looked at her, she suspected he saw the truth. When he sighed and looked away, she knew he had.

"Pay close attention," he began. "What I'm going to say is very important. The facts are that you haven't told me anything. I've made guesses that you haven't confirmed. You haven't asked me to help you. We met on the road three days ago. It looked to me from the beginning as though you could use some help, and I'm offering it to you now in the form of a ride and a place to sleep. You can take it or leave it."

Margaret Ann understood immediately. He was saying that if she was caught, he could not be charged with harboring a fugitive from justice. She couldn't blame him for being careful, yet his cool calculations about the impulsive act of helping a criminal escape the law were a little startling.

"What happens— What if I don't want your help?" she asked.

"I get off at the next exit and let you out."

"That simple?"

"That simple."

She shook her head, puzzled. "Then why didn't you wake me up this morning to tell me all this? Why hide my things and take off like you did?"

She could see he was exercising caution in his response. Finally, he answered with another question.

"Did you happen to notice whether anyone saw you climb into this truck last night?"

Margaret Ann's eyes widened. Lord, he was more paranoid than she was!

"I understand," she answered slowly. As another thought occurred to her, she frowned. "What time did you start driving?"

"Four o'clock."

"You didn't sleep at all?"

"You worried I'm going to pass out at the wheel?"

"No, but—" She glanced out the window at the sunshine pouring down on the mountain peaks and casting shadows deep in the gorges below them. She had never seen more beautiful country, but at the moment, her interest in the scenic splendor of the Rockies was nil. Looking at the digital clock on the radio, she saw it was already two-thirty. "Where are we? We must be pretty far from, uh . . . well, couldn't you stop for a while to sleep?"

He shook his head. "I'm all right. And if you want to stay with me, we'll drive straight through."

"All the way to—" She broke off.

"To Seattle? No, I won't get that far. But, my quiet little sneak—" he glanced at her "—we both know that's where I'm heading, don't we?"

Margaret Ann had the decency to blush, and Peter's mouth sloped into a grin. It was the first really overt expression of emotion she'd spotted in him, and it was a shocker. Hands down, he had the sexiest grin she'd ever seen—gorgeous white teeth set off against a piratical black beard. She knew she was staring, and her blush deepened, but the import of his next words did not escape her.

"We'll stay at a motel tonight," he continued. "After this drive, I'm going to need some time out of the truck. In the morning, I'll unload in Seattle, then drop down to Portland to pick up a load that's headed for Kansas City. From there, it's Saint Louis, then back east to Harrisburg, Pennsylvania, then all the way south to Mobile. After that, I'll be in the South and Southwest mostly, until the end of September. In case it isn't obvious, I don't sit still for long. I push myself pretty hard—too hard, probably—but there's something to be said for it. The faster you move on, the fewer people there are who know you've ever been there."

It was perfect, and Margaret Ann knew it would be idiotic to turn down this offer. But she had to know why he was making it. What did he expect from her in return?

There was one possibility, but she dearly hoped she was wrong; she did so want him to be different. Different from the man she was running from, who never gave anything to anybody without strings attached.

"What if I say yes? What do you want from me?"

They were coming to the top of a long uphill grade. Peter glanced in his side-view mirrors as he set the gears to begin downhill. Margaret Ann watched the muscles in his bare arm ripple, and when she lifted her gaze she found him watching her.

His words were quiet and easy and tender enough to make her want to cry. "I told you, Margaret Ann. I don't want anything from you. I don't want the seven hundred dollars you've got in your wallet, and, as much as I regret having to say it, I'm not going to ask you to sleep with me, either. The idea has crossed my mind, and I'm sure it will again. But let's face it, the last thing you need is a lover."

Margaret Ann didn't know whether to be relieved, flattered, insulted or what. She told herself she absolutely was not disappointed. Clearing her throat, she croaked, "Are you always this . . . honest?"

"You wanted to know if I expected you to have sex with me, didn't you?"

"Well . . ."

"Didn't you?"

"Yes."

"So now you know."

"But I still don't know why you should care what happens to me."

He didn't answer right away. In fact, so many minutes passed that Margaret Ann began to think he wasn't going to say anything. Then, as they reached the bottom of one grade and began the long climb up the next, he asked her a question that brought her gaze back to his face in a hurry.

"Have you ever been in prison?"

Something in his tone made her hesitate and search his hard profile, this time, taking serious note of the silver strands that marred the perfection of his black hair and beard. What was it she had thought about him? *Something in his eyes that looked like wisdom, an awareness of things beyond her own experience.* In an instant of stunning clarity, she understood.

"No, I haven't. But you have, haven't you?"

He nodded. "I spent two years in a state correctional facility, and I assure you, it's not the sort of experience you can chalk up as one of life's interesting detours. You don't learn anything from it worth learning. Not a day goes by that doesn't eat away at whatever integrity and self-esteem you've got left. It doesn't matter whether or not you actually committed the crime you've been sentenced for—your whole environment reinforces the idea that you're a bad person, and after a while, you start to believe it." He paused for a moment, a muscle in his cheek flexing. "I don't want you to go through that, Margaret Ann. If there's a way out of the mess you're in, I'd like to give you the chance to find it."

There it was. She had all the answers she needed. Anything else she might ask—why he'd gone to jail, for instance—would only be to satisfy her curiosity. Unfortunately, her inquisitive impulses had always been strong.

With her eyes narrowed in speculation, Margaret Ann asked, "How can you be so sure I don't deserve to go to jail?"

Peter frowned, but after a moment his mouth twitched into a smile. "Think of it like mint jelly. I just know."

Wouldn't it be wonderful, she mused, if all of life were so simple? She could be a murderer, but for some reason, Peter Lericos's intuition had decreed she should not be punished. If, indeed, he was telling the truth. It did occur to her that this whole thing could be an elaborate trap.

The next instant, though, she had to dismiss the notion. It *was* like mint jelly. As easily as he had passed judgment on her and found her innocent, she could look at him and known that he wasn't going to hurt her. She had known it that first night.

She sighed. "All right. I guess I can hang around maybe for a day or two, until my feet are better. But, Charlie, there's one thing."

"What's that, Wonder Woman?"

"Do you ever stop to eat—like in a restaurant?"

"Not if I can help it."

"Then, we've got to stop at a grocery store."

"You one of those people who gets picky about their brand of peanut butter?"

"No. I'm one of those people who absolutely cannot handle canned stew, Cheez Whiz or SpaghettiOs for breakfast."

Chapter Five

I t'll do."

Peter's pronouncement about the dingy motel room they had entered filled Margaret Ann with dismay—no more so, however, than had her first sight of the hostel when they'd pulled into the parking lot. With its peeling paint, battered doors and two rusty trash cans flanking the single row of rooms, it had not looked promising. It was the kind of out-of-the-way place where things could go on you'd rather not hear about. It was the kind of place where each room boasted one double bed—and little else. It was the kind of place where no one inquired about anyone else's business. Margaret Ann understood exactly why Peter had chosen it, but that didn't make her any more comfortable.

She watched him as he dumped his canvas bag and her knapsack on the scratched dresser, then tore off his T-shirt and pried off his running shoes.

"There's shampoo and soap in my bag. You're welcome to use them. I'll shower in the morning." He stopped, hands at his belt buckle, to stare at the saggy double bed. An instant later he pulled the belt from the loops in his jeans and added, "I'm going right to sleep."

It was a wonder to Margaret Ann that he was still able to walk. He had to be exhausted.

"Do you need anything?" He turned, his eyes making a rapid trip over her as she stood stiffly by the closed door.

Margaret Ann shook her head nervously.

"Still hungry?" He took a step toward her.

She inched backward, trying to pretend being in a bedroom with him was the most natural thing in the world, and wondering why the intimate confines of his truck hadn't seemed as...intimate. "I-I'm fine," she stammered.

He gave her one of his penetrating looks, as though to say he wasn't fooled, before turning to empty his pockets onto the dresser. Loose change clattered along with his keys and wallet.

"The keys to the truck are here," he told her, "in case you want anything out of it. But wait until dark if you decide to go out. Okay?"

"I don't need anything." She wrung her fingers, then lifted one hand to swipe the hair back from her face. "But, uh, if I do, I'll wait. I promise."

He didn't seem worried. With a brief smile in her direction, he walked over and sank onto the edge of the bed. For a moment he rested an elbow on his knee while he rubbed his face. Then, taking one of the pillows from beneath the spread, he punched it several times before falling onto his back and slowly lifting his long legs onto the bed. Crossing his arms above his head, he let out a sigh. His eyes closed, and Margaret Ann guessed it wasn't more than a minute before the steady sound of his breathing indicated he was asleep.

What on earth had she done to earn such trust?

He had dismantled his precious schedule for her, driven miles out of the way to find this godforsaken motel where she could be safe for the night, had even given in to her cries of starvation to stop and buy them both fried chicken and salad for dinner. All afternoon, though they had spoken little, he had been patient and kind. She wished, just once, he would get angry, snap at her, for it was becoming impossible to maintain her churlish armor in the face of his relentless compassion.

She looked at the man lying on the bed with both awe and foreboding, acknowledging something she had been trying to ignore. She liked him. She liked him too much. It was also true that the sight of his indecently sexy body caused warm, melty feelings inside her that were both shocking and unwanted. Shocking because she had thought her interest in males had been permanently crushed. Unwanted because, of all the times she could have picked to discover her sexual response was still functional, this had to be the worst.

Tearing her gaze away from what she could not have and probably should run from, Margaret Ann eyed the canvas bag on the dresser.

Shampoo, he had said. Heaven knows, she needed it. But did she dare use it?

She had done nothing to earn Peter's trust, though he had done a great deal to earn hers. It was a small step on her part, one she would have to take anyway, sooner or later. She studied the bag a moment longer before walking to the dresser. Then, locating the shampoo, she gave Peter a last measuring look and headed for the shower.

* * *

Peter awoke slowly and without alarm. Rolling to lower his feet to the floor, he absently scratched his chest and yawned. Half-asleep, he found his way to the bathroom. When he returned, he shucked his jeans, leaned over and pulled the bed covers down, stopping short when he realized something—or, rather, someone—was missing.

His eyes found her in the darkness. She was scrunched up in the saggy armchair beside the bed, staring at him.

"There you are." He put a knee on the mattress, stretched across it and snagged her wrist in his hand. "Come to bed, Margaret Ann," he said, tugging her toward him as he lay down.

She tried to pull away, and he heard her say something about the chair being comfortable, but he didn't let go of her. Sooner or later they would have to deal with sleeping in the truck, where the bed was even smaller than this one. Besides, he wanted her next to him.

"Shh," he said, when he had succeeded in drawing her from her nest. "Quiet, now. Don't want to listen to you moaning tomorrow 'bout the stiff neck you got sleeping in that chair. Lie down here."

She was babbling on about letting her go, but he heard her breath catch in her throat when he tucked an arm around her waist, bent his bare leg against her bare thigh and drew her back flush against him. It felt good. She was small and soft and smelled of his shampoo. She was also trembling like a leaf. In his sleepy-haze state, which he was loathe to give up, he gently stroked her hair as his voice rumbled in the darkness. "It's all right, baby. Close your pretty eyes and go to sleep.... Mmm.... Just go to sleep. I'm right here...."

Peter hung on the edge of sleep, murmuring half sentences and unintelligible sounds until he felt her trembling stop. Then, with a sigh, he drifted into contented oblivion.

Margaret Ann, however, was wide awake. The panic that had wracked her a moment ago, when Peter had pulled her into bed, was gone. And she had fought off tears evoked by his incredible tenderness. But she lay for a long while, thinking how strange it was that she should feel so at home lying with a man she had met only four days ago. Sad that it had never felt like this, lying with the man to whom she had been married for six years.

Red. Not copper or chestnut or strawberry blond but a pure breathtaking red. Peter blinked in bewilderment at the sight that greeted him when he opened his eyes, and when his vision cleared a little, he saw that the wild profusion of bright curls that lay on the pillow beside him was actually an extraordinary combination of colors ranging from the whitest gold to the darkest auburn. The result, though, was red, and he was enchanted.

His enchantment deepened when Margaret Ann stirred in his arms, stiffened in awareness, then jerked around to face him. And the puzzle came together. The freckles and the peachy skin, the blue eyes, the pale lashes and brows—all of it made perfect sense.

"Perfect," he whispered, and he reached up to catch a curl that had caught in his beard, rubbing it as though he were fingering silk. Her full lips parted, and his gaze dropped to them as he tried to remember when the last time was he had awakened like this. Warm and mellow and hungry for the woman beside him.

Then his eyes rose to meet hers, and he saw two things: desire—not a burning passion, but a curious yearning that flickered on the surface of her sapphire gaze—and beneath that, fear. Not the immediate, desperate thing he had seen that first night, but something deeply rooted and ready to flare up if he made the wrong move.

Dropping the hair he had wrapped around his finger, Peter smiled, "Good morning. Or maybe I ought to make that, 'How do you do?' I have the strangest feeling I've just met the real Margaret Ann Miller."

"Don't jump to any conclusions, Charlie." She squirmed backward, putting some space between them, and frowned.

Peter grinned. "You mean there's more? Is that gorgeous red stuff out of a bottle, too?"

At her indignant look, he chuckled.

"No, this isn't out of a bottle, too. But there are disguises . . . and then there are disguises."

"Ha! Are you going to let me in on the rest or keep me guessing?"

Her eyes narrowed thoughtfully. "I think I'll keep you guessing. It'll even the score. You guess what there is about me that's not what it's supposed to be, and I'll go on wondering why you're hiding under all this hair." Reaching out, she tugged on his beard.

"Ow!"

"Why do you wear it, anyway?" she persisted. "Are you ugly or something underneath it?"

"I don't like shaving. And, no, I'm not ugly."

Margaret Ann's next question was not so easy, and she asked it with her eyes riveted to his.

"Why were you in jail?"

Peter hesitated only an instant. "I was convicted of murdering my wife."

He never lied about his past, and he couldn't lie to Margaret Ann, but the instant the words were spoken he wished he could take them back. Her reaction was immediate and, at first, exactly what he had expected. Her face drained of color, and her eyes registered shock. Next, he figured, she would start talking about how much better her feet were and how she had to be getting along now. He steeled himself against the blow.

But then she said the most amazing thing, something that no one else—not a living soul outside of his family—had said to him. And Peter knew the moment the words left her mouth that he was lost.

"That's the craziest thing I've ever heard. How could anyone have been stupid enough to believe it?"

It was several moments before he trusted himself to speak. When was the last time anyone had offered him such perfect innocent faith? Had anyone ever? His first reaction, as he stared into Margaret Ann's deep blue eyes, was to feel he didn't deserve it. The next was to wonder if he actually might cry. The next was to realize that he could easily fall in love with her.

When he spoke, his voice was strained. "It wasn't a matter of any one person believing it. The evidence presented to the jury appeared conclusive. They found me guilty."

She shook her head slowly, then frowned. "But you said you were only in jail for two years. How did you get out?"

He hesitated, waiting for her to realize who he was and that she already knew the answers to the questions she was asking. All it would have required was that she had heard or read the news. He had given her enough information, but, amazingly, she still wasn't making the connection.

Keeping his answers deliberately vague, he replied, "I was given a life sentence. But evidence was found that exonerated me. My conviction was overturned, and I was released."

They stared at each other a minute longer, Margaret Ann's eyes full of questions Peter knew she wanted to ask.

And for the first time since he had been arrested, he genuinely wanted to explain himself.

When she remained silent, however, he rolled away, disappointed yet aware he had to no right to be. Pushing himself off the bed, he spoke as he walked toward the bathroom.

"Let's get going. It's late, and I want to be out of Seattle by noon."

Chapter Six

Back on schedule, they were heading south toward Portland by eleven forty-five. Margaret Ann was glad to be traveling again; hiding in the sleeper while Peter stripped freight from the trailer onto the warehouse loading dock in Seattle had made her feel too much the fugitive. He hadn't told her to stay out of sight, but it was part of their unspoken agreement that she would do so. Riding beside him now, on a sunny day, with the dense forests of the Northwest surrounding them, the summer-scented wind rushing through the open window and the notes of Copland's *Appalachian Spring* pouring from the tape deck, the last hellish days seemed unreal. As unreal as the notion that the strong arms in which she had slept last night belonged to a man who had been found guilty of murder.

For at least the dozenth time since they had left the motel, Margaret Ann cast a furtive glance in Peter's direction. Murder? This man? The one who ate peanut butter

only because it reminded him of home? Maybe she would
have believed it if he had said he'd gotten one too many
speeding tickets. But kill somebody? Kill his wife? Not a
chance.

Thoughts of Peter living through such an ordeal tor-
tured her. How had he felt? Angry couldn't begin to touch
it. What about the despair and helplessness he must have
suffered? Two years was a long time; it would have seemed
like eternity when he had thought it would go on until he
died. And, to have had to face the grief over his wife's
death, all the while fighting for his own life! The *bitterness* he must harbor toward the people who had done it to
him! In some ways, that would be the worst.

Margaret Ann knew about rage and despair and helplessness. And she knew about bitterness, too. She knew
what it was to sit in a courtroom and hear lies told about
her that she had no way to disprove. And, like Peter, she
had paid a terrible price because others had believed those
lies. She had lost her son. Granted, that was not the same
as going to prison, but it was another kind of nightmare,
one she had finally been unable to live with another day.

She was beginning to wonder if Peter identified with her
as strongly as she did with him. Was his willingness to help
her based on an affinity he felt with a victim of circumstance? But he had no way of knowing her circumstances.
Did he?

That thought worried her. But what disturbed her more
was that she hardly cared what he knew or didn't know.
Worse, if there were more scenes like last night's, she might
well end up crying on his shoulder and telling him everything, after all. That was the kind of person he was, the
kind of confidence he inspired in her.

Unfortunately, she knew another man who had the same
effect on people. For him, though, it was all an act. Every

grain of common sense and all her best instincts said that Peter's essential goodness was no act. He was so real, at times it took her breath away. Yet a part of her—the part that had been wounded by the other man—was afraid of being duped again by a man whose charisma drew her like a magnet and made her want to pour out her soul to him. It was a good thing, she concluded, that she had no real choice. For to confide in Peter totally could be disastrous—for her, for Jimmy, for Jane and for Peter, as well.

"You know, Margaret Ann, there's something I've noticed about redheads."

Peter's too-casual tone captured her attention, and she sighed, weary of the role she felt forced to play in this drama.

"What now, Charlie? Are you going to start philosophizing about my hair?"

Disregarding her comment, he continued. "Redheads never get away with anything. People see them once and remember them. Now, that hat of yours is pretty disreputable looking, but it does the job of hiding your hair."

They were turning onto a two-lane road that appeared to head into a small town. It must be time for a break, she concluded, turning in her seat to reach into the sleeper compartment for the black felt hat Jane had given her. "Now he doesn't like my hat," she muttered.

"And those jeans you've got on. They look like they belong to your big sister. How many times have you got them rolled up?"

"Forty-seven. Want to count?" Margaret Ann stuffed her untamed curls under the brim of her hat, which was every bit as disreputable as he had said it was.

"Are baggy jeans part of this superior disguise I'm not supposed to notice?"

She shot him a look and caught him grinning at her.

"It occurred to me the other night," he went on, "that your outer attire didn't exactly go with your silk and lace underthings, now, did it?"

Margaret Ann felt the heat rising in her face and looked away. "My, my, Charlie, you're getting smart," she said, then quickly turned the tables on him. "Are you smart enough to know it's lunchtime and that I haven't eaten since 6:00 a.m., when you bought those stale doughnuts?"

"They couldn't have been too bad—you ate three of them. For such a little squirt, you've got an awfully big appetite."

"Yeah, well, my appetite's not anywhere near as big as your head."

"And my head's not anywhere near as big as your mouth."

"My mouth's going to keep on running, too, if you don't feed me. And see if you can manage to find a place that's got a real bathroom."

They had, in fact, pulled into the parking lot of a small diner. There were a few cars in the spaces in front of the building and several trucks parked in the side lot. To Margaret Ann's surprise, Peter ignored the truck parking and maneuvered the rig around to the back of the low white building, bringing it to a halt five feet from the outside of rest room doors.

"Is that good enough for you?" he inquired.

She gave a cocky shrug. "Don't you think the owner might have something to say about your parking this monster *in*side the back door?"

"If he does, I'll sic you on him. Now, be a good girl while I'm gone, and try not to to chew up the upholstery."

"'Do this. Don't do that.' You should have been somebody's mother."

"Thank the Lord I'm not yours!" Peter exclaimed, jumping down out of the cab.

"My mother didn't complain."

"Yeah, but I think she gave up too soon."

"She died when I was fifteen."

He halted in the act of closing the door, and a strange piercing silence sprang up between them. Margaret Ann sat scowling, but her lower lip quivered when she found Peter watching her.

Such fierce tenderness—his eyes were on fire with it. It burned through her pitiful defenses and made her throat tighten. He climbed onto the step and stretched across the seat to capture her hand. And when he raised it to brush the backs of her fingers with a kiss, letting her feel the warmth of his lips and the softness of his beard, she nearly came apart.

"Your mother did a fine job, Margaret Ann," he said. "I can't believe any woman would be ashamed to call you her daughter."

A tear ran down her cheek, but she didn't care. Shaking her head, she whispered, "How can you say that? You don't even know me."

He looked down at her hand, his thumb tracing the delicate bones in her wrist. "I know you better than you think I do," he told her. "I know as much about you as you do about me. And the truth is, we know each other pretty well." His eyes rose to hers, and he smiled, a gentle, knowing smile. Then he let go of her hand and jumped down from the step, tossing her a wink before he closed the cab door.

Astonished, speechless and thoroughly confused, Margaret Ann gazed after Peter until his long strides took him around the front of the diner. She remained dazed until her eyes traveled to the corner of the small building and focused on the telephone booth.

Suddenly, all thoughts of Peter vanished and those she had been warding off about Jimmy came rushing in. It had been too long since she had talked to him, and it would be at least ten minutes before Peter returned. The phone was less than fifteen feet away. So close it was irresistible. If she kept her hat on and made it quick, probably no one would notice her.

Still, she cast anxious glances over her shoulder the entire time she was dialing the number and waiting for the operator to verify the collect call.

"Jimmy's asleep," Jane told her. "He and Mark were up at five this morning with me, feeding chickens, milking the cow, weeding the garden and generally carousing. They crashed an hour ago in front of the TV. Wait a sec', and I'll wake him up."

"No, don't." Margaret Ann swallowed her disappointment. "Leave him alone, Janey. I just wanted to know if he was okay."

"He's fine," her friend assured her. "But are you sure—"

"Positive. I've only got a few minutes, anyway."

"Where are— I mean, uh, are you all right?"

Margaret Ann squeezed her eyes closed. She hated it that Jane couldn't ask where she was.

"I'm doing pretty well. I'm riding with a trucker who's got this thing for ratty-looking women with blisters on their feet."

"A trucker?" Jane sounded appalled. "Margaret Ann, you haven't told him anything, have you? He doesn't know who you are?"

"Of course not," Margaret Ann replied. "But he knows I'm in some kind of trouble."

"And he's helping you?"

"He's a nice man, Jane. And he's got his reasons."

There was a brief silence.

"Margaret Ann, I know this is going to sound preachy, but are you sure about this? I mean, do you really think you need, well, you know, to get involved with somebody?"

"I'm not sleeping with him, Jane. I'm only riding in his truck. Look, I can't stay on the phone long. He'll be back in a minute. Tell me if there's been any news."

"I'll say there has." Jane's tone was both ominous and disgusted. "You made the front page of yesterday's morning paper. Your dear ex-husband is really pulling out all the stops. I heard him last evening on the six o'clock news."

"Jimmy didn't see it, did he?"

"No, I sent him and Mark upstairs. It was a quick piece, an interview. The jerk made this big emotional pitch, begging you to bring *his* little boy home. Said he'd do anything, let bygones be bygones and all that garbage."

"He's making it look good for his adoring fans," Margaret Ann muttered.

"Well, if I didn't know better, I'd have bought his line. He's one of the slickest talkers I've ever heard."

"Tell me something I don't know."

Jane hesitated, then spoke carefully. "He said he'd be willing to drop the charges if you came back with Jimmy."

"It's a lie," Margaret Ann declared with absolute certainty. Larry Silver wanted her dead—*needed* her dead. Ultimately, nothing less would do. And she was terrified that he had arrived at the same conclusion regarding their son.

"What are they saying about where I've gone?" she asked.

It gave her some satisfaction to hear that, apparently, her efforts to leave a false trail had worked. Jane said that news reports placed her everywhere from Pennsylvania to Montana. Her credit cards had been turned in by a fast-food restaurant employee in South Dakota, her driver's license by a motel manager in Wisconsin, though he had no record of having rented her a room. The Montana state police thought she had been seen in the area of state road 191 and Interstate 90; a trooper had identified her, and they doubted that a woman traveling a mountain highway on foot could have gotten very far. On the other hand, the trooper wasn't absolutely certain the woman he had thought was Marge Silver was, in fact, she. The best news was that a train station employee in Toledo remembered selling tickets—two of them—to a Margaret Ann Miller for a train bound for Florida.

Nobody was sure where she was or where she was going, yet there was evidence that she had been in half a dozen different places, and Margaret Ann was greatly relieved that she was on the way to achieving her goal. Which was, very simply, to disappear. Permanently.

With a promise to Jane to call again when she could, Margaret Ann hung up the phone, turning in time to see Peter rounding the corner of the restaurant, a large brown bag in his arm and a brawny, older man at his side.

Peter hesitated when he saw her. The stranger, who was talking a blue streak and waving his hands in emphatic gestures, kept on walking. Peter's eyes flickered to the phone, then returned to hers. He began walking again, and she tried to hurry back inside the tractor. But it was too late.

"I tell you, Pete, it's a helluva thing! For two bits, I'd toss it in and—" The man stopped short as he caught sight of Margaret Ann climbing into the truck. "Say, now." He slapped Peter's back companionably. "What's this? You sweet-talk some little lady into riding shotgun for you?"

Placing a hand on her arm, Peter stopped Margaret Ann when she was halfway into the cab. He helped her back out, and she tried not to look startled when his arm draped around her shoulders and tucked her close to his side.

"Walt, this is Maggie."

Maggie? Another name to add to her list? This one wasn't so bad, Margaret Ann decided, offering Peter's friend a nervous smile.

"Walt hauls for American Roads," Peter explained.

The man's barrel chest seemed to expand as he added, "Logs, mostly. Been at it thirty-five years."

"Hmm." Margaret Ann tried to sound interested. She didn't know whether or not she was supposed to speak— or if Peter was furious at having found her out of the truck. He might have expected her to use the rest room; he would not have expected her to stand by an outdoor phone in a public parking lot in broad daylight.

Still, he didn't sound angry. He didn't *feel* angry, either. His body was warm and relaxed, the way it had been last night, his arm hanging loosely around her shoulders as his fingers toyed with a lock of her hair, their hips bumping when he shifted his weight from one foot to the other. Margaret Ann was well aware that his posture declared her his woman. It was a show for Walt's benefit, yet a voice inside her head whispered that it could be for real if she wanted it to be.

An impossible notion, but a shiver of awareness curled through her. Oddly enough, there was no fear attached to it. Peter felt the tremor and must have assumed there was, because his hand dropped to the small of her back, stroking a little, as though reassuring her.

"Say, Maggie, I'm sorry I kept your man inside so long." Walt tapped Peter's shoulder with a meaty fist. "I haven't seen Phoenix here for nigh onto six months, and, well, you know how it is when a couple of truck jockeys get to shootin' the breeze."

"Oh, that's okay." Margaret Ann smiled. *Phoenix?*

Walt's tone was reproachful as he said to Peter, "Give me a shout when you're out here again. You know, you ought to keep your ears on once in a while. Never can tell what you might be missin'. 'Sides, it's downright unsociable. Paul says you don't need a CB, for all you use it."

"It's true." Peter grimaced. "I hardly ever turn the thing on. You know how it is. I'm still new at this business, and I'm not much good at small talk."

With an expansive wave that encompassed the Kenworth, the older man laughed. "Well, looks to me like you're sure good at *something*. She's a beauty—and worth every penny, I'd bet."

Peter said his thanks, then, with a quick look at his watch, added, "Hey, I hate to say it, but we've got to get moving."

"Sure." Walt nodded briskly. "I'm late, myself. Nice meeting you, Maggie. You take care of my buddy, you hear?"

Margaret Ann cleared her throat. "Uh, sure. I will."

Peter drove back onto the interstate, the bag containing their lunch sitting on the floor between them, untouched, like the silence that had descended after Walt's departure. They had traveled several miles before Margaret Ann got up the nerve to say what she thought needed to be said. And, for once, her tone was sincere.

"I'm sorry."

Peter's eyes remained fixed on the road. "It's not your fault Walt was there. Don't worry about it."

"That's not what I meant."

"You don't have to be sorry about using the phone, either."

"I thought if I made it quick, it would be okay."

"It's all right, Margaret Ann."

"I don't want to cause you any trouble. Really. Maybe it would be better—"

"I said it's all right. I parked by the phone deliberately."

She broke off, and her head snapped around.

"I expected you to use it," Peter said.

He met her gaze, and again she felt the impossible strength of his tenderness in the way his eyes moved over her features. When he turned his attention back to the road, his tone still carried the message.

"I did the same thing last night when I stopped to buy dinner. And again this morning when we stopped for fuel."

"You—" She shook her head. "I don't understand. You mean, you *wanted* me to use the phone?"

Peter was silent for a moment, the beard covering his jaw ruffling as he chewed a corner of his mouth. Reaching down into the lunch bag, he pulled out a cup of coffee and tore the piece of plastic from the cover that made a hole for drinking. He took a couple of sips and set the cup in the holder on the console before he spoke.

"Four days ago, the day after we met, I ate lunch in a rest stop outside of Chicago. I went to buy a newspaper, and you were there, making a phone call. I heard you talking."

That announcement alone was enough to make Margaret Ann feel faint. But before she had time to wonder exactly what he had heard, Peter told her, and she nearly had a heart attack.

"I heard everything. I know you've got a little boy named Jimmy and that you've hidden him with a friend named Jane. I would have told you I knew from the start, but I didn't want to frighten you any more than you already were."

When she could only stare at him, her face white and her breathing shallow, he reached over and took her hand. He did that a lot, she thought, touched her at the very moment she was most vulnerable.

"It's all right, Margaret Ann," he told her. "I know about Jimmy, and it's all right. You can call him anytime you want. We'll find a phone."

She didn't know what to make of this. Gradually, the terror subsided, but it was still impossible to think. Her brain was burned out from figuring angles, anticipating problems, worrying about who knew what. Finally she gave up and simply followed her heart. Peter was her friend. She hadn't asked him to be, but she accepted the knowledge that he was in the same way a person accepts her parents or siblings. When he began asking questions, she closed her eyes, sank into the seat and answered with the truth.

"How old is Jimmy?"

"He turned six last month."

Peter muttered something under his breath about innocents being dragged into adult problems, then fell silent. He had finished most of his coffee before he spoke again, and she belatedly realized that he was struggling as hard as she was, not quite certain what to say. The tack he chose startled her.

"One of the first things you learn in prison is the pecking order," he said. "How you get treated by guards and other prisoners depends a lot on what you've done, what crime you've committed. The ones who suffer the worst treatment, though—get beat up or raped or even killed—are the child molesters. Nobody, not even the most hardened criminal, can seem to tolerate the notion of a child being physically abused."

Margaret Ann wanted to make one thing very clear. "I didn't break Jimmy's arm."

"You think I don't know that?" Peter finished his coffee and reached behind his seat to throw the cup in the trash, catching her gaze as he did so. "But you're afraid that the man who did will do worse if he finds Jimmy, aren't you?"

"He isn't going to find him," she replied, her tone adamant. "Nobody is. And no matter how nice you are or how much you help me, I'm not telling you where he is, either."

"Believe me, I don't want to know. Your son's location is your ace in the hole. Your bargaining power."

"There aren't going to be any bargains."

"If you're caught, bargains might be the only way out."

"I'm not going to get caught. I'm going to disappear."

He cocked one eyebrow. "Right off the face of the earth, huh?"

"In a manner of speaking, yes." She gave her red curls a toss and lifted her chin.

There was a brief pause, then Peter began in an oddly casual tone, "This, uh, person who broke your son's arm. What is he to you?"

The question made Margaret Ann's stomach churn. "My ex-husband."

"He's Jimmy's father?"

She could hardly bring herself to nod, and her voice shook as she said, "The court gave him sole custody. For the past year, I've been allowed to visit Jimmy for four hours every other Sunday afternoon. I was never allowed to see him alone."

Peter was appalled. "What in God's name happened in that courtroom?"

"A witch trial," she stated flatly. "He lied. He produced 'evidence' that made me look like a drug-using streetwalker who shouldn't be allowed within ten miles of any child. The social worker believed him. The judge believed him. By the time he and his lawyers were finished, I think even *my* lawyer believed him."

Peter drove in silence, an elbow resting on the steering wheel as he stroked his beard. Then, sighing heavily, he murmured. "How the hell did you ever get involved with that pig?"

A good question, Margaret Ann thought, one she had been trying to answer for herself for a long time. "Oh, he's a charmer," she said, sarcasm dripping from every word. "The original Dr. Jekyll and Mr. Hyde. And I was young and stupid and blinded by a good religious upbringing that didn't teach little girls to watch out for men like him."

"I take it your mother had died by the time you met him," Peter concluded. "But what about your father? Wasn't there someone around to warn you about him?"

"My father died when I was ten," she replied, relieved to be on relatively safe ground. "He was a welder. There was an accident at the plant where he worked. Afterward, my mother and I lived over her sister's restaurant. Mom baked cakes and pies. After she died, I stayed with Aunt Dorothy and helped out in the restaurant after school and summers. Mostly I cooked, but sometimes I waited tables. Even though it was a truck stop, lots of locals came in. That's how I met him. The restaurant was near the water, and he kept a boat close by. He came in frequently."

"And you dated him?"

"Yes." Margaret Ann methodically ran a fingernail over the seam of her jeans as she recalled events of her ill-fated youth. "He was the first man who'd asked me out that Aunt Dorothy actually approved of. Even the fact that he was older than me didn't bother her. She thought a man his age would be more settled and apt to have marriage on his mind. He was so nice. Nice to her, nice to me, nice to everybody! He spent lots of money on me, bought me things, took me places. It never occurred to me that he wasn't sincere."

Peter made a derisive noise. "When did you get your first clue?"

"Oh, there were plenty of clues, if I'd wanted to notice." Her mouth twisted in a grimace of self-disgust. "He always took me to out-of-the-way places. We never went anywhere he'd see people he knew. I was a secret. But I didn't realize that. I guess the first time I ever considered something might be wrong was when I told him I was pregnant."

There was embarrassment in admitting she had been so naive, but Peter's expression held no accusation; it was filled with anger—anger at a man who had seduced an innocent, uninformed girl. Still, she felt some compulsion to explain.

"I only went to . . . to his house once. I was in love with him—or thought I was. Which shows you how blind love is, because I went on thinking I loved him, even after he told me I should have an abortion because he wasn't going to marry me."

"So why did he?"

Margaret Ann closed her eyes. The truth stopped her. She knew very well what had changed Larry Silver's mind about marrying her. But she couldn't tell Peter, no matter how compelled she felt to trust him, not without risking everything.

The appalling fact was, there were people, evil people, who existed in a world of no moral values, where power was money made off other people's pathetic suffering. She had stumbled ignorantly upon the secrets of that world, and because she had, Larry had shackled her to him. When she had woken up to the full horror of his crimes and tried to break free, he had made sure no one ever would believe a word that came out of her mouth. He had ruined her credibility, and she had no proof, not a single piece of evidence against him. Yet he had still felt it necessary to hold their son hostage to ensure her silence. Well, he no longer had Jimmy, but if anything went wrong, if he ever found her—or, perhaps even worse, if any of his terrible friends found her...

No. She could never tell Peter or anyone else of the horror she had lived with. So she concocted a watered-down version of the truth that would satisfy Peter's question.

"He was a successful real-estate broker," she said. "But he was shooting for a career in politics. The pregnancy came at a critical time in his career, and he realized he couldn't afford a paternity suit."

Peter gave her a dubious look. "He told you that, and you still married him?"

"He didn't tell me anything except to pledge eternal love. He let me stew for three days, thinking I'd been dumped and wondering what on earth I was going to do. Then he took me out to dinner at the most expensive restaurant in town, apologized and told me that, of course, he loved me. He'd been shocked when I told him I was pregnant. I should forgive him for being so insensitive. Then he produced this enormous diamond ring and made the prettiest proposal speech you've ever heard."

"And you bought it."

"Yes," she snapped. "At eighteen, unmarried and pregnant, with a sick aunt and nowhere else to go, I bought it."

"I'm not blaming you," Peter said quietly. "You weren't the first teenage girl to be seduced by a bastard who knew the right things to say. But, Margaret Ann—" he hesitated a moment "—have you thought about going back and fighting him through legal channels?"

"No way."

Peter let out a resigned sigh. "Yeah, I kind of got that message, overhearing your talk with Jane. But you're not alone, you know. There are a number of cases like yours going on right now, some of them well publicized."

Margaret Ann eyed him warily. "What do you mean?"

"Women hiding their children from their ex-husbands. In most instances the mothers are accusing the fathers of sexually abusing the kids. Of course, some of those women are in prison for kidnapping or contempt of court—or both. It varies from state to state, but a number of courts are refusing to hear evidence against the father—refusing even to set bail—until the woman agrees to produce the child."

"They can't put me in jail if they can't find me."

"You can't run forever," he shot back.

"I don't plan to. I'm only going to run until I'm, let's say, lost."

"Then what?"

"What do you mean, then what?"

"Well, you must have something in mind—beyond disappearing off the face of the earth." His hand swept grandly across the steering wheel toward the horizon. "What are your plans, your dreams? What are you going to *do* with your life?"

"All I want is some peace. A place I can raise my son and—" her voice quavered "—and be happy."

"How are you going to eat? The money you're carrying won't last forever."

Margaret Ann hesitated, but his prodding had triggered a need inside her to prove she was not without prospects—though she didn't know whether it was Peter or herself who required the proof.

"I teach," she answered.

Peter's dark eyebrows shot upward, and his mouth twitched with poorly suppressed amusement. "Oh?"

"I have a degree in classical studies, and I'm two semesters away from completing the course work for my doctorate."

"A doctorate!" His eyes sparkled as they widened in astonishment. "In classics! You mean, like Latin?"

"And Greek. I've taken classes in philosophy, history—all aspects of ancient Greek and Roman culture. But I'm most interested in languages. Primarily Latin."

"Lord have mercy," Peter muttered. "All of a sudden I smell incense, and my knees hurt."

Margaret Ann smiled at the memories his comment evoked, memories of the many hours she, too, had spent kneeling in church on Sunday mornings.

"So you teach this stuff, huh?"

"Part-time. I teach second-year Latin at a private girls' school."

"Are you going to finish your degree?"

"Yes."

"Hmm. And do you have your transcripts with you?"

His question caught her off guard. It also made her nervous. "No. No, but I'll send for them."

"Whose name are you going to have put on them?"

Her mouth hardened. "I'll worry about that when I have to." A surge of anger made her add, "Listen, Charlie, if I can't work it out to get my credentials verified without giving away where I am, well, that's the way it goes. I'll shovel dirt for the rest of my life sooner than go back."

"So you're not very committed to teaching, then."

Her anger mounted. "I am so committed to it."

"But you're not willing to fight for it."

"*Fight* for it? Listen, going to school and teaching are about the only things that kept me sane the past eleven months, since I lost Jimmy. I've wanted to teach since I was twelve, and I'm going to keep doing it, too! I don't know what I'll do, but I'll—I'll work it out. I'll find a way. I'll..."

Peter let her angry words trail off into silence before he glanced over to see her fighting back tears of frustration. Then he spoke.

"So it's like that, is it? You've worked your butt off for a career that's never going to get off the ground. A damned shame, isn't it, Margaret Ann?"

Her eyes were brimming, but she returned his gaze defiantly. "Is that how *you* feel?"

"I think it's a sin you spent all that time and—"

"I'm not talking about me," she interrupted, and he gave her a puzzled look. "You didn't always drive a truck, did you?"

He glanced away quickly and, an instant later, uttered a terse "No."

She studied his closed expression. "I met enough truckers at Aunt Dorothy's to know you don't fit the mold."

"Are we back to the mint-jelly theory?"

"Maybe." Her defiant attitude softened a little. "Actually, I was just remembering what you told that man, Walt. You said you were still new at this business."

Peter shrugged and made a big deal out of passing a slow-moving car in front of them. "So I haven't always been a gypsy trucker. That doesn't mean I'm running from something. Prison has a way of changing your life, whether you want it changed or not."

"I imagine it does. But I want to know if you're driving this truck rather than face the creeps who called you a murderer. Rather than make your life your own again."

His lips formed a thin line in the thick blackness of his beard, but he didn't answer.

Margaret Ann's eyes narrowed, and she spoke softly. "Tell me something, Charlie. Who's Phoenix?"

"It's my CB handle. The name I use over the radio. All truckers have one."

"You're not *from* Phoenix, are you?"

"No."

"Then we're talking mythological birds."

"Yes."

"And you chose the name yourself."

"Yes."

"Hmm." Her gaze drifted over him, over the lines that marked the corners of his eyes, the silver highlighting his black hair—those threads of vulnerability that some people might have chosen to hide but that he chose to flaunt, letting them grow to a length that said he didn't care who noticed them. What sort of man had he been? Why didn't he want to be that man again? Was the life he had now truly better than the one he had lost? Or was there another reason he couldn't—or wouldn't—reclaim that past existence?

There was a lot about him she didn't know. In another sense, though, Margaret Ann felt as if she were seeing him clearly for the first time, seeing the hunger in him, the vibrant spirit beneath the controlled—or was it sad?—exterior. Cool on the outside, hot on the inside. The image planted itself in her mind, and she wondered why it had taken her so long to get it straight.

"So," she said, "has the phoenix risen?"

Amber eyes flashed to blue ones, but, in the next instant, he looked away.

"Let's say it's rising."

"Hmm." She studied him a moment. "I wonder."

Then she ducked into the sleeper, leaving him to drive alone.

Chapter Seven

It began raining at dusk in southern Idaho's Snake River Valley. The interstate that followed the path of the river was a dark road, and the lights of oncoming vehicles, bouncing off the wet asphalt and colliding with the Kenworth's own beams, reminded Peter of his godson Alex's video race-car games. The Kenworth's windshield was the video screen, the steering wheel was his joystick, and he was up to level three—high speed. Except the last time he'd played with Alex, he had crashed out at level two. At nine-thirty, after fifteen hours of driving, it seemed wise to quit.

He glanced at Margaret Ann sitting quietly in the seat beside him as he turned into a roadside pull-off. "I've about had it," he said.

When her only response was a nod, Peter sighed and maneuvered the Kenworth across the unlighted lot without further attempt at conversation. She hadn't spoken more than a half dozen words since that afternoon—since she had neatly turned his strategy to draw her out into a surprise attack on him, then left him to brood.

The pull-off was small, no more than a scenic picnic spot, and the Kenworth shared it with two other trucks—a tanker and a flatbed piled high with logs. The rain was coming down in sheets, but Peter felt an urgency to get out and walk. Once he had parked, he ducked into the sleeper long enough to grab a waterproof poncho from the closet.

He pulled it on as he climbed back into the front seat, grabbing the door handle as he said, "There's an extra one of these if you want to get out"

"No, I'll—" Margaret Ann's gaze flickered to his briefly. "I'll stay here. Thanks, anyway."

He nodded, jumped out of the truck and strode quickly away. He felt as if he were going to explode and knew if he'd spent one more minute in that truck with her, he would have done or said something stupid.

"Has the phoenix risen?" What the hell kind of question was that?

Peter hunched his shoulders against the wind-driven rain as his compulsively honest conscience forced a response. It was a damned good question, and it was killing him not to be able to give her the answer she deserved—the real answer, not a cryptic half-truth designed to keep things between them as impersonal as their bizarre circumstances would allow.

The end of the gravel lot came quickly. Peter reached it and kept going to the edge of the woods, where he hooked his elbow around the wet trunk of a young aspen and pulled to a halt. He stood for a minute, breathing hard, though not from exertion. Then he swung around, leaning a shoulder against the tree as he stared at the Kenworth, its long shape barely visible in the dark and the rain, and he thought about the woman waiting there for him to return.

What was he going to do with her? She didn't know what she was letting herself in for, indulging her curiosity about him in order to put off facing her own predicament. She had no way of knowing the thin line they were walking. He knew, though, and the responsibility was his to keep them from falling over the edge.

But things weren't going the way he had planned. He was supposed to be winning Margaret Ann's trust so he could convince her the best course of action was to turn herself in and fight Larry Silver in court. He was supposed to be maintaining his distance, keeping a clear head and not letting his own feelings get in the way of her needs. Instead, he was falling in love with her. And he had no idea how to stop it from happening, even if he had wanted to. The fact that he did not indicated how poorly he had learned the lesson Alyce's death and going to prison had taught him.

Stay cool. Don't get pushy. And keep communications light. Those were the rules he had made for himself, and he was convinced his happiness—perhaps his survival—depended upon strict adherence to them. But how did you keep things light with a woman who was running from the law? How, without getting pushy, was he supposed to convince her it was critical she turn herself in? And as for staying cool . . . forget it. Around Margaret Ann Miller, he didn't seem to have a cool bone in his body.

Neither did she, for that matter. She was fiery and quick. She knew how to get to the heart of things—and of people—with a look, a few well-chosen words. And she did it as easily as breathing. She shot his "Mr. Good Guy" act all to hell. With her, he seemed capable only of being . . . himself. And, Lord, it felt good. Good, like the rain beating down on his face, like the smell of wet leaves and forest earth. Good, like Margaret Ann's big blue eyes and freckles and outrageous red curls.

He had called her Maggie that afternoon, and of the names she had collected so far, it fit her best. She was Maggie, all right—fresh as paint and full of life. At the moment, she was also very fragile, quick to scare, ready to scratch if she was cornered. Ready to break under the burden she was carrying.

He wanted to help her carry that burden. He wanted to take it from her and into himself. He wanted to take *her* into himself, to let go of the reins and be with her, know her, let his heart and his body pour into hers until the enormous emptiness inside him was gone. Until his overpowering need for real intimacy was filled. Mother of God, how he wanted that.

He wished she would call him by his name. Just once, he wanted to hear her say it. In calling him Charlie, she was refusing to acknowledge him in a personal way and thereby keeping a barrier in place between them. And he resented that barrier like hell.

He knew how to tear it down, though. It was as much a part of his nature as it was hers to know exactly the words to say or the thing to do to cut through a person's defenses. And it scared him not to know if he could resist doing so. For the truth was, he needed her. Needed her unquestioning faith in him, that blessed precious belief, which she had expressed so succinctly, that anyone who had entertained the notion that he might be capable of murder was out of his mind. He had been starving for so long, he hadn't realized how huge his need for that kind of faith had become; when she offered it to him, he'd discovered he was ravenous.

Still, it would be an enormous mistake to allow that fragile barrier between them to collapse. Experience warned Peter that he was letting himself in for grave disappointment. The lessons of a lifetime had shown him that his expectations were unreasonable and that no normal person—man or woman—could live up to them. Alyce had taught him better than anyone how frightened people were of his intensity and how little they understood it. And he'd had plenty of time in prison to come to grips with the fact that such intensity would only go wanting in a world where most people interacted largely through form and pretense.

He had learned form easily, years ago, but he wasn't good at pretense. He simply didn't know how to have a casual friendly relationship. After his tragic experience with Alyce, he had thought it better to have no close relationships at all than to risk repeating history. If he didn't get involved with people, he couldn't intimidate anyone, and they couldn't disappoint him. Living alone in a truck had seemed a good way to stay out of trouble.

He hadn't bargained on Margaret Ann Miller.

But he couldn't let his needs and desires get in the way of what had to be done. If he wasn't careful, he would scare her off, then she would be caught and tried. Under those circumstances, he had no doubt that Silver would find a way to win. Margaret Ann would lose. And so, consequently, would her son. His own needs were unimportant compared to hers. He would survive. She might not.

Still, as he walked slowly back across the lot, he could not dispel the thought that he had stumbled upon a woman who could satisfy him, body and soul. And it made him angry and incredibly sad to know he would never have the chance to find out.

When Peter climbed into the truck, Margaret Ann was ensconced in a corner of the bunk with a book. Her knees were drawn up, the book resting on them. She was reading Tom Wolfe's *The Bonfire of the Vanities*—or pretending to, at least.

"I'm going to sack out," he told her, hanging his dripping poncho behind the driver's seat in the cab, then sitting on the edge of the bunk to remove his wet shoes.

"Oh," she said in a tiny voice. "I'll move up front, then."

"You can stay where you are."

"I'm not tired, and I thought I'd read for a while."

"Fine."

"But the light will bother you."

"No, it won't."

"You're sure—"

"It's okay, Margaret Ann. Read as long as you want."

He pulled off his T-shirt and glanced at her. She was staring over the top of her book at his naked torso. He saw her gulp before her eyes rose and she caught him watching her. Dropping her gaze quickly to the book, she frowned in concentration, but her cheeks were flushed, and her efforts to squirm farther into the corner of the bunk were ridiculous.

Peter's lips thinned as he stuffed his T-shirt into the laundry bag and stashed it on the closet floor. He stripped off his jeans almost defiantly. He didn't know who he was more angry with, himself or her, but if she was still afraid of him after last night, there wasn't much he could do about it.

Yanking the sheet and spread down, he climbed into bed, rolled onto his stomach and shoved his arms under the pillow. His legs stretched down under the covers and immediately encountered her feet on top of them. She wiggled out of the way with a mumbled apology, and he closed his eyes.

A minute later, he raised his head and looked back over his shoulder at her. Her eyes were very busy scanning a page of print.

"Are you planning to read all night?"

"Maybe. This is good."

"And besides that, it beats having to face the problem of where you're going to sleep."

She turned a page.

Peter rolled onto his side and propped himself up on an elbow. A minute passed before he heaved a sigh. "Margaret Ann, you've got to lie down sometime. The bed's big enough for both of us, and there's no reason we can't share it." On a dry note, he added, "I didn't bite last night, did I?"

Another page turned.

"I'm not scared of you, Charlie."

Peter studied her.

When he didn't say anything else but simply lay there looking at her, Margaret Ann glanced up. Her eyes flickered over his body, covered to the waist with a sheet. When she returned her attention to her book, she spoke with a hint of her usual caustic tone—her way of reassuring him.

"Go to sleep," she said. "You're scheduled to log nearly seven hundred miles tomorrow. You need your beauty rest."

Peter rolled onto his stomach once more, muttering, "Maybe I should teach *you* to drive this rig."

"That'll be the day."

"Well, it would solve the bed problem. I'd drive all day, and you could drive all night."

"Dream on, Charlie."

Dream on, is right, he thought. Dream about the woman he wanted but couldn't have.

A clap of thunder, directly overhead, brought Peter awake with his pulse racing. It was dark inside the sleeper, and his eyes went automatically to the doorway, expecting to find some light, however dim, filtering in from outside. The curtain was down, though, and he sat up to open it. He thought he'd find Margaret Ann huddled in the front seat. But she wasn't there.

Panic gripped him for a moment, but it fled as the next flash of lightning illuminated the interior of the truck. She was curled up on the floor, in the narrow space between the bunk and the doorway to the cab. She had her clothes on and was using her knapsack for a pillow.

Peter shook his head, torn between exasperation and tenderness. "This is crazy," he grumbled, reaching down to touch her shoulder. He said her name a couple of times, but she didn't respond, so he put a foot on the floor on the far side of her, braced his other knee on the mattress, and slid an arm under her to lift her into bed. "Come on, Margaret Ann. Get up here before you—"

His first warning of what was about to happen came when he felt her body tense. The second came when her hand clamped around his wrist. He knew what was coming next, felt himself being thrown off balance, and he reacted instinctively.

Two seconds later she was on her back beneath him, the length of his body pinning her much smaller one to the floor.

"Don't!" Her high-pitched cry was barely coherent.

"Margaret Ann!"

"Don't, please! Don't hurt me!"

"Hurt you? I was only putting you in bed!"

If there'd been room, he'd have simply gotten out of her way, but in the cramped space, all he could do was restrain her frenzied attempts to do him bodily harm.

"Stop it, Maggie! You're going to cripple us both!"

"Oh, no! No! Not again! Please, not again!"

Her keening helpless moan, the way she said "not again," got to him. And in a flash of clarity, Peter understood. She was fighting in her sleep. And she wasn't fighting him.

Instantly, his hold on her changed. He let go of her wrists and didn't try to stop her from flailing at him, gritting his teeth a couple of times when her wild punches connected. All the while he spoke to her, quiet soothing words, anything he could think of to bring her out of the nightmare she was reliving.

He knew the moment she came fully awake. Her breath caught on a choked sob, and every muscle in her body tightened. There was a terrible silence, the only sound their labored breathing. They lay in an impossible tangle of arms and legs; Margaret Ann's T-shirt had ridden up, and Peter's heart pounded in his chest where it was pressed to her overheated skin. He waited for a sign from her, expecting some biting remark meant to put him in his place and give her back her pride.

Instead, what he heard shattered his cynicism, and she said it in a voice so shaky, so vulnerable, it broke his heart.

"Peter?"

His eyes closed, and he lowered his forehead to rest against hers. "Yes, baby, it's me."

"What are you doing?"

"Putting you to bed."

"You . . . you scared me."

"I know. I'm sorry. You were asleep."

"Oh."

Peter levered off her, drawing her with him to sit in the V his thighs made as he sat back on his heels. Her hands clutched his, fingers trembling as she hung on. She wasn't trying to push him away.

Lightning slashed an erratic pattern in the sky overhead, and in the brief flashes slanting through the doorway, Peter saw her face turned up to him, her eyes liquid and defenseless.

"What did he do to you, Margaret Ann?" he asked.

She held his gaze for an instant. Then, pulling her hands from his to wrap her arms around her waist, she turned her head aside. "Ask me what he didn't do. It would take less time to answer."

The bitterness in her voice tore through him. He knew the kind thing would be to let it go at that; he had already forced her to say more than he had a right to know. But kindness wasn't going to keep her out of prison, and he needed to know exactly what weapons she possessed to nail Larry Silver to the wall.

"He beat you?"

A nod.

"Raped you?"

Another nod.

"Are there hospital records of your being treated for injuries?

"Yes."

"And the rape? Was it medically verified?"

She looked at him with a cold intensity that sent gooseflesh racing down his limbs. "Do you have any idea how hard it is to prove you were raped by your husband?"

Yes, he knew, and if the husband was a popular figure who held the public's sympathy, it would be harder still.

"Why didn't you use the hospital records in the divorce trial?" he asked.

"I...I tried. But he said I broke my ribs falling down the stairs. It was true. I did fall—because he pushed me. But he—he said I was high on drugs and fell because I couldn't walk straight."

Peter swore under his breath. "How often did this go on?"

She was silent a moment, then spoke in a tiny voice. "Only once. He only hurt me one time."

Physically, Peter added silently. But what about emotionally? The answer was obvious. He steeled himself to go on, knowing the anguish he was causing her. "Why did he attack you that time?"

When she didn't answer, he figured he had pushed her too far. Then her hand fluttered, and she spoke in a rasping whisper.

"I provoked him. I made him angry."

"And that's when you left him?"

"Yes. Well, no, I . . . I left a couple of months later."

"Why did you wait?"

Her head dipped low. "I—I don't know. He said he'd—" She broke off, shrugged, then finished in an embarrassed murmur. "I let him talk me into staying."

She was lying. Not about Silver attacking her. Oh, no, that was so real, Peter could almost see it happening. But the picture was incomplete. There was something she was hiding that had to do with why she hadn't left Silver immediately after he attacked her—or, for that matter, long before.

Peter wasn't familiar with the psychology of battered women, women who seemed to seek relationships with men who abused them either physically or mentally, but he didn't think Margaret Ann fit the mold. He remembered watching her disable the guy in the rest stop that first evening, and he would lay money that Silver's attack had provided the impetus for her to learn self-defense. It seemed unlikely she would go to such lengths to protect herself if she were truly addicted to the victim role. It seemed far more likely that Silver had somehow made it impossible for her to leave him—trapped her. But how? And why?

There were more questions than ever, but Margaret Ann had had enough for one night. And so had he.

Lightly he ran the backs of his fingers down her arm. "I have trouble sleeping sometimes," he said quietly. "Things bother me. Noises, locked doors, feeling closed in. Strange as it seems, though, since the first night you climbed into my truck, I've been sleeping better. Maybe it's because I know you're as wary as I am. It's as if my subconscious feels safe enough with you around to shut off for a while." He reached for her hand and laced his fingers through hers. "It was good last night, holding you. It's been a long time since I slept that well. Come lie beside me and let me hold you again."

Her gaze dropped to their entwined hands. "I—I don't know if I can," she whispered.

"You did it last night," he prodded gently.

"You didn't give me a chance to think about it."

"I'm not going to hurt you, baby."

"I know," she said, her voice quiet but clear. Her face tilted up, and her eyes searched his in the darkness.

Peter smiled and gestured toward the bed. "Come on, Maggie. It's late. Time we got some rest."

Her lashes lowered then, and he heard the hint of a smile as she muttered, "'Maggie,' my foot."

She liked the name, he thought, pulling her with him when he stood. He held on to her hand and drew her down to lie beside him, And as he had last night, he pulled her close, wrapping his arms around her protectively. Possessively.

Once, he'd been found guilty of murder when he had been innocent. But as he lay there in the darkness, thinking about the woman in his arms and of the things she had been forced to suffer, he wondered what he would do if he ever had the chance to wrap his hands around Larry Silver's neck.

Chapter Eight

For the next three days, Peter drove with a single-mindedness of purpose that exhausted Margaret Ann, simply watching him. They were in Kansas City by ten o'clock Saturday night, where he got rid of the 897 cartons of paper in his trailer at an all-night loading dock. The following morning they took off for Saint Louis to pick up a shipment bound for Harrisburg, Pennsylvania. They spent Sunday night in a rest stop east of Columbus, Ohio, and were headed for Harrisburg by 6:00 a.m. Monday.

There were no probing dialogues. Neither were there further arguments over sleeping arrangements. Margaret Ann read, listened to music and performed the necessary housekeeping chores while Peter drove. He told her tales of truckers he had met. He made her laugh over stories about his large Greek-Italian family. They groaned together over memories of nuns and parochial school. And occasionally, she discovered, he liked to plug a tape of golden oldies into the deck and sing along in his own rich baritone.

As pleasant as the company was, Margaret Ann would have gotten stir-crazy cooped up in the truck except that Peter always managed to arrange breaks before she felt trapped. Her silent question as to whether she would have to bathe forever in the Kenworth's tiny sink was answered when he introduced her to the amenities provided for professional truckers, men and women both, by interstate rest stop facilities.

Peter also made certain she had the chance to talk to Jimmy every day, and for that alone she was grateful to him. It was clear, listening to Jimmy's enthusiastic reports of his adventures with Jane and Mark, that he was happy, and that went a long way toward reassuring her that the final hideous incident with his father had not done irreparable psychological damage. She wasn't even certain he understood that anything was seriously wrong; children were such forgiving souls when it came to their parents' sins.

With her mind easier about Jimmy, along with the growing belief that, if no one had found him yet, they weren't likely to, Margaret Ann began to relax and enjoy the ride in Peter's sumptuous rig. In fact, she rather liked traveling this way. No luggage to haul in and out of motel rooms. Hot meals when they wanted them. A refrigerator handy for snacks. Good music. A comfortable bed. And strong arms that held her close to a solid warm body as she slept every night.

More and more she found herself fantasizing about that increasingly familiar masculine body. She knew Peter wanted her. She also knew he would cut off his own hands sooner than touch her in a way that made her feel sexually threatened. Indeed, the resolute control he exercised over his emotions astounded her, for she was learning what an acutely sensitive man he was and how strongly he felt about nearly everything. It wasn't so much the things he said or did; there was simply an energy about him, a sort of dynamic presence that let her know on a minute-to-minute basis exactly where he stood. To the part of her that needed almost constant reassurance that she wasn't being a fool for trusting him, it was very encouraging. He was clearly incapable of being anything but completely, almost excruciatingly, honest. And the honest truth was, he wanted to make love with her.

Yet he did not even try. When he held her at night, she felt cherished. It was as though they had been lovers for so long that merely being together, lying beside each other in the darkness, satisfied some basic need for intimacy that surpassed passion. The passion was there, though, a constant thread that wove itself into every word or look that passed between them.

It was new to Margaret Ann, this hot longing that stirred inside her when she looked at Peter, but at twenty-five, it seemed about time she learned what it was to look at a man's mouth and wonder what it would be like to kiss him, to study his body in jeans and a T-shirt and imagine it unclothed. To watch that same virile body engaged in mundane acts—driving a truck, lifting a crate, climbing a loading dock ladder—and picture it, naked and hard, moving toward her with purposeful intent.

There the fantasies stopped. The only experiences Margaret Ann had had beyond that point were ones of embarrassment, disillusionment and numbness—and one frightful time of pain. Those weren't feelings she could attach to Peter, so rather than taint her imaginings of lovemaking with him with memories of Larry Silver's cold selfish lust—or his violence—she imagined nothing at all. But she did wonder.

They arrived in Harrisburg ahead of schedule, at eleven on Monday morning. But the loading dock at the company where Peter had to drop his freight was backed up, and it was hours before they were able to leave. Then the dock foreman at the warehouse where he was to pick up a shipment bound for Mobile couldn't find the cartons corresponding to Peter's manifest, and another hour was wasted while Peter fought—and won—a battle to prevent the foreman from having the wrong cartons put into his trailer.

By the time they left Harrisburg, heading south on I-81, it was seven-fifteen, and Peter was grumbling about the day being a total waste. Realizing he wasn't in a good mood for conversation, Margaret Ann got the book she was reading from the sleeper and brought it up front. She read for a long while, thoroughly engrossed, before the dwindling light made it hard to continue.

Closing the book, she glanced up to see the rolling foothills of the Appalachian Mountains stretching along the horizon to the right. It was a familiar view, one that brought pleasant things to mind. Taking Jimmy for day trips to Harpers Ferry, West Virginia, or to Catoctin Mountain National Park. Sometimes they would simply go driving down the Skyline Drive, and while they rode, they would sing songs her mother and father had sung when she was little.

Lost in the memories, Margaret Ann nearly missed the road sign on the right.

HAGERSTOWN 1½ MILES. Her heart raced. That was the exit for Jane's place. She hadn't been paying enough attention to realize they would be passing it—hadn't even realized they had crossed the Maryland line. To be so close. It was suddenly imperative to see her son.

"Uh, Charlie," she began as casually as she could manage. "Are we going to eat sometime soon?"

"Not until we stop for the night."

"But I'm starving."

"I put some sliced ham in the fridge yesterday. Why don't you make a sandwich?"

"I don't want a sandwich."

"Yogurt?"

"Yuck."

"SpaghettiOs?"

"Please!"

"I don't want to stop again, Margaret Ann. We lost too much time today."

"Maybe you should, uh, you know, call it a loss. Start over tomorrow morning."

"If I did that every time I lost hours like I did today, I'd be broke in a month."

"Well, but *one* time wouldn't hurt, would it?"

With his eyes on the road, Peter was concentrating on the traffic, which was picking up as they approached the outskirts of Hagerstown, Maryland. He was preparing to launch into a speech about how hard it was for independent truckers to make a living, but then he glanced at Margaret Ann, and the words died, unspoken.

Her legs were drawn up, bare feet flat on the seat. One arm was wrapped around her legs, and she was chewing on the knuckles of her other hand. Her eyes were frantically searching the road ahead of them.

Something was wrong. She was anxious for him to get off the highway and stop. But why? They came to an exit for Hagerstown, and Peter passed it with one brief shudder—a tribute to his memories of the Division of Correc-

tions facility located there. The DOC wasn't the sort of
place one went back to visit for old times' sake. He knew
why *he* was bothered by this stretch of road, but when
Margaret Ann swiveled in her chair, hands and face practically pressed to the window as she strained to look back,
it hit him what was going on for her.

She stared at the road behind them for several minutes.
Then, with a tiny whimper, she faced front again, wrapping her arms around her shins and dropping her head to
her knees. Her hair fell forward to screen her face, and she
sat huddled in a tight dejected-looking ball.

Choosing his words carefully, Peter said, "You talked
to Jimmy this morning, didn't you?"

Her muffled "Yes" was barely audible.

Peter's gaze darted back and forth from the road to
Margaret Ann as he tried to think, tried to figure out what
he should do.

"Tell me, what sort of place does your friend Jane
have?"

"A farm."

"Is she married?"

"Widowed. With a five-year-old son."

He hesitated, then asked, "Are there other people
around?"

"No. It's not a working farm."

He hated making her nervous by probing, but he needed
to know how great the risk was. "How do you know her?"

Margaret Ann lifted her head and leaned back against
the seat. Her eyes drifted closed. "I went to school with
Jane, but we lost contact when I got married. When I arrived on her doorstep with Jimmy, I hadn't seen her in over
seven years."

"And your ex-husband doesn't know about her," Peter
concluded.

Margaret Ann didn't bother to reply.

"You hadn't seen her in seven years," he went on, "yet you knew she would help you."

Again she remained silent, and Peter shot her a quick look. Her lower lip was caught between her teeth, and as he watched, she covered her eyes with trembling fingers.

"How long had Jimmy been with you before you took him to Jane's?"

"I don't know. A few hours, I guess."

A few hours—after nearly a year of seeing him on alternate Sundays for a four-hour, supervised visit. A few hours—and then to have to leave him, broken arm and all, in another woman's care.

Peter couldn't stand it. To hell with trying to keep himself clean. To hell with calculating every damn move. He was going to do the right thing, and to hell with what happened later.

"Margaret Ann, do you want to see him? I can get off at the next exit and go back. You don't have to tell me where he is. I'll park wherever you say. You go to Jane's. Stay as long as you want. I'll wait for you."

He looked over to find her staring at him, her lips parted in astonishment. She made no effort to convince him he had guessed wrong.

"I can't," she whispered. "I can't do it. I did want to, but—" She broke off, shaking her head. "It's too soon. I've got to wait until I'm sure they've stopped looking. If anybody saw me, if I was recognized, they'd find him. They'd take him back to... to his father, and... No. No, it's better this way."

"Are you sure?"

She straightened, making a show of pulling herself together, but her voice was thick with tears. "Jimmy's fine. He's happy and... and he's safe, as long as I stay away. I can't risk seeing him only to make myself feel better. I can wait. Soon he and I will be together. And nobody is ever going to take him away from me again!''

Hastily, then, she whirled and disappeared into the sleeper.

Worried, torn and damned close to tears himself, Peter moved quickly into the right lane of traffic. He searched with growing impatience for the sign he wanted, then, seeing it, slapped on his blinker and peeled off into the lot of a tourist information center. There wasn't another vehicle in sight at this hour, and he parked in the back corner, the nose of the tractor pointed toward the mountains and the setting sun.

The orange-red ball balanced on the Appalachian ridge, casting its final rays through the windshield of the truck and the doorway to the sleeper.

Peter found Margaret Ann lying on the bed, her face buried in the pillow, her slender shoulders quaking with sobs. Easing down to sit beside her, he brushed her hair away from her face with a gentle hand.

She stiffened instantly and choked off her cries. He wondered if he should leave her alone, but she suddenly turned over and flung herself against him, arms clinging, face pressed to his shoulder. And Peter felt his heart burst. Such precious tears. He despised the reason for every one of them even as he gathered her close, but he was more grateful than he could have expressed that she entrusted her tears to him.

"Don't tell me not to cry."

His hand stroked a slow, repetitive pattern down the back of her head and across her shoulder.

"I have to cry! I can't stand it anymore. I just... can't... stand it!''

Her fist hit his shoulder, and he captured it, bringing it to his lips, prying her fingers open to kiss them.

"Why don't you tell me it's going to be all right? Tell me to stop this! Tease me or—or make me mad or *something*! Oh, please," she begged. "Please, tell me something to make it stop hurting!"

Peter buried his face in her hair. "Oh, Maggie, I wish I could. I wish I could tell you it's going to be all right. I wish I knew it would be."

"It has to be! Oh, dear Lord, it has to be! I want my baby! I want my little boy!"

"I know. Oh, Maggie, I know."

A violent shudder racked her. "I've been so scared. Almost a year—every day, I've been waiting, wondering if I'd get a call, and he'd . . . he'd be dead."

Dead? Lord Almighty! Peter clenched his teeth against the fury inside him. She'd had enough of this, and so had he. And they were going to put an end to it right now.

"Maggie, we'll go back and get him," he said. "I'll take you both somewhere where nobody will find you. I've got a friend with a cabin in Oregon. It's in the woods, nobody around for miles." Her cries had subsided as he spoke, and he finished quietly. "Paul won't even question it if I tell him I want to use the cabin, be alone for awhile. You'd be safe there for as long as you wanted to stay."

When Margaret Ann lifted her head to look at him, shock had replaced the misery on her face. Her eyes were a brimming, vivid blue as she whispered, "You'd do that for me?"

Peter drew a deep breath. "I must be losing my mind, but, yes, I think I would. I'd rather see you turn yourself in and beat the bastard to a pulp in court, but if you won't—or can't—then I'll help you disappear. I can't stand by and watch you go to jail for what amounts to protecting the life of your child."

"I think you really mean it," she breathed.

He was as shocked as she was, but he really did mean it. Talk about burning your bridges. A silence fell between them as they looked into each other's eyes, and Peter knew that Margaret Ann saw more deeply into him than anyone ever had or, perhaps, ever would. At that moment, any price he had to pay to keep her safe seemed worth it.

Finally her lashes lowered, and she shook her head. "I can't let you do it," she said.

"I swear, I wouldn't tell anyone where you are."

"No, but your conscience would kill you."

He smiled sadly. "I'm willing to risk it." His fingertip trailed down her cheek, hooked a wet curl and tucked it behind her ear. "Margaret Ann, your son needs you. And you need him. And you both need to have this madness over with so you can get on with your lives."

Her breath caught on a sob she couldn't hold back. The tears started flowing again, and Peter pulled her head down to his shoulder once more.

For a long time he simply held her, rocking her in his arms, his cheek against her hair. He thought about what it would be like, going away with her to start a new life. He thought about holding her like this for years to come. And as he sat there, cradling her in his lap, dreaming dreams that he began to envision could possibly come true, the last barrier between them crumbled, his control slipped and something happened that, thus far, he had refused to allow.

When her crying stopped abruptly and she went rigid, he knew she had become aware of the undeniable change in his body. Cursing silently, he spoke to reassure her before she bolted.

"Maggie, don't be scared. You've been lying here against me, all warm and soft. You feel wonderful." His fingers brushed across her neck. "But, baby, I've had a lot of practice restraining my impulses. I'm not going to start making demands just because you let me hold you and I got hard."

Her face burrowed deeper into his shoulder, and Peter knew she was embarrassed, but that was infinitely better than terrified. Miraculously, she didn't pull away.

A minute later, though, she drew back, slowly lifting her eyes to his. Her lips were parted, red and moist, the most desirable thing he had ever seen, and it was a mighty effort not to lower his mouth to hers. He was startled when her gaze dropped to his mouth, as though he had spoken his thoughts aloud and she was considering them. But that shock was nothing compared to what he felt when her hand crept across his shoulder and she reached up to touch his lips, her fingertips delicate and curious as they traced the firm lines, discovering also the softness of the beard that surrounded them.

He couldn't breathe. He was afraid to move. He watched her, his look intent and wary, as she shifted in his embrace until her face was only inches from his. Her fingers remained lightly covering his mouth while her eyes flickered to his, questioning, testing, then dropped once more. He couldn't believe she would do it.

But she did. In hesitant little steps, with her fingers smoothing across his lips, coming to rest on his cheek, her head came closer...closer... So warm. So incredibly soft. Her lips trembled against his, and a sound escaped him. His breathing was jerky and labored, and his entire body shook. There were a thousand reasons he had to stop this, but before he could think of one of them, her lips moved against his in a caress so sweet it tore a groan straight out of his soul.

"Margaret Ann, wait! What are you— Baby, stop!" He turned his head aside, but she followed him, her fingers now buried in his beard as she feathered kisses across his jaw. "Dammit, this isn't a game."

"I'm not playing games."

"Well, you aren't solving anything, either! God, Maggie.... Oh, baby, don't do that. On top of everything else, you don't need this, too!"

She paused to look at him with not-so-innocent eyes and slowly shook her head. "You are so wrong. I think this is exactly what I need."

Her lips caught his, and Peter was incapable of pushing her away. He kissed her back, not fully, not as he wanted to, only torturing himself with what he might have, allowing himself to know the responsiveness of her lips, the pliancy of her body as she molded herself to him. His control took a serious beating when her mouth opened hotly and her tongue touched his lips, asking him to give her what she wanted. What she *thought* she wanted.

He wrenched away, gasping. "Margaret Ann, will you think! What if you get pregnant? I don't have—"

"It's safe," she cut him off. "I won't get pregnant."

"No!" He gripped her shoulders and threw his head back, his eyes squeezed closed in pure agony. "You don't understand. You can't begin to know what you're asking for. If I make love to you—" he drew a quick painful breath "—I couldn't take it. I couldn't take seeing you scared of me."

When he looked at her again, her eyes were filled with amazement.

"You foolish man," she whispered. "Is that really what you think? Don't you know by now that I could never—

not in a million years—be afraid of you?'' And with her eyes holding his entranced, she took his hand in hers and placed it fully, deliberately, on her breast.

"Ah, God, Maggie...."

"Touch me," she said. "I want you to touch me... like this...."

His fingers sank into the irresistible softness of her, and she sighed, then arched sharply when his thumb rubbed her taut nipple.

"Peter," she breathed, her words coming in panting bursts. "I want to know how it feels to be touched.... I want to know how it feels to... make love. Show me. Please, Peter. Show me."

There wasn't a power on earth but her that could have stopped him then. His arms enveloped her, his body curled over hers, and on a long, hoarse groan, he took her down.

And from that moment on, Margaret Ann knew it was true: she hadn't begun to know what she had been asking for. It was like riding the crest of a tidal wave. Before she had even grasped that it was approaching, she was swept up and tossed to the top of it. His arms were completely around her, his mouth was devouring hers from every conceivable angle, there wasn't an inch of her that wasn't covered by some part of his powerful body, and she was staggering under the sheer, blinding ferocity of his passion. Passion that possessed him utterly and, like the surging wave, drove him toward one end: to possess her— utterly. The passion left no room for thought or reason, no space for doubt or fear. It simply took over every one of her senses and filled her with the awareness of a single truth: his need. His need for her.

He spoke of that need in earthy, carnal words as his mouth tasted her face, her throat, her shoulders and breasts, never leaving her, always moving, moving over her

ribs and her belly, her thighs and upward until it returned
to reclaim her mouth once again. Such hunger! There was
no finesse in it, not even tenderness; clothes were torn off
when they got in the way, until she was naked and he was
half so, and she couldn't have said how it happened. Nor
was there apology or restraint in the slow, erotic rhythm of
his hips against the nest of curls at the juncture of her
thighs. Even through his jeans, the message conveyed by
the hard ridge of his sex was flagrant. Emphatic. Shameless.

She should have been frightened—the thought occurred to her fleetingly—but she wasn't. Even in the white-
hot center of this passionate storm, she never dreamed of
stopping him. She wanted it. She wanted *him*.

When had his passion become her passion, his need, her
need? When had her body become this trembling, moaning thing that craved every hot, devouring kiss, every
trembling movement of his hands over her flesh? The feel
of his body shuddering under her own hands, the heady
male scent of him, the sounds he made, were wildly excit-
ing, for all of it said he wanted her in a way she had never
been wanted before. When his hands splayed flat on her
belly, glided unerringly between her legs, and his fingers
slipped inside her, she cried out, her hips lifting and falling to the rhythm of his stroking caress.

His mouth broke its moist suction on her nipple, and his
cheek pressed into the pillow of her breast. Here, he
paused to whisper, "I've dreamed about this. Dreamed
about how you'd feel inside. But I only imagined." His
eyes closed, and he swallowed hard. "God, Maggie, now
I know."

"Peter..." Her hands trembled over his hair and face,
down over his chest as she reached for his belt. "Peter,
please...."

He was off her then, kneeling over her while he dealt with his belt buckle and yanked open his jeans. While he stood for the instant it took to kick his jeans and briefs aside, she lay beneath the heat of his relentless gaze and stared at his heaving shoulders and chest—the sculpted muscles, the dark skin covered by a sheen of sweat. Her gaze wandered downward, following the arrow of black hair, until it encountered the awesome proof of his virility—and there it stopped.

She couldn't help herself. She drew a quick breath, and her eyes widened. Every fear she'd ever had, all those she had thought she could never attach to Peter, began to well up inside her.

But then he was lifting her chin, his other hand catching her hand and drawing it downward, wrapping her shaking fingers around his swollen flesh.

"Look at me, Maggie," he rasped. "Watch my face. Watch what you— Ah, God . . ." The breath left his body in a rush, and a spasm of pleasure flickered across his features. "I'm yours, Maggie. Feel what you can do to me."

Lord, yes, she felt it. Felt it deep inside her own body, where an unbearable ache was building. She wanted him. Oh, how she wanted him! The feel of his hand guiding hers over his silky, taut skin was more erotic than anything she'd ever dreamed of. The thought of having him inside her took her breath away.

Falling forward on one arm, he hovered above her as she continued to caress him. He was letting her see how much power she had over him, his honesty as merciless in this as it was in everything else. And it was a stirring sight. By the time he lowered his body to hers, the muscles in his thighs were quivering, and he was breathing in shallow gulps. When his thighs pressed hers wide, she offered no resistance. She understood entirely that this was about need. Their need for each other.

The need drew them closer and closer, until she felt the moist heat of her own desire against the back of her hand, still wrapped around him. At the stunning contact of his sex with the hot wetness of her own, she came undone. Her hand fell away on a moan, and her body arched toward him, her breathing thready as he held back from completing the union.

"This is the first time, Maggie." His words were husky, close to her ear. "First time for you. For me. Nothing came before...this." Slowly, then he slid into her, whispering, "It can be everything you ever wanted it to be. Reach for it, baby. Make it yours."

Her fingers dug into his flanks, and her legs locked around him. He rocked against her. Then she was moving and he was moving, and each movement brought him deeper into her until she was filled so entirely she was aware of nothing but that and the indescribable pleasure it gave her.

"Love, Maggie." His mouth searched for hers to breathe words against her lips. "No pain. No fear. Just love."

And it *was* love. She knew it to the very end, when the wave broke and came crashing to the shore, carrying both of them with it. She knew it when she cried out his name and he caught her in his arms to lift her off the bed and crush her against his chest. She knew it from the initial riveting shock of pleasure to the last ripple of satisfaction. For those few blessed out-of-time moments, she knew what love could be.

Gradually, Margaret Ann become conscious that she was upright, her arms and legs wrapped around Peter as she straddled his thighs. She was clinging to his shoulders with a strength that made her fingers hurt. His face was buried between her breasts; her lips were pressed to his temple, where she could feel his pulse race. Both their bodies were slick with sweat.

She whimpered when, by slow agonizing degrees, he lowered her to the bed once more. He didn't release her, though, nor did he withdraw from her as he rolled to his side and held her against him, the idea of separation clearly as painful for him as it was for her.

He had been right, she thought again before exhaustion overcame her. It was indeed love they had made. Whether that meant he truly loved *her* she didn't know and could not allow herself to believe. Nor could she admit to loving him. She had no future, no right to love anyone. But he had taught her what loving was between a man and a woman, and that was a gift she would treasure.

In the morning, when Peter awoke, Margaret Ann was gone. He found a note lying on the driver's seat.

Please, try not to be angry with me. I had to go. If I stayed with you, I'd let you take Jimmy and me to Oregon—or wherever else you wanted to go. And I can't let you do it. I can't let you ruin your hard-won life trying to help me save mine.

Peter waited all day at the rest stop, knowing she would not come back but unable to give up the possibility. He was worried sick, thinking about what would happen to her. But when darkness fell, he faced the fact that she was not going to return. And there was nothing he could do about it.

He warmed up the diesel and got back on the highway, heading south toward Mobile. A couple of hours later, when the CB crackled and the familiar voice of another trucker sent his greetings to Phoenix, he ignored it.

There was no Phoenix. It was lying in ashes.

Chapter Nine

Summer was scorching its way through the South and across the plains states, where Peter had contracted for a series of short hauls that took him through the last weeks of July. It was nine o'clock at night on the second of August and he was in Little Rock, Arkansas, when he picked up a call over the CB that his brother was looking for him.

Although Nicholas had been typically skeptical about relying upon a citizens band radio to reach Peter in case of emergency, he had bought one and learned to use it. At the time, Peter had laughed at Nick's disparaging remarks, knowing that a collect call for Phoenix through the truckers' mail was a reliable enough means of communication. But he wasn't laughing when he picked up the pay phone on the outside wall of a McDonald's; his brother had never tried to reach him and wouldn't unless something were wrong.

"Nick, it's me."

"Peter? Lord, it worked! You got the message!"

"Yes. Is everybody all right?"

"Everybody's fine," Nick assured him. "Mom and Dad just got back from the ocean. Maria and her crew came back with them, because Thad had to leave for two weeks of reserve camp. Sandy and I are sweating it out here with our brood. We're hot but healthy."

Thus relieved, Peter was only mildly curious. "So, what's going on?"

Nick spoke in measured tones. "I have some news I thought might interest you. They picked up Marge Silver early yesterday morning. A plainclothes officer identified her in a drugstore in Ellicott City and made the arrest."

When the only response was long-distance static, Nick said, "Peter? You there?"

"Yeah." It was a hoarse utterance.

"Are you all right?"

Peter mumbled something affirmative. "Was she alone?"

"Yes. And I gather they can't get a word out of her about where the boy is. Silver's beside himself. Claims he's worried she's killed the kid. He—"

"The *bastard*!" Peter's fist hit the brick wall beside him, and he let out a string of oaths that elicited horrified looks from a few passersby. Swearing didn't help, though, and he was trembling with rage as he growled, "She snatched Jimmy because Silver broke the boy's arm. She's terrified he's going to kill him."

Nick hesitated, then whispered, "And you believe her?"

"Like I'd believe you."

"Oh, Lord."

"You know how I've always felt about Silver?"

"Yes."

"Well, lately I've been thinking I'd like to take him by the..."

The particular parts of Larry Silver's anatomy upon which Peter wished to wreak his graphically described vengeance left little doubt in Nick's mind as to what the man had done. For good measure, Peter added, "He pushed her down a flight of stairs, broke her ribs—I don't know what else, but there are hospital records."

"How bizarre," Nick muttered. "I don't remember any of that from the press coverage of their divorce. I never would have guessed that Baltimore's fair-haired boy was the type to physically abuse a woman or child."

"Neither would I. It's not his style. But save that for later. Tell me where they've got her."

"City Jail."

"Damn! Already?"

"They brought her in to Central District and ran her straight through a bail hearing. I started looking for you as soon as I heard. Peter, I've got to ask. Do you know where Jimmy Silver is? Because if you do—"

"I didn't ask, and she didn't tell me. What's bail set for?"

"Ninety-thousand. Peter, for God's sake! When are you going to tell me how you got involved in this?"

Peter took a deep breath. "Soon. But do me a favor." He pressed the bridge of his nose and thought quickly. "Ask Mom to open the house for me—hire somebody to clean it, stock the fridge. Oh, and try to get the phone turned on. Let's see, it's Tuesday night. It'll probably be Thursday morning before I can get there. I'll call from Security Mall. You'll have to pick me up—I can't drive the rig in town. Bring my car, and I'll drop you off on the way into town. I guess you'd better bring me something to put on besides jeans—and cash out of my account. I'll want to go straight down and get her out of that hellhole. God, I hate making her wait."

"You're coming home."

"Yes."

"Because of Marge Silver."

"Her name's Margaret Ann. Margaret Ann Miller."

"Well, I'll be damned," Nick said softly. "You mean there's still something out there worth fighting for?"

Peter smiled a little. "It's not a some*thing*. It's a some-*one*. 'Bout a hundred pounds, red hair, blue eyes and freckles. And if I get there and find even a scratch on her, the warden at City is going to have a riot on his hands."

"I get the picture," Nick said.

And Peter figured he probably did.

As a warehouse night crew unloaded his trailer, Peter put out messages to Paul Flatt, Walt Saddler and a few other truckers who would cover his hauls for him. By 1:00 a.m. he was free of all upcoming obligations.

Traveling east on I-40 throughout the night, he spent a long time thinking about his brother's comment: *"You mean there's still something out there worth fighting for?"* The answer was yes, and it was called love.

Since Margaret Ann had left him nearly three weeks ago, he had been driving the Kenworth into the ground, exhausting himself so he couldn't wonder too hard why he was even bothering to get out of bed in the morning. But in a way, that punishing behavior was only an extreme version of what he'd been doing before he met Margaret Ann. He had been missing his sense of purpose—and running from the void—for a long while. Since the day he'd been arrested for murder and the process of betrayal had begun.

When the process ended the day he was released from prison, all remnants of the idealism that had motivated him in his youth were gone. Any naive myth he'd harbored about justice and truth and loyalty had been destroyed. He had been betrayed by the justice system, to which he had committed his life's energies. He had been betrayed by his colleagues and neighbors and friends, who'd all looked at him with horrified fascination, thinking, not, "Of course, he's innocent," but, "Golly, I wouldn't have believed it, but *maybe* he could have done it." And he had been betrayed by the woman who, for ten years, had been his wife. Yet he had found it easier to forgive her than the others—perhaps because it was hard to remain angry with someone who had paid the price of her foolishness with her life.

For the past year, he had been drifting. Recovering, he had thought. His logbook told a different story, though, one of a man desperate to fill up every minute of every day, driving back and forth across the country at a furious pace, as though he had to be somewhere in a terrible hurry. But there was nowhere he'd had to be. And there was only one place he had truly wanted to go.

Home. He missed his street and his house and the crab apple tree in his backyard. He missed sultry summer nights, lying in the hammock on the porch. He missed the kids riding skateboards down the sidewalk and the dogs barking in Mrs. Morley's yard next door. And he missed his family desperately. But the thought of returning to Baltimore, of facing his old friends, his old life, had been unbearable. The bitterness inside him lay like a slowly melting block of ice that froze hard every time he considered going back. And he still wondered how he'd ever get past it.

But Margaret Ann had given him a reason to try.

Perhaps it was crazy to become involved with her again, when she had made it so clear she didn't want him involved. But hadn't that been because she had thought conspiring with her against the law would ruin his life? If her note told the truth, if it wasn't really what he most feared—that she had left because the fierce intimacy of their lovemaking had been more than she could handle—then there was still a chance. A chance that he could get her out of this mess and.... And then what?

Would Margaret Ann consider a future with him? Did she even begin to love him the way he loved her? To think about it under present circumstances was crazy. But he would fight for Margaret Ann's freedom to choose her own future. And when he had won that battle, he would fight for her love if he had to.

The Baltimore City Jail was as depressing a place as a person could find anywhere on earth. A huge building of gray stone turned black with city grime, it saw the very worst side of life; prostitutes, drug users and dealers, murderers, thieves and all manner of other criminal types comprised the overcrowded population. The place was bug infested and hot. The smell alone was enough to make a person gag. And after three days inside this dismal place, packed in a cell with five other women, Margaret Ann truly believed she was on the verge of losing her mind. She was dirty and sick and exhausted from heat and from all the crying she'd been doing. She had no idea what time of day it was, or even which day it was.

When the guard came and unlocked the cell door, telling her someone has posted bail and she was being released, her only thought was that there must be a mistake. She followed the guard along the dingy corridor, half-dazed and not even vaguely curious about how this turn of events had come about. There was no one with the financial means who would do it for her; the only monied people she knew were Larry's friends.

And what difference did it make? Either she was in jail, or she was dead. Maybe she'd be dead even in jail. It gave her a measure of peace to know that Jimmy was safe, but she would never see him again. And she was having a hard time believing that her life was worth much.

The guard opened a door that led into a large glass-enclosed room where prisoners were visiting with friends and relatives. A long row of tables, divided by a wall of bars, separated the inmates from their visitors. Margaret Ann blinked in discomfort at the bright light that filled the room, and when the guard who had brought her stepped aside, motioning her on, she hesitated, thoroughly bewildered. There were guards lined up along the walls; the prisoners and their visitors were all engaged in quiet conversations. And there was one dark-haired man in a gray suit leaning against the wall closest to the locked gate that led, eventually, outside.

When the guard left her, the dark-haired man straightened and took a couple of steps toward her. Embarrassed, Margaret Ann kept her eyes on the floor, knowing what an unwashed, unkempt mess she was and wishing the man would have the decency not to gawk. But he went on looking, and finally she was compelled to cast a quick nervous glance at his face.

The fleeting look was followed instantly by another, one that became a long, disbelieving stare. His features were barely recognizable without the beard. But the shaggy, dark hair was the same. And the clear, amber eyes, Margaret Ann knew very well, indeed. Gasping, she whispered his name, overcome with a rush of joy so strong, tears sprang to her eyes. In fact, the surprise of seeing him was so great, it only dawned on her slowly that this clean-shaven man in the light gray suit, whom she had known as a truck driver, was familiar in another way. And he was not a trucker at all.

When the whole truth of who he was finally hit her, her knees went weak and her head reeled. The happiness left her face, replaced by undiluted shock, and for a moment she actually ceased to be exhausted and even forgot where she was or what she was doing there. It was outrageous, unreal. Except that he was quite real, standing there, regarding her steadily from halfway across the room. And all at once she felt like a fool, standing where *she* was, staring back at him.

Reacting instinctively, defensively, Margaret Ann whirled away, wrapping one arm around her waist and burying her face in her other hand. Behind her, she heard Peter's footsteps as he came slowly toward her. Then his hand touched her elbow.

"Come on, Margaret Ann. You have to sign a receipt for your things. Then we can go."

Go? Go where? There was a war in progress inside her as she allowed him to guide her through the motions of retrieving her knapsack. Then he was escorting her through the electronic gates and all the guards, through the tiny waiting area jammed with people who'd come to visit prisoners and, finally, out into the noisy, glaring, asphalt heat of downtown Baltimore. Her feet were moving forward, but that was the only proof she had that her trust in him was greater than her feeling of betrayal. He had lied to her. Aside from which, she was trying to grasp the impossible notion that she had been bailed out of jail by *the* Peter Alexander Lericos.

Crusader, freedom fighter, world changer. Brilliant attorney for the American Civil Liberties Union, whose

reputation for winning important cases had gained him
recognition throughout the region and beyond. The man
who had forced one of the city's biggest law firms to pro-
mote its female attorneys to partnership when they'd
earned it. The man who had put an end to George Lyle's
development company's discriminatory housing practices
in the Overland community. The man who'd made it possible for ten thousand Angels of the Golden Light to have
their annual devotional celebration in Langston Park,
much to the city's discomfort. Those were the ways Balti-
moreans knew him. Or *had* known him, before he went to
prison. To some he had been a hero, to others, a royal pain
in the neck. Larry had called him names far more vul-
gar—but then, George Lyle, who had been financially ruined in the suit Peter won against him, was Larry's friend.

Margaret Ann's memory of Peter's murder trial was
sketchy; his wife had died in a fire, which he had allegedly
set. There had been witnesses. What Margaret Ann did
recall clearly was how delighted Larry had been when Peter was found guilty. But her own life had been in such
turmoil then, she'd had little attention for anything but
taking care of Jimmy, going to school and wondering how
in heaven's name she would ever get out from under Larry
Silver's supreme control. That she had known Peter's
name all along but had had only the vaguest sense the night
she met him that Lericos sounded familiar, told the entire
tale of how badly her mental state had suffered the last
years of her marriage.

Peter led her to a black Corvette on a side street near the
jail. He opened the door, but she hesitated before getting
in. Looking at the car, then at him, she shook her head in
an effort to clear it. The color and caliber of the car were
right, but it should have been a Kenworth tractor. And he
should be wearing jeans and a beard. It had not escaped

her notice that he wore a suit and *no* beard awfully well, but he looked like an entirely different man. And it was going to take some getting used to.

Not that she would have the opportunity to get used to it.

The cold reminder of her extremely precarious position should have depressed her, but sheer exhaustion, made worse by the sweltering heat, was taking over; she was too numb to care about anything. As she wilted into the bucket seat, the part of her brain that was still functional harbored one thought only: she had to find a phone. Beyond talking to Jane, nothing mattered. There was no room in her head for wondering how Peter had gotten there or why he had come. Besides, as angry as she was at him, she had never been so happy to see anyone in her life.

They were several blocks up Calvert Street before Peter broke the silence.

"Are you okay?" he asked in that quiet gentle voice that always put a lump in her throat.

"Fine," she mumbled.

"It's going to be all right now, Margaret Ann."

Her eyes closed, and she pressed her lips together against the pain. He was trying to be kind, but she hadn't a prayer of anything ever being right again.

"I'm sorry you had to be in that stinking place so long," Peter went on. "I was in Arkansas when my brother, Nick, got ahold of me. I came as fast as I could."

When she remained silent, her gaze fixed straight ahead, Peter drew his own conclusions.

"You're mad I didn't tell you who I was."

Silence.

"I expected you to guess a dozen times," he said. "A lot of people do. Some of them ask. Some just stare and wonder. In the beginning it got to me a little, so I grew a beard." He paused a moment, then let out a sigh. "I don't know, maybe I should have told you. But I was afraid it would freak you out, first wondering if I might murder you in your sleep, then worrying that I might turn you in." He glanced at her. "I'm sorry, Margaret Ann. I swear, I never set out to deceive you."

"You've known about me all along, haven't you?" she asked. "Who I was, who my ex-husband was...everything."

"Since the night in Montana, yes."

"How?"

"I recognized your Baltimore accent and called Nick for the local news headlines."

She gave him a startled look. When she saw the corner of his mouth twitch slightly, she scowled and looked away. "I don't have an accent."

"Oh, yes, you do," he returned, "when you're very tired or when you've been crying. But I wouldn't worry about it. It probably doesn't come across in Greek and Latin."

"What are you doing here?"

It was close to noon, and traffic was heavy on the northbound artery through town. Peter negotiated around a delivery truck double-parked in their lane as he answered. "That's up to you. Originally, I had hoped I could convince you to turn yourself in. I would have given you the names of some good defense attorneys and kept in touch to make sure things were going the way they ought to go. Now, well—" he snorted softly "—it's too late for that. I'll still give you the names, if that's what you want. But I'd much rather take care of it myself."

She shook her head, blinking to keep her eyes open. "What are you talking about?"

"Representing you—if you'll accept the offer of my services."

That woke her up. "You want to be my lawyer?"

"I know. It's a shocker. But it isn't *quite* like the guy down at the auto body shop offering to take out your tonsils."

"Oh, no! I didn't mean—"

"You'll get used to it. Blue jeans and beard. Suits and briefcases—" he shrugged a little "—they're all just trappings."

"It's not the way you look, for heaven's sake. It's, well . . ."

"If you're worried I won't remember what I'm doing—"

"Of course not! I just didn't think you'd—"

"I was reinstated to the bar when my conviction was overturned. I *am* licensed to practice law."

"That's not what I meant!"

"So, it's settled, then."

"I can't afford you."

"Yes, you can."

"You posted my bail."

"I put up the usual ten percent in cash and posted bond for the rest. I've got the money, Margaret Ann. Unless you're planning to take off, don't worry about it. Now, quit stalling and tell me why you don't want me to take the case."

Because I don't want to fall in love with you. I can't let myself fall in love with you. But you'll look at me with those incredible eyes and say something wonderful, and I'll be lost. And I'm scared. I'm just plain scared of giving any man that much power over me.

Margaret Ann bit her lower lip against speaking the words aloud. Almost immediately another thought occurred to her—the automatic question that popped into her mind whenever she was faced with a major decision:

What would Larry do to her? It was a safe bet he would not be pleased to learn Peter Lericos was her attorney. It would threaten him. And threatening Larry was a dangerous game.

Margaret Ann brooded in silence over the impossible situation. She was being offered the best legal counsel a person could want but was afraid to make use of it. Yet she couldn't think of a single logical reason to reject it.

She had no idea what Peter was thinking or feeling about her, but honestly she didn't care. At the moment she didn't even care that she might be making a fatal mistake. She needed him desperately, needed his strength, his tenderness. And he was here. She didn't have it in her to send him away.

Margaret Ann drew a shaky breath. "I never did understand this thing you've got for lost causes. But I'm not exactly in a position to be telling somebody else how to run their life, so—"

"You're not exactly in the best shape to recognize whether or not a cause is lost, either," he shot back. "You need to rest and take care of yourself. And you need to stop worrying about Jimmy."

"I'm not worried about him." The calmness of her reply brought a dubious look from Peter. "He's safe," she said simply.

"Well, we'll talk about it later.... Margaret Ann, are you sure you're okay?"

"Yes," she lied.

"Nobody got rough with you in there?"

"No." At least that was the truth.

"And you're not sick?"

"No." Another lie. She felt dizzy and nauseated and close to fainting.

Peter pulled into a parking space before Margaret Ann even realized where they were. When she looked at the familiar turn-of-the-century structure with the wide covered porch and the third-floor dormer that was her living-room window, it seemed as if it must have been another woman who had lived there. The one who went to graduate school and taught giggling fifteen-year-old girls the finer points of Latin grammar and practiced karate five times a week at the YMCA.

"How did you know my address?" she asked when they were walking up the front steps.

"It's on your ID card. Remember?"

Yes, she remembered, but it boggled her mind that he did, too. Was there anything that escaped this man? she wondered. But she already knew the answer was no.

He found her key in the bottom of her knapsack and went in ahead of her. The house had been split into three apartments, and they walked up the stairs to the third floor, which was hers. She waited for him to unlock her door, then watched in bewilderment as the door swung open on its own. Peter was inside before her brain registered what he had noticed immediately. The handle was broken off and the frame splintered where the door had been pried open.

The place was a shambles—drawers ripped out of her old oak desk, flowered couch pillows lying on the floor, clothing from her dresser strewn everywhere. The room had been searched from top to bottom.

Oddly enough it didn't surprise her, but it shook her out of her stupor and sent fear racing along every nerve ending in her body. Nothing, in fact, could have scared her more effectively than this flagrant violation of the small private space she had made for herself. What would she do when Larry came again? Or would he? Maybe he would simply tell his despicable friends what she knew and let *them* worry about how to get rid of her.

Peter was standing in the middle of the living room, surveying the scene. "What was he looking for, Margaret Ann?"

He turned to her as she stood trembling inside the doorway, and she saw the anger in the set of his jaw and the grim turn of his mouth. The beard had softened features that, undisguised, were both harsh and arresting. She stared at the cleft in his chin, thinking how natural it seemed that he knew it was Larry who had done this.

"I have no idea," she answered, her voice breaking.

"See if you can tell if there's anything missing."

She didn't have anything worth taking, but she began hesitantly to pick her way around the room, stepping over clothing and papers, trying to remember where they had been. When she came to her desk, she stopped, stared for a moment, then frowned. The pages of her June phone bill were scattered on the desktop, the chair and the floor. And her Rolodex was empty. She looked but didn't see the cards on the floor or anywhere else.

"My Rolodex is empty, but I can't think why he would—"

"Was Jane's number written anywhere he could have found it?"

She shook her head. "I called Information from a phone booth to get it." He was probably right, she thought. Larry was desperate to find Jimmy and had come here looking for clues.

"I'm not leaving you here."

Peter's announcement brought such enormous relief, she thought she might cry. She avoided his gaze, not wanting him to see how upset she was.

"Can you find some things to pack?" he asked.

"Where are you taking me?"

"Home." He picked up a cushion and tossed it onto the couch.

When he turned back to her, she said in a tiny voice, "Your home?"

His tense expression softened somewhat, and he stepped toward her. Taking her hands in his, he said, "Yes. My home. I'm not leaving you here alone. But first we have to get one thing straight." He paused, his eyes searching hers. "The days in the Kenworth are over, Margaret Ann. For now, I'm your attorney."

She tried to lower her face, but he lifted it with the pressure of his fingers under her chin.

"You're in one helluva lot of trouble, lady. It's not impossible—not half as bad as you're imagining it to be—but it's going to take everything you and I have got between us to get you out of this. And that's the only thing we're going to think about right now."

Maybe it was the only thing *he* was going to think about. But as Margaret Ann gazed up at him, studied the strong masculine features and tried to connect them to the man she had come to know so well, she realized it would be impossible. He had given her the only fulfillment she'd ever had as a woman, and he had made it beautiful. He had also given her more warmth and caring than she had known for many years. Even in a muddle of exhaustion and raw nerves, she knew it would be inconceivable to forget that he had been her friend, her lover.

Yet what he said was true: the days in the Kenworth were over. She had lost her son and her freedom. She had lost the future she had hoped to steal. And she had lost any chance to share that future with a man she had dared to imagine she might love.

She lowered her gaze, unable to look him in the eye any longer.

"Get your things, Margaret Ann," he said. "I'm taking you home."

Chapter Ten

There was a dog barking. A breeze was whispering across her bare skin. Margaret Ann awoke feeling rested and strangely content—a pleasant fantasy that lasted all of five seconds. Full consciousness brought with it the familiar knot in her stomach, and she groaned, wishing she could go back to sleep and forget the whole thing.

But she was wide awake and starving. And she had to call Jane.

As she rolled onto her back and opened her eyes, her gaze began wandering over the sprigs of violets on the wallpaper, the deep embroidered flounces on the pillow-cases, the cherry-wood four-poster and the lace curtains that blew gently at the windows.

This was Peter's home. He brought her here, had shown her to this room, given her towels from the linen closet and left her to shower while he went to make her something to eat. How long ago had that been? She had no idea. She had fallen onto the bed, wrapped in a towel, with her hair still wet.

The towel was now a damp lump beside her. She was lying on top of the white eyelet spread, nude. And her hair was dry. She did not remember turning on the window fan or pulling the blinds. Clearly, she had fallen asleep before Peter returned. Had he come back before or after she discarded the towel?

The thought of him watching her sleep, unclothed, was at once erotic and disturbing. It was as though he were both a lover and a stranger. But he was neither. He was her lawyer.

Why he even wanted to speak to her she didn't know. She winced, remembering sneaking away after the night they had shared. It had been a terrible thing to do. But then, maybe their lovemaking hadn't affected him as powerfully as it had her. Maybe he looked upon it as...as what? A pleasant encounter? The natural course of events? No big deal? She wouldn't have guessed he would treat sex casually—he certainly didn't *have* sex casually. But what did she know about the average man's attitude toward sex?

One thing she did know. Peter had wanted her, but he never would have made love with her if she hadn't practically begged him. That he had given in hardly constituted a vow of undying devotion.

Neither did offering to represent her in a court of law.

Margaret Ann recognized the irony that, in bringing her to stay with him, Peter had undoubtedly postponed Larry's plans for her. But how was she going to stand seeing him, talking with him...wanting him? And this time, she couldn't run away. Not only would Larry be watching her like a hawk, but worse, Peter had put up her bail and would surely be in deep trouble if she disappeared. No, she was stuck here. With him.

And he wanted to be her lawyer.

Margaret Ann was tempted to climb under the covers and stay there. Instead, she sat up and reached for the robe she had left lying on the foot of the bed. Before she could deal with her confusion over Peter, she had to eat and talk to Jane.

Tying back the lace curtains at the windows and raising the blinds, she saw it was morning. Discovering she had slept almost an entire day made her feel even more disoriented, and she hurried to dress.

The luxury of the experience did not escape her, however. It felt wonderful to be clean, to put on makeup and to fuss with her unruly hair until it was a somewhat tidier mess of curls pinned back in a wide barrette. Her clothes felt wonderful, too—the textures of white linen slacks and a soft cotton blouse after weeks of wearing Jane's old jeans and T-shirts. By the time she slipped on a pair of sandals to go in search of food and her host, she felt almost normal.

Margaret Ann came upon Peter in the kitchen, and seeing him was a shock all over again, knowing it was he yet feeling as if she were looking at a stranger.

The people with him were definitely strangers. She stopped in the doorway to the bright, high-ceilinged room to observe Peter leaning against the counter with his arm around a short, plump woman. There were two unfamiliar men, as well—an older man with snow-white hair and a younger one, who had to be Peter's brother. The two men were sitting at a big oak table under a wooden ceiling fan that was swishing away the August heat. Everyone was listening as Peter talked.

"—not making promises, Dad. Let's see how it—" He broke off, catching sight of her, and his mouth curved into a slow, easy smile. "Well, hello, sleepyhead," he said, starting toward her. Then his eyes skimmed over her. "Make that Sleeping Beauty. Is this another Margaret Ann I'm meeting?"

That helped. If he looked different, so did she. It evened the score a little. His safari shorts, bright red T-shirt and bare feet helped, too. No lawyer suits today.

Margaret Ann smiled hesitantly under Peter's warm regard, her gaze darting to the others, who all looked at her expectantly. She felt like an intruder, but as odd as it seemed, they were smiling at her. She let Peter take her hand and lead her into the room.

"Margaret Ann, come meet my mother. And do me a favor, will you? Tell her I haven't been starving to death."

Had he told his parents how they had met? It would be easier not to have to lie about it, but what would they think of her? Margaret Ann was uncomfortable and couldn't duplicate Peter's light attitude, but she said a polite hello to the older woman as Peter abandoned her at the counter to go pour her a cup of coffee.

Carmen Lericos, whose black hair was crowned with a striking silver wave that swept back from her face, gave Margaret Ann a knowing look. "Don't bother reassuring me about my son's eating habits, dear. I know he's been surviving on jelly, canned stew and instant coffee. It doesn't look like it's hurt him, but I'm sorry if he made you suffer with it."

"Oh, and Margaret Ann suffers in silence, too." Peter winked as he handed her a mug of black *brewed* coffee, then returned to his position against the counter, between the two women.

Margaret Ann would have tried to give him a flip reply, but she suddenly noticed that Mrs. Lericos had been crying. And in spite of the gentle maternal reproach in her tone, the older woman stuck close to Peter's side. He put an arm around her shoulders as he introduced Margaret Ann to his father.

Alexander Lericos was a big robust man, with an expansive graciousness about him. He nearly waxed poetic, in fact, as he told her how he had often enjoyed meals at her aunt's restaurant on Eastern Avenue, years ago when he had kept a boat on the Gunpowder River.

Finally, turning to the man lounging in the captain's chair at the head of the table, Peter said, "And this is Nicholas, the other attorney in the family. Nick's a federal persecutor. And right now, he's very glad to see you and to have this whole business out in the open, so he can stop worrying about whether or not he really knows things he isn't supposed to know."

Nick shot him a pointed look but when his gaze shifted to Margaret Ann, he smiled. "It was worth losing a few nights' sleep to see my brother, after a year of wondering when I'd ever see him again. So, how do you do, Margaret Ann? It's nice to meet you."

Peter gave her ribs a gentle poke and leaned down to speak in a loud whisper. "Catch that? You're a star. You've single-handedly brought the black sheep home when all else had failed."

He hadn't been home before this? Not even once? Not in…? It had to be three years. Margaret Ann tried to take in that startling news as she listened to the family make plans for a homecoming dinner in Peter's honor.

"Tomorrow will be fine, Mom." Peter gave his mother's shoulders a squeeze. "It's too bad Thad had to leave straight from vacation for Reserves, but I'll see him when he gets back. I'm not going anywhere, probably for quite a while."

"Good! We'll eat at five." Mrs. Lericos looked at Margaret Ann. "And, of course, you'll come, too, won't you, dear?"

Margaret Ann began to decline, not wanting to intrude on what was sure to be a family celebration, but Peter spoke first.

"Say yes."

"Oh, I really don't think I should—"

"Yes, you should."

"But you'll all want to be, well, together, and—"

"If you don't go, I don't go."

Her gaze flashed to his.

"I told you I wasn't going to leave you alone," he said quietly.

Her eyes widened. "But that was because of…well, the mess in my apartment. I didn't think you meant—"

"If you'd woken up this morning and come down to find an empty house, how would you have felt?"

Scared. The word popped into her mind, and she saw his eyes darken as he caught the message.

"I'm not walking out the door unless you're with me," he said. "And you're not going anywhere without me."

She shook her head. "But, Peter, that's silly. You can't—"

"No," he interrupted. "It's not silly. So get used to it." As she gaped at him, he gave her a heart-stopping smile. "Now, be a good girl and tell Mom you'll come."

"Please do, Margaret Ann," Mrs. Lericos put in.

Mr. Lericos cleared his throat. "I don't suppose you know how to make cheesecake like your mother's."

Margaret Ann tore her gaze away from Peter and looked from one to the other of his parents, her cheeks warm. "As a matter of fact, I do. After my aunt died and the restaurant was sold, I sold Mom's recipe to a bakery that supplies cakes for some of the local restaurants.''

''*Flo's* cheesecake?'' Nick straightened his chair.

She nodded.

''And you know how to make it?''

She nodded again.

He leaned forward, pinning her with eyes very much like his brother's. ''What would it take to persuade you to bake one for dinner tomorrow?''

''Better make that two,'' Mr. Lericos put in. ''I'll want one for myself.''

''Oh, you two,'' Mrs. Lericos scolded. ''Margaret Ann can't be bothered baking cheesecake at a time like this. For heaven's sake!''

''I'd love to do it,'' Margaret Ann insisted. When Mrs. Lericos peered around Peter to give her a skeptical look, she nodded her reassurance. Then a thought occurred to her. ''But you probably had something special planned, and—''

''Oh, no!'' The older woman waved a hand. ''They'll all tell you I'm not much of a baker. It would be an enormous help, if you truly don't mind.''

''I don't. I'll do three, so you'll have leftovers.''

Nick said he had to get to work, and Mr. and Mrs. Lericos had errands to run. Since Margaret Ann hadn't had breakfast, Peter left her to her own devices in the big country-style kitchen while he went to say goodbye to his family.

After his parents had driven away, Peter leaned against a porch column and looked at his brother. ''So, what do you think?''

Nick leaned against the opposite column and folded his arms. ''Silver must be some kind of lunatic if he thinks he can get anybody to believe that sweet little freckle-faced thing beat him up.''

Peter chuckled. ''When I met that 'sweet little freckle-faced thing,' she was in the process of flattening a guy easily twice her size.''

''You've got to be joking.''

''Nope. He was trying to pick her up.'' The smile left his face. ''But something's wrong, Nick. That's not the real Margaret Ann you met in there.''

''She looked all right to me. Damned good, in fact. Does she get better?''

''I'm serious.''

''I can tell.''

Peter gave Nick a look of strained patience, and Nick sobered.

''She's given up,'' Peter said.

''Well, she *did* get caught.''

''No, you don't understand. She thinks the fight's over when it hasn't even begun.''

''For Lord's sake, Peter.'' This time it was Nicholas who was impatient. ''What do you expect of the woman? Five weeks on the run, three days in a rat-hole jail cell, finding her apartment ransacked—how do you think she's going to feel?''

Peter looked for a way to explain the nuances of Margaret Ann's manner that made him certain he was right. ''Nick, I've seen her scared. Really scared,'' he said. ''And I've seen her exhausted and worried and totally strung out. But I've never seen her . . . *hopeless*. She thinks she's a lost cause and that I'm crazy for bothering with her. And when she got a look at that apartment yesterday—'' his frown became a brooding scowl ''—she seemed ready to sit down and wait for Silver to come do the same thing to her. Tear her to shreds.''

Nick remained skeptical. "But that was yesterday. Things might look different for her today."

Still brooding, Peter watched a robin digging worms in his front lawn. "I want to know why."

"Why what?"

"Why Silver tore her place up like that. The police had already searched it—I checked—and it's damned sure they didn't make that mess. Why would he go through it himself? And why wasn't she the least bit surprised that he had? I think she almost expected him to do it. She's still terrified of him, even though she hasn't got a reason to be anymore."

Nick was silent for a moment. "It doesn't make a lot of sense, does it? The worst has certainly happened."

Peter looked at his brother. "No. Not the worst. The worst would have been if she'd had Jimmy with her when she was arrested."

"Is she going to turn him over?"

Hesitating, he lowered his gaze before replying. "I don't know. I'll talk to her about having a guardian *ad litem* appointed. If she knows there's somebody impartial looking out for the boy, and that he won't go back to Silver while the litigation is pending, maybe I can convince her."

Nick sighed. "Well, if anyone can do it . . ." He let the sentence trail off and, a moment later, said quietly, "What I want to know is how you're going to handle this."

"The defense?"

"Uh-uh. Being in love with her."

Peter's gaze flashed to his brother, and his lips curved in a crooked smile. "I'm not going to handle it. *It* handles *me*."

"Yeah. I noticed." Nick returned his brother's slow smile. "I've got to say, the two of you together, uh . . . sizzle."

Peter laughed, neither surprised nor embarrassed. It was such a pleasure to be having this conversation with his brother, to be looking at each other face-to-face and talking about things that mattered.

Besides, there was something reassuring about Nick's perception. It took two to sizzle, and maybe that meant his feelings for Margaret Ann weren't one-sided, after all. For a brief moment when she had first seen him the day before her expression had made him think his fears were groundless, but then she had closed up on him. He had tried to make it clear that he had no expectations of her, that he was here to help her. But she hadn't looked sure she wanted his help. And, now, well, it was hard to tell anything with this restrained polite creature who didn't even look like the Margaret Ann he knew. But then, he didn't look much like the man she knew, either. The whole thing was disorienting. Did they have to get to know each other all over again?

Lord, he hoped not.

"It'll be all right," he said finally, the broad statement meant to cover all concerns he or Nick might have.

But Nick reminded him of the one concern he was trying to avoid, and there was no teasing about it.

"What are you going to do if she's convicted?"

"She's not going to prison."

"Coming from you, that's certainly one of the more ridiculous things I've ever heard."

"I mean it. I'm going to win this case." Peter shoved away from the porch column to pace as he spoke. "Nick, look, the charges are crazy. Silver claims she threatened him with a gun. But where is it? The police report I read says the only gun in the house was his, and the only fingerprints on it were his. Then he claims she tried to beat him to death. But he's not dead, and the report of his injuries don't indicate he was anywhere close.''

"What about kidnapping?" Nick put in. "She did take the boy unlawfully. You say she was protecting him, but why didn't she go to the police?"

"She had reason to think they wouldn't believe her. And when we charge Silver with rape and battery, we're also going to add malicious prosecution, defamation and intentional infliction of emotional distress to the list. What he did to her in their divorce trial was malicious slander. The statute of limitations is still good, and I'm going after him on it. I'll bet Silver's lawyers will recommend he drop the charges—fast. If they don't—or he won't—well, that suits me fine. By the time I'm finished with him in court, she'll have the whole damned city rooting for her, and Silver will be leaving town with a bag over his head. That's *if* he doesn't go to jail when the state decides to prosecute him for obstruction of justice.''

"And if *she* doesn't end up in jail for contempt of court because she won't produce the kid."

Peter whirled to a halt in the middle of the porch and leveled a look on his brother. "She's not going to jail."

Nick remained cool. After a minute, he said, "You're not thinking of doing something stupid, are you? Like getting back in that truck with her and taking off?"

Peter sucked in a breath, held it for an instant, then let it out in a rush. "No. I already offered her that alternative. She turned it down. She said she didn't want me to ruin my life trying to help her."

Nick studied him closely. "You know what, brother? I think this time you're in trouble."

But Peter knew the only real trouble would be if he got Margaret Ann acquitted...and she still turned him down.

When Peter returned to the kitchen, Margaret Ann was sitting at the table, eating French toast as she read the newspaper.

"Looks good," he said, pouring himself a mug of coffee and settling into the chair across from her.

"Mmm." Margaret Ann gave him a quick glance over the top of the paper.

"Are you feeling better today?"

"Much."

"I brought you lunch yesterday, but you'd already fallen asleep. I didn't want to wake you."

The paper crackled as she turned a page. "Thank you for not."

"Hmm. Were you comfortable upstairs? If there's anything else you need—"

"No, I'm fine. The room is lovely. Your whole house is lovely."

"Thank you. I'm glad you like it." His finger traced the rim of his mug.

"I like your family, too."

"Thank you again. So do I."

"Your brother looks like he could be your twin—except for being younger, of course."

"Actually, he's less than a year younger than me."

"Oh," she stammered, clearly embarrassed.

"It's all right, Margaret Ann. My gray hairs don't bother me."

The color in her cheeks deepened as she attacked the food on her plate. "You don't have gray hairs. They're silver."

"Well, whatever."

"I've always thought they were . . . very attractive."

"Thank you."

"You're welcome."

How long could they keep this up, Peter wondered, before one or both of them cracked? He and Margaret Ann sitting there, all groomed and proper, across the breakfast table from each other, exchanging polite inanities, was too much to take. When she spoke again, her too casual tone caught his attention.

"I thought your house had burned down."

He studied her for a moment, then answered. "No. There was a lot of smoke damage. Some things were a total loss, but paint and wallpaper and cleaning fluid took care of the rest. I did a lot of the work myself, while my trial was going on. It kept me busy."

"Does someone live here—to take care of things, I mean?"

"No."

"It just sits empty."

"Yes. My family keeps an eye on it."

"Why haven't you sold it? Did you plan to come back someday?"

"I wasn't planning anything," he said. "I just wasn't ready to give it up."

Her fork hovered above the next piece of French toast. "Because of your wife? Because it had been your home together?"

When he didn't answer right away, she looked up to meet his disbelieving gaze. There was no guile or meanness about her expression, though, not that she would ever be deliberately cruel. "You really don't know, do you?" Peter concluded.

She frowned. "Know what?"

"About Alyce. About why my conviction was overturned."

Margaret Ann shook her head, picking at the food on her plate. "No, I... You must have been released from prison about the same time I was getting divorced. I wasn't paying much attention to the news then."

"I was convicted mainly on the testimony of two neighbors who said they saw me drive away from the house at the same time they saw the fire. I'd gone fishing for the weekend. I was alone at a cabin out in Cumberland and didn't have an alibi."

"Yes. I knew that. So who did the neighbors see?"

"An arsonist. A clumsy arsonist. He had a build like mine, and he drove a black Corvette like mine. I'd put the house in Alyce's name, so she'd always feel secure. She hired the guy to torch it for the insurance money so she could run away with her lover. Unfortunately, the bastard wasn't careful enough to check inside first. Alyce was in bed, asleep. She never woke up."

Margaret Ann blanched, her fork clattering to the plate, and Peter watched the shock and horror play havoc with her features. Once he would have given anything to tell her what it had been like for him. Losing his wife in such a violent way, then being convicted of murdering her. Sitting in prison, despairing that Nick would be able to keep his promise to find the truth. Finally, his brother telling him what Alyce's checkbooks and personal phone directory had, at last, revealed. Purchases at men's clothing stores, all delivered to the same address. A man no one had known about. A man no one, not even he, had known about. A confession torn from the man's guilty conscience and another search for an arsonist, who had been on his way to jail for something else and was all too happy to trade a confession for immunity on other charges.

What he had most wanted to explain to Margaret Ann, though, was his own uncertainty. The terrible fear that maybe it *had* been his fault—partly, at least. Why hadn't he known about Alyce's lover? More than that, why had he married someone so unlike himself, someone so cool and remote, then spent ten increasingly unhappy years trying to coax and prod her into matching him emotionally? He had failed, of course. But he hadn't known how badly. He hadn't known in the beginning, when Alyce would laugh and say, oh, he was simply too much for her. Nor had he realized later, when she had grown increasingly distant, that she was actually threatened by him. So threatened she had found it easier to attempt burning the house down than to tell him she wanted a divorce.

Once he had wanted to tell Margaret Ann how it was to be afraid of getting close to a woman for fear of intimidating her as badly as he must have intimidated Alyce. But the Margaret Ann he had wanted to tell called him Charlie and knew exactly how to put him in his place. He wasn't sure he hadn't done it again, frightened another woman with the intensity of his need for emotional, as well as physical, intimacy. Margaret Ann had met his need beyond his wildest dreams. But then she had run away.

To ask her now, when she was unable to run, if, indeed, he had made another mistake, would be grossly unfair. It was for her sake that he had to maintain the distance between them that their attorney-client relationship would provide. Which was why, when Margaret Ann continued to stare at him, her eyes full of questions, he quickly put a lid on the subject.

"So, let's talk about plans for the day," he said, forcing a matter-of-fact tone. "We've got business to take care of, if you think you're up to it."

She blinked a couple of times, confused. Then her look became wary. "What kind of business?"

"We need to get a locksmith over to your apartment, but first I want you to file a breaking-and-entering report. And we need to talk about the charges you're going to file against Larry Silver."

When she simply looked at him as though he had lost his mind, Peter explained patiently. "The bottom line on how to get out of the mess Silver's created for you is to create one for him. He's filed serious criminal charges against you. You have clear grounds to file equally or more serious charges against him."

"Charges like what?" she whispered.

"How about if we start with rape and battery?"

Peter could almost see her want to crawl under the table, and he wondered how he could bring himself to go through with this. She looked so small and fragile, so utterly feminine, with her curls clipped back demurely, little wisps of them fluttering around her face. She had done something to her eyes that made them look huge and very blue. Only his rage that a man had dared to touch her with anything less than respect and love hardened his resolve.

"This is important, Margaret Ann," he said. "I know it won't be easy, but if it helps, I don't think it's ever going to come to trial. I think Silver's lawyers will want to drop the charges against you. We'll negotiate a settlement that gives you full custody of Jimmy and be done with it."

"Larry will never drop anything." She shuddered visibly, and when he would have argued, she shook her head. "No. I can't do it. I told you what my divorce trial was like. It would be bad enough talking about . . . about what he did to me. But to have to do it *knowing* no one is going to believe me—"

"*I* believe you."

That brought her eyes snapping to his, and he watched as a deep blush crept into her cheeks.

An instant later her lashes lowered. "What will you do? Tell them how I attacked you in my sleep when you were trying to put me in bed?"

Peter grimaced. "I think we'll let that ride. It would open up a subject we don't want to discuss in court, if we can help it. But there's another way to get at the truth, and that's to file these charges. Besides the rape and battery, there are things called malicious prosecution, intentional infliction of emotional distress, and defamation. In other words, Silver lied to win the divorce suit against you, and you've suffered because of it. When the state's attorney is informed that Silver committed perjury, the state may well decide to prosecute him, too."

Peter made a dismissive gesture. "But it's unlikely it'll get that far. Silver is a public official. He can't afford to have stuff like this smeared all over the news if there's even a remote possibility he could lose. Which, I promise you, he damned well would. But whether he drops the charges against you or we have to go to trial, one way or another, it's time to end the lies. And this is the way to do it."

When she continued to stare at her coffee in tight-lipped silence, he went on. "There's something else we have to talk about. I need to know how you're going to respond when the court orders you to produce Jimmy."

Her reply was succinct. "The only thing I'll say about Jimmy is that he's happy and healthy."

"Are you willing to discuss conditions? For instance, tell them where he is if they put him under court protection and agree he won't go back to Silver while procedures are pending on your case?"

"No." She met his gaze squarely. "They made the wrong decision about my son's welfare before, and I'm not going to trust them to get it right now. He's safe, and he's going to stay that way." Suddenly her eyes narrowed, and she added, "I don't understand how you, of all people, could suggest that I *should* trust them. Not after what they did to you."

Peter knew what she was trying to do, turning what she perceived as an attack on her into one on him, and he couldn't let her get away with it. Not this time.

"I was convicted by a jury, Margaret Ann," he said, his gaze never wavering from hers. "A jury appointed by due process of law. And those people did the best they could with the evidence they had before them. If I'd been on that jury, presented with the same evidence, I'd have delivered the same verdict."

Peter realized what he had said, realized how convinced he sounded, and it stunned him. He had told himself the same thing many times—and it was true—yet he hadn't really believed it. But for Margaret Ann, he *had* to believe it. The justice system had failed her in the past, and she was convinced it would fail her again. It was critical that he have faith where her faith was lacking.

He had pushed her far enough, though. Her expression was closed and definitely frightened.

"Think about it," he said on a lighter note as he got up to carry his empty mug to the sink. "We don't have to make any monumental decisions today. It's Friday. Maybe by Monday—"

"Friday! Friday the what? What's the date?"

He turned to see her shuffling madly through the newspaper, looking for the date. When she found it, her breath caught for a second, then her shoulders fell and she uttered a sound of dismay.

"What's wrong?" Setting his mug in the top rack of the dishwasher, he walked over to stand beside her. "Did you forget somebody's birthday?"

"It's nothing."

He put a forearm on the table and leaned over, catching her wrist in his other hand as she tried to hide her face.

"What is it, Margaret Ann? What did you miss that's so important?"

In a show of indifference, she rolled her eyes and sighed. "I was supposed to register for classes. *Last* Friday was the final day to do it."

"Well, that settles that!" Peter rapped his fingers lightly on the table as he straightened. "I'll change my clothes while you finish your coffee, then we'll go."

"Go where?" She was looking up at him with eyes that made his heart melt.

"To school," he said, and he began hustling dirty dishes into the dishwasher. "We'd better get rolling, too, if we have to convince somebody to accept your late registration. Knowing the way bureaucracy works, that could take all day."

She didn't move from her chair. "They'll never do it."

"Can't hurt to try."

"But it's silly for me to bother. I mean, if I'm going to be . . . well, I wouldn't get to finish the semester, anyway, probably."

"I knew you couldn't be serious about this business of teaching Latin. I mean, how could anybody really take a dead language seriously?" His back was to her, but he heard the warning in her sharp comment.

"It won't work, Charlie. You can throw out the bait, but I'm not biting."

Peter grinned, delighted to know his Maggie was alive and well, after all. Slamming the dishwasher door closed, he pivoted to spear her with a look. "Get off your duff, Margaret Ann. You didn't work all these years for a Ph.D. only to quit two semesters from the end. You're going to sign up for the damned courses, and you're going to finish them. And I don't want to hear another noise out of you about it."

Her slender neck stretched in perfect indignation, but she got up. Snatching her plate off the table, she strolled over to stick it in the dishwasher, slamming the door closed once more. With the dishwasher between them, she planted one hand on the counter, the other on her hip, and glared at him. "All right, mister big-shot lawyer. I'll sign up for the darned courses. But let's get one thing *real* clear, here. Just because I let you bully me into wasting a semester's tuition doesn't mean I'm going to do everything you want me to do."

"I'm certain you'll let me know when I've reached the limit."

"You bet I will."

"It's nice to know you'll never let me be, well, you know, a macho pig, or anything like that."

"Humph!" She tossed her head and gave him a look that said he was close.

At least she was fighting again, thank God. Peter watched as she turned and sauntered out of the room, his eyes alight with sensual appreciation as they followed the swaying of her hips. He couldn't figure out why she had *him* pegged as the one she should be fighting, but it was obvious that she did—and that he had his work cut out for him.

Chapter Eleven

Margaret Ann felt like a freak in a sideshow. Peter took her to Johns Hopkins campus, then downtown so he could update his professional wardrobe and get his hair trimmed to a slightly more conservative length. They went to an elaborate kitchenware store to buy springform pans for making cheesecake, then to a grocery store for ingredients. And at every stop, people stared until Margaret Ann was tempted to cross her eyes and wriggle her nose to entertain them as she had Jimmy when he was a baby.

With her face so recently in the news, people recognized her immediately, and their scandalized expressions made their opinion of her crystal clear. Margaret Ann decided she had better get used to it, and that she would do well to take a lesson from Peter. When people who had been glaring at her recognized him, their expressions became surprised, curious and decidedly suspicious. But if it upset him, he didn't show it. He smiled. He chatted with salesclerks in the stores. He talked baseball with the man who trimmed his hair. And he shamelessly seduced the registrar into letting Margaret Ann take the courses she needed.

Margaret Ann was impressed with Peter's fortitude. It wasn't as though they lived in a city like New York or Chicago, where one might blend in with the woodwork, where fame—or infamy—might be here one day and gone the next. Baltimore was the sort of town where you were born and stayed until you died. Where almost no one *rented* houses, and lawn services had a hard time making it because folks fertilized their own grass. Where, years after the fact, you'd meet somebody in a checkout line who was the classmate of your older brother's best friend's fiancée and who remembered seeing you at the wedding. A big small town that had seen its share of public scandal, in Baltimore everyone knew everyone else's business. And Margaret Ann could almost hear the dinner table conversations that those who had seen her and Peter that day would be having. "You'll never guess who was at the Rotunda Mall, walking around looking like he owned the place. And you won't believe who was with him!"

Margaret Ann went through a grueling day at Peter's side, knowing it would have been unbearable without him. He made it possible. He even made it fun. She was happy to be with him. Proud, in fact. And before long she wasn't paying attention to what other people were whispering or to the looks they gave her; she was thinking about how handsome and engaging Peter was. She was noticing that everything he did, he did the way he drove a truck—with style, determination and success. She was realizing how easily he could make her laugh, or make her mad. How he knew the things to say that would make her want to cry.

One question bothered her, and she had to bite her tongue to keep from asking it. How could any woman have been crazy enough to betray him the way his wife had? Clearly, she decided, Alyce Lericos must have been, in fact, crazy. Nobody in her right mind would try to burn down a house rather than ask for a divorce. For that matter, no woman in her right mind would want another lover if she was fortunate enough to have Peter. What kind of marriage had his been to have ended so tragically? What had it been like to get his ticket out of prison stamped with the knowledge of his wife's betrayal?

No wonder he had decided to live in a truck. No wonder he hadn't wanted to come home. Her estimation of what it was costing him to go through this day with her rose steadily, as did her estimation of his courage.

When they arrived back at his house, she had to ask, "How do you do it? How do you manage to act as if nothing ever happened?"

Handing her a package out of the back seat, he closed the car door and his brow furrowed in thought. "A very smart woman once asked me if I was driving a truck rather than face the creeps who'd called me a murderer. And I think I knew even when she said it that she was right." He looked down at her, one heavy eyebrow arched. "Except they aren't creeps. They're my friends and my colleagues and the people I went to school with. Some of them are people I've represented in court. And I'm tired as hell of being mad at them. It's easier to smile." And he did so as he grabbed another bag off the roof of the car and motioned her to start with him up the walk.

Margaret Ann bit her lower lip against the sudden urge to cry. He humbled her and inspired her and made her want to throw her arms around him and tell him how happy she was that he had decided, at last, to make peace with himself and his home.

They were halfway up the front walk when the screen door on the neighboring house banged and a woman came out to pick up her evening paper off the porch.

"Hello, Mrs. Morley!" Peter called. The woman looked toward them, her startled expression visible even at a distance, and he raised a hand in greeting. "Nice to see you again!"

"I think she's going to faint," Margaret Ann muttered as they took the steps to the porch.

"She might," he agreed. "She and her husband are the two who testified against me. But I'm not moving, so they'll have to get used to seeing me. They'll get over it. People don't die of embarrassment."

He couldn't be real, Margaret Ann decided. No man could be that forgiving, could he? Could she be that forgiving, if she were in his shoes? If she won her battle and was able to bask in righteousness, could she rebuild her life without resentment?

No need to worry about it—she'd never get the chance to find out.

After dinner, Peter planted himself in front of the television to indulge in the rare luxury of watching Orioles baseball. Margaret Ann joined him, but her mind was not on the game. She studied Peter—sprawled in the overstuffed chair, one leg draped over the arm and a can of light beer in his hand—and decided this would be a good time to call Jane. She had been waiting all day for an opportunity to do so without Peter knowing. As he had noted, the days in the Kenworth were over, and ethically he might be bound to inform the court if he knew she had talked to her son.

First, though, she had to find a phone. She already knew there wasn't one in the kitchen, the living room or her bedroom. The door to Peter's study was off the living room, and he would see her if she went there. So, with a sigh of feigned boredom, she rose from her chair, strolled across the wide foyer and casually headed up the stairs.

Peter had always liked baseball, had played it through college, but he had never been a slave to any sport the way some people were. He was well aware of the instant Margaret Ann got up to leave the room. He even knew where she was going, and his feelings about the matter were ambivalent, to say the least.

Legally, as long as he didn't know where Jimmy was, he was okay. And it was not his job to drag, force or otherwise wrest the information out of Margaret Ann. Not that he could have.

But he wanted her to tell him. For purely personal reasons, he wanted her to come to him with all he needed to know in order to save her from what could be a very grim sentence. There were so many unanswered questions. And the biggest one was why Margaret Ann still seemed reluctant to let him help her. Peter understood why, back on the highway, she would have been wary of letting anyone help. But now? What possible reason could she have for still being suspicious? What reason had he given her not to trust him? He might have scared her with his out-of-control lovemaking, but he had made it clear he was on her side in her battle with Silver.

It made him angry that she didn't trust him. It also hurt. And when he thought about the possible consequences of her continued refusal to cooperate with him, he got a panicked feeling in the pit of his stomach. Trying to be objective, he had thought about suggesting she get another attorney with whom she might feel more comfort-able. But he knew as surely as he knew his name it wouldn't make any difference. If she wouldn't talk to him, she wouldn't talk to anybody. That certainty reassured him only slightly. And in the long run, he didn't know whom he was angrier with—her for not trusting him, or himself for taking it personally.

Either way, he was in foul humor by the time he switched off the set and went looking for Margaret Ann. It was eight o'clock. She'd had time to make her calls, and he had put this off long enough. He needed answers, and, one way or the other, he was going to get them.

Margaret Ann found what she was looking for on the night table in what was obviously Peter's room. The enor-mous sleigh bed was made with his usual flair for preci-sion—with his running shoes kicked carelessly beneath it. Feeling like a trespasser, she entered the room, looking at the creamy-white walls graced with original watercolors by a local artist. Oriental rugs partially covered the random-width pine floors, and a carved oak mantel dominated the fireplace on the wall across from the bed. The room was as lovely and comfortable as the others in the Victorian house, and she wondered—not for the first time that day— how Peter could have been happy living in a truck when he had this sitting here waiting for him.

But then, she knew why he had chosen the open road in a tractor-trailer over his house on its quiet wooded street in the Roland Park section of Baltimore.

Margaret Ann perched on the side of the bed, studying the phone as one might a live wire from a downed utility pole. She had lived for too many years with a phone tap— one of Larry's handy ways of keeping tabs on her—not to wonder if it was safe to dial Jane's number. Had there been time for Larry to hear she was out of jail? Did he know where she was? Had he had time to infiltrate Peter's telephone line? The answers were yes, maybe and probably not. In any case, she had to risk it; Jane was undoubtedly frantic, wondering what was going on. And later, communications might become impossible.

She picked up the receiver and dialed the call collect. The operator barely had time to leave the line before Jane burst into tears.

"Oh, dear Lord, Margaret Ann! Oh, thank God.... Thank God, you're—"

"Janey, it's okay. I'm all right."

"I—I saw the news, and..."

"I know. It must have looked pretty awful. Does Jimmy know?"

"No, I haven't told him. I didn't know—I've been so worried." With obvious effort, Jane pulled herself together to ask, "Where are you?"

Margaret Ann glanced around the room, her eyes coming to rest on the white shirt and tie hanging on the knob of the open closet door. Her mouth slanted in a dry smile. "Remember the trucker I told you about? The one I was riding with a few weeks ago?"

"Yes."

"Well, Jane, you aren't going to believe this, but..."

And she told her friend what had transpired after her arrest and who her friendly truck driver had turned out to be.

If anything, Jane was more stunned than she had been. "You're right. I don't believe it. I mean, I do, but..."

"I know," Margaret Ann agreed. "I'm having a hard time getting used to the idea myself. Maybe if he'd kept the beard—"

Jane wasn't listening. "It's like— Why, it's—" Suddenly her amazement became an excited stream of words. "This is wonderful! Margaret Ann, if there's anybody who can help you, it's Pete Lericos. Oh, honey, do you have any idea what kind of reputation he had? When Brian was working as a court reporter, we used to follow all the big civil liberties cases, and I don't think your 'truck driver' ever lost one! Sometimes when a trial was scheduled in Baltimore or D.C., Brian would go just to watch. He said it was like watching Olivier perform on stage—that there wasn't anybody who could handle a jury or psych out a judge as well as Lericos. Oh, Margaret Ann, this is too good to be true!"

Too good to be true? She had expected Jane to know who Peter was, but she hadn't been prepared for Jane's enthusiastic reaction. Surely her friend was missing the point. She had to remind herself that Jane knew only what Larry had done to Jimmy and that he was a crook who did business with other crooks, nothing more.

"You don't understand," she said. "Having an attorney with a record like that is only going to make things worse."

"Margaret Ann!" Jane exclaimed. "How could having a good attorney—no, a great attorney—make things worse?"

Margaret Ann closed her eyes. In her mind she had trudged over this same ground over and over, it was as if she'd had dug a trench. "Jane, I told you about Larry because you had a right to know why I needed somebody to take Jimmy. But I can't tell anyone else what I told you."

"Well, for heaven's sake, why not?"

"Because I don't have any proof!" Her tone was both impatient and bitter as she added, "You don't just go around saying wildly popular elected officials are criminals, unless you've got evidence. And when you're the man's ex-wife, who everybody—including the court—thinks is so bad she shouldn't be near her own child, you don't expect anybody to take you seriously enough to go looking for evidence you haven't got!"

"Pete Lericos would take you seriously."

"So what if he did? What could he do but stir things up, make Larry madder? Think, Jane! Even if you *do* have evidence, you don't say things that implicate crime bosses unless you're prepared to have plastic surgery and move to the outback! They'd find me floating in the river, the victim of an 'unfortunate accident.' And the only satisfaction anybody would get out of it is that Larry would probably be dead, too, when his friends found out he'd let me live all this time, knowing what I know."

"But, Margaret Ann!" Jane began. Then, abruptly, her tone became disgusted. "This is ridiculous. Pete Lericos wouldn't do anything that would get you killed. You've got to trust him."

Trust him. Lord knows, she wanted to. And in many important ways, she already did. What she didn't trust was the situation and Peter's ability to control it. Larry Silver was a deeply evil, extremely powerful man and Margaret Ann had lived too long under his threats to believe that salvation was possible. She had no faith in justice. And justice was what Peter Lericos, Attorney-at-Law, was all about.

"I don't know," she murmured. "I'll think about it. I'm still pretty confused, I guess. I'm not sure about anything right now."

"Oh, honey," Jane replied, "I know it must be awful. You take it easy and try not to worry."

Worry. That brought her to the hardest part of this call. "Jane, I need to know... If I wind up in jail or—or if anything happens to me, are you still willing to keep Jimmy?"

"Absolutely. I made a promise, and I'll keep it. And I won't start regretting it, so don't even think that." Jane hesitated, then continued on a quavering note. "He's a wonderful little boy, Margaret Ann. And I swear to you, I'll love him like he was my own."

Tears were running down Margaret Ann's cheeks as she reaffirmed her half of the bargain. "And I promise I won't tell anyone your name or where you are. Oh, Janey, I'll never be able to repay you for this. Not in a thousand years. And to think of the danger I might have exposed you to—"

Her friend cut her off. "None of that, Margaret Ann. We've been over this already. I make my own decisions, too, and you've exposed me to nothing I'm not ready to handle."

Margaret Ann was forced to concede the point, and she whispered gratefully, "Because of you, Jimmy is safe, and I don't have to worry about him anymore."

"Good," Jane said firmly in spite of the emotion that made talking difficult. "Maybe with Jimmy off your mind, you can start worrying about yourself for a change. And if you've got the good sense you used to have, you'll let Pete Lericos help you." She paused briefly, then sighed. "Gosh. I can hardly believe you got so lucky as to run into him like that. And he's been driving a truck!"

"A very big, very nice truck," Margaret Ann put in with a tiny smile.

"It's unbelievable." Jane sighed again. "But then again, maybe it's not. The press was pretty ruthless with him, even after he was let out of prison." Her tone was disparaging as she grumbled, "People do such weird things when they're feeling guilty. They put a man in prison, then, when they find out they made a mistake, they look for things to say about the guy that make it sound like the mistake was *his* fault.''

Margaret Ann uttered a derisive laugh. ''Well, they made one huge mistake with Peter. He's a good man, Jane, and I don't understand how anybody could think differently.''

''Actually, I do understand it,'' Jane replied. ''He's a risk taker. Even a rabble-rouser, for a good cause. You know how it is with people like that, people with real principles. They put themselves on the line for things they believe in, and people think they're wonderful and call them heroes. But let there be even a hint of scandal, and everybody's ready to burn them at the stake. Your friend Peter got burned worse than most.''

Burned to ashes. Burned like the phoenix, whose name he had borrowed. Burned to rise again from the cinders of his own destruction. The image came to her, and suddenly Margaret Ann could think of nothing else. *''So, has the phoenix risen?''* she had asked him. *''Let's say it's rising,''* he had answered. And she had had the gall to suggest he might be lying. Even worse, as he had so clearly reminded her that day, she had all but accused him of being a coward for refusing to face the people who'd called him a murderer.

Some coward. Some incredibly stupid mouth she had.

''You must mean a lot to him, Margaret Ann. But I guess you realize that.''

Jane's quiet words made her grow hot with embarrassment—then cold as a numb, bleak feeling stole through her.

Maybe it wasn't *she* who meant a lot to him. Maybe it was what she represented. That would explain why Peter was here, clean-shaven, wearing a suit and ready to step back into the courtroom. Why, finally, after staying away the entire year he had been out of jail, without even a single trip home to visit his family, he had decided to return. Why he had been able to go through that day with her, smiling.

Although the cynical part of her, the part that had been hurt by another man, was satisfied to have solved the problem so neatly, she felt tears of disappointment stinging her eyes. Irrational foolish tears.

No, there were no vows of undying devotion required. He wanted to be her lawyer. He had taken her ignorant remarks as a challenge—the motivation he needed to get past his bitterness and face the city and its people who had turned on him so abruptly, so viciously. And it was suddenly quite clear in her mind that, in defending her, Peter would be defending himself. She could almost hear him summing up: "You made a mistake with my life, but you're not going to make the same mistake again. I won't let you send another innocent person to prison."

Except that she wasn't innocent. Not in the eyes of the law.

Jane interrupted her thoughts, asking if she wanted to speak to Jimmy. Margaret Ann was about to say yes, when a noise behind her made her jerk around. Peter was standing in the doorway, watching her, his expression inscrutable.

Her eyes didn't leave his as she told Jane, "I have to go."

"Don't you want to speak to—"

"Not now. I have to go."

Jane hesitated. "Somebody's there?"

"Yes."

"All right, but what should I tell Jimmy? Do you want him to know..."

Margaret Ann's gaze followed Peter as he slowly crossed the room to stand in front of the window, his back to her, his hands shoved in the pockets of his slacks.

"Uh..." Margaret Ann pressed a hand to her forehead. "Look. Don't say anything. I'll—I'll think of something. Just...don't say anything. I've got to go."

Chapter Twelve

The phone receiver slipped in her sweaty hand as Margaret Ann rattled it back into its cradle. She was in no shape for a confrontation with Peter, and her only thought was to leave the room as quickly as possible. She started to get up, mumbling an apology for intruding.

"The phone was turned on two days ago."

Peter's flat statement made her hesitate, though she remained poised for flight. He turned to study her, his eyes a blazing gold in his otherwise dark countenance. His look was calculating and fierce, and it held not a scrap of mercy. It was a look he had never given her, and with a sinking feeling, she knew this was not her tender, compassionate truck driver.

"It ought to be okay," Peter said with a glance at the phone. "But I don't know if I'd trust it not to be tapped."

She thought about trying to lie. *Oh, I was just touching base with a distant cousin who I thought might have heard*

I'd been arrested. But lying was pointless. Saying anything was pointless.

"If your apartment is any indication," Peter went on, "I'd guess Silver's desperate enough to try anything to find Jimmy. But you already know that, don't you?"

Margaret Ann stared at him, her mouth open to speak, but she didn't know what to say. "Yes, well," she stammered, "Larry's a rather, uh, determined man when he gets fixed on something. Look, I'm really worn out from all the walking and shopping today. The heat, you know. I think I'll . . . well, maybe just go to bed."

"Tell me . . ."

She looked at him wearily.

Peter arched an eyebrow. "What happened the night you took Jimmy from Silver's house?"

Margaret Ann hesitated another second or two, then settled tentatively on the edge of the bed, knowing her time had just run out. She told herself it was okay; he was only asking for the story she'd told Jane, so she knew what to say without having to think. And it was, after all, the truth—as far as it went.

"It was Saturday," she began, her voice no more than a whisper. "Larry called in the afternoon to say I couldn't see Jimmy the next day. He told me Jimmy was sick, but he wouldn't let me speak to him."

"Had you cause to think something might be wrong before this?"

"Jimmy had called on Wednesday and again on Thursday. He wasn't allowed to, but he did. The second time, he was crying, but he wouldn't tell me why."

"So you were worried."

"Very."

"Had Silver ever hurt Jimmy, to your knowledge?"

She shook her head, rubbing her palms up and down over her slacks. "I called several times. At ten o'clock that night, Larry said if I called again, he wouldn't let me see Jimmy the next visit, either. I was . . . scared. I went to the house. Larry was furious when he saw me." She stopped for a moment, then continued in a monotone. "Jimmy was in his room and must have heard Larry yelling. He came to the top of the stairs, and when he saw me, he ran down. Larry grabbed him by the arm and pushed him down. Jimmy screamed. I knew his arm was probably broken because of the way Larry had twisted it, but Larry was yelling at him to get back to his room—that if he didn't, he'd be sorry. He started to pick him up by the back of his shirt and drag him toward the stairs." Again she paused, this time drawing a ragged breath. "I...tried to stop him. He let go of Jimmy and swung at me, and—" She gestured vaguely. "It wasn't something I planned. When he tried to hit me, I— Well, I did what I had to do to stop him."

Margaret Ann looked at Peter, but he turned away and began wandering around the room, pausing only to give her a brief glance.

"Go on," he said.

"I couldn't have walked out of there without Jimmy," she continued. "I didn't try to kill Larry, like he says I did, but I did disable him so he— So I could get Jimmy away. When I picked Jimmy up off the floor and made him run with me, Larry was on the floor, groaning and sort of half-conscious. I made sure he would be all right. Then we ran."

She stopped, looking at Peter for some reaction, but he remained silent. "Jimmy was trying hard to be good, not to cry," she continued. "I got him to Jane's and stayed long enough to dye my hair with some rinse she had and to throw some of her old clothes into a knapsack with a couple of sandwiches. She gave me what money she had in the house, which was a lot, because she'd sold one of her horses that day to a man who'd paid her in cash. Then I . . . well, I left."

She glanced at Peter. "That's all there is. I met you the following night."

Peter returned her gaze for a moment, then asked, "What reason do you think Silver had for canceling the visit? Was he angry with Jimmy for something?"

Margaret Ann hesitated, chewing the corner of her lower lip. "I'm not sure," she said finally. It was true. Jimmy had only given her a foggy story, and the rest was guesswork on her part. "Jimmy told me he was being punished. But he didn't know why, and I couldn't make sense of what he said. Something about walking in on Larry without knocking."

"Does Silver love Jimmy?"

"No. I mean . . ." She shook her head, flustered. "I mean, I don't know how he really feels about him. He mostly just—" she cast her gaze around the room and ended up looking at her lap "—ignores him."

"He *ignores* him?" Peter shot her a dubious look. Then he sighed in a way that said he wasn't surprised. "The night I called him from Montana, Nick told me a little about the press coverage of your divorce—how hot Silver was to keep Jimmy. It seemed unbelievable to me. He never struck me as the devoted-father type."

Stopping in front of the fireplace to lift a porcelain figurine off the mantel, Peter looked at the rendition of a small child fishing and frowned. "But, you know, when I saw your apartment, it occurred to me that, for a man who doesn't love his child, Silver is damned anxious to get

Jimmy back. As eager as he was to keep him from you in the first place. Why is that, Margaret Ann?''

Because my son is where I'm most vulnerable, and Larry knows it. He used Jimmy to control me, so I couldn't try to ruin him. The words pounded so loudly in Margaret Ann's head, she was sure she had spoken them. But that was impossible. *Speaking* was impossible.

She was scared. So scared her whole body was shaking, inside and out, freezing cold in spite of the muggy August heat. She could barely see the pattern on the carpet, where her eyes were fixed. There was nothing rational about the terror. Nothing having to do with thinking or common sense or even trusting Peter. Her reaction was primitive, a reflex that had been drilled, threatened and finally beaten into her with vicious clarity. Very simply, if she spoke, she died. Just like that. Her fear-numbed brain did not register the details of how it would happen. It could be instant. A lightning bolt from the sky. She would say the words—and drop dead.

And so she could only raise her eyes and stare at Peter, hoping he might read the answer, for she simply could not give it to him any other way.

It was as though she had made a sound—maybe she had—for he looked at her suddenly, his gaze darting across the room to lock with hers. If his expression had held even a trace of the tenderness of which she knew he was capable, she might have come apart then and there and somehow managed to whisper or croak or scream something to let him know she was trying. Trying with all her might to see out of this dank oppressive hole she was in. To see light at the end of the tunnel. To see herself in the future—happy, trusting, full of plans and dreams, the way she had been, once . . . a long time ago, it seemed.

But the tenderness wasn't there. His countenance was hard and unrevealing, not cold, exactly, but distant. And his attitude only confirmed her belief that, however well-intentioned he might be, his persistent interest in her was professional.

His eyes narrowed in thought. Then, a moment later, he placed the figurine he had been holding back on the mantel and spoke in measured tones.

"Let's try a different question. Why did Silver marry you?"

When she didn't answer immediately, Peter held up a hand. "Never mind. Let me see if I can sort this out. You told me you were pregnant, and he was afraid of a paternity suit. But any legal problems a paternity suit would create could have been solved by marrying you and getting a quick divorce. And since we've already established that Silver wasn't in love with you—" Pausing, he looked at her to ask, "Do you want to change your mind about that?"

For an answer, Margaret Ann squeezed her eyes closed.

"Well, then, it's rather strange, don't you think?" Peter began pacing again as he explained. "I've known Larry Silver for years. Got to see him in action quite a bit when I was working on the Lyle Development case. He's driven by ambition. He would want a splashy wife. Somebody with the social background he lacked and the savvy to handle political situations. Somebody he could use. Somebody whose image furthered his career. He *wouldn't* want a naive eighteen-year-old from east Baltimore, no matter how beautiful or sweet or smart she was. And if it's strange he married you to begin with, what's even stranger is why he made it so difficult for you to get a divorce. He turned your suit against him into a public spectacle. A scandal. Why? To keep the son you say he ignores? The son whose arm he broke in a fit of anger?''

Peter halted in front of the window to look directly at her. "What the hell is going on here, Margaret Ann? Why is Larry Silver so interested in destroying you?''

He wasn't bothering to wait for her answers anymore. Abruptly his demeanor became even more aggressive, his words coming harsh and fast.

"Why did Silver beat and rape you? I've lived with rapists, Margaret Ann. I don't believe for a minute Larry Silver is that crazy. Mean? Vindictive? A con artist? Yes. But not crazy. He'd have to have reason for resorting to that kind of violence. He'd have to think it would serve a purpose he couldn't accomplish any other way. What was he trying to prove? What lesson was he trying to teach you? And why—after he abused you to the point of screaming nightmares, to where the mere thought of a man touching you makes you shake so hard your teeth chatter—*why*, in God's name, did you wait *two months* to file for divorce? How in bloody hell did you let yourself get 'talked into' staying in that house even one more *day*?''

Her face was buried in her hand, and her body was rocking back and forth, slowly, steadily, an unconscious motion. When Peter moved to stand directly in front of her, she felt the impact of his presence, his anger, his frustration close in around her. He grabbed her chin, forcing her to look at him.

"You tell me, Margaret Ann! You tell me what kind of hold he's got on you! You tell me why you aren't willing to lift a finger to fight him!''

"There's nothing to fight for.'' The whisper was torn from her by the sheer force of his will.

Peter's eyes grew wide. "Nothing to... *Nothing to fight for!*'' he shouted. "What the *hell* kind of thing is that to say?'' Letting go of her chin, he strode to the center of the room and whirled to face her. "What about your *life*? What about your *son*? Margaret Ann, how are you going to explain to Jimmy that his mother is going to prison for the next twenty years?''

When her lower lip trembled, Peter swore crudely. "Silver might as well have his hands around your throat—you can't even speak! And if you can't talk to me, how are you going to talk to a jury? Or maybe you aren't planning to talk to them, either, huh? Maybe we should enter a guilty plea and forget it. Maybe you can waive your right to a trial, let them sentence you and get it over with. Would that make you happy?''

It would make Larry happy. And that might keep her alive. With all the unreasoning single-mindedness of a woman who has been too long terrified, Margaret Ann looked at Peter as though he had offered her a free ride to paradise.

He drew a quick breath. "God, I think it *would* make you happy. Lady, I'm not sure I know you. The woman I met back on that highway would be ready to scratch Silver's eyes out sooner than let him win this. That woman had guts! She was ready to give up the career she'd worked for, her home, everything familiar to her, rather than lose her son again.''

She muttered something.

"You had *what*?''

"I had—" She gasped. "I . . . I had a chance then.''

He stared for an instant, then his face twisted in total bafflement. "A *chance*? A chance to what? Disappear off the face of the earth?''

A terrible silence preceded Peter's stunned whisper. "Wait a minute. That's it, isn't it?''

He crossed to her quickly, propped one knee on the bed, planted a hand behind her and hovered, his face only inches from her ear. "Disappearing wasn't simply *a* chance—it was the *only* chance. Getting acquitted of these charges isn't good enough. But why would that be? Why would staying out of prison not be good enough?"

He arrived at the answer with hardly a pause for breath. "Because you'd still be where Silver could get his hands on you. Because the only way you're going to be safe is if you can *disappear*. Just like you told me you planned to do. Just like you told Jane that day on the phone when I overheard. 'It's the only way,' you said. 'The only way Jimmy and I will ever be safe. Believe me, Jane, he won't give up.' I remember every word, Margaret Ann. Every word!"

Yes! she screamed silently, wanting with all her heart to tell him he was right. Wanting to beg for his help. Dying because she could not. She could not.

She was going to be sick. "I—I can't stand..." She tried to speak. "I've got to...to..." She moaned, uncaring what he thought as she flung herself off the bed and ran out of the room.

Peter shot up, a hand out to catch her. But, instead, he swore and pivoted away. Feet planted wide, he stood staring at the ceiling, the sweat dripping off him, and every muscle in his body taut. He had no business being near her in this state. No business to have done what he had just done, willfully, with calculated intent. But he hadn't asked her anything she should not have been able to answer. And the fact that she could not—had indeed been quaking-with-fear mute—told him everything he needed to know. He had his answers. Oh, yes, he had his answers now.

Well, not quite all of them. Silver was blackmailing her—that much he was certain of. But he didn't know why.

And before she would tell him, he had to undo what he had just done.

With a ragged sigh, Peter relaxed his stance, and, running a hand across his jaw, he turned and started out of the room. He wondered if he would be able to convince Margaret Ann to open her door and let him in, but as he reached the doorway to his own room, he saw her leaving hers. He watched as she walked quickly down the long hall. She nearly ran down the stairs, and a few seconds later, the front screen door banged closed.

Peter followed, but he didn't rush. She hadn't been carrying a suitcase, so she wasn't going anywhere. He even hesitated at the bottom of the stairs, wondering if perhaps he should leave her alone. He felt an urgency to reassure her, to hold her and tell her he was sorry, that now, finally, he could say he knew it would be all right. But he doubted she was ready to hear any of it, and it was a sure bet she didn't want to talk to him. He had started to turn around and go back up the stairs when the sound of screeching tires sent a chill of alarm coursing through him.

He was out the screen door in seconds flat. A few seconds later he was slamming back into the house, snatching his car keys off the hall table and racing to the study to grab the phone. He dialed 911 with fingers that could barely find the buttons and reported the necessary information in a voice he didn't recognize as his own. Then he dropped the receiver on the desk and ran for his car. And as he tore off down the street, he prayed as he had never prayed in his life that he hadn't just seen Margaret Ann for the last time.

Margaret Ann landed in the back seat of the big car, knowing exactly what was happening and wondering if she would ever get out alive. She scrambled into the far corner, her eyes locking in the dimness of twilight on the man who lounged casually on the other side.

He smiled at her. "Hello, Marge. You're looking well—quite well, in fact, under the circumstances."

She was shaking so hard she had to clench her teeth before she could speak. "Let me out of this car, Larry."

Silver's vote-winning smile didn't waver. "That was some stunt you pulled, sweetheart—laying me out like that. I was impressed. Maybe you'd like to try it again, with Joe, here, standing by to, uh, even the odds." He nodded toward the young man driving, the one who had poked a gun in her ribs and thrown her into the car.

"I said, let me out."

"What's the matter? Are you afraid your final hour has arrived?"

"Has it?"

He let her wait for the answer, taking the time to put out the cigarette he'd been holding. When he was relaxed once more, with his arm draped across the back of the seat, he said, "Let's talk about something else, first. Like, for instance, where our son is."

Margaret Ann's voice was the clearest it had been in the past hour. "I won't tell you." Then, with an utterly weary sigh, she added, "You should have let me go, Larry. You know I haven't got any proof against you. I wouldn't have told a soul anything. All I wanted was to take Jimmy and get away from you."

Silver grimaced. "That may be, Marge, but I have to sleep at night. Think of that, sweetheart. We depend so much on each other to be predictable. You know exactly what I'll do if you don't play the game. And it's only fair that I have the same assurance. Now, for instance, take the matter of the legal counsel you've retained."

Margaret Ann's eyes narrowed. Larry Silver was one of the handsomest men she had ever known, with his beach-boy blond hair and perfect features, but the ugliness inside him made him repulsive to her. "What about him?" she said.

"Cut the bull, Marge. What are you trying to do, hiring Pete Lericos?" The smooth charm that was Silver's chief asset shut off abruptly, and his lips curled in a derisive sneer. "How the hell did you even track him down? He hasn't been back in town since he was sent up."

"It's none of your business," she snapped defiantly, then cringed when she saw the familiar quirk of his eyebrow and the slow, mean smile that went with it.

"Marge, everything you do is my business. You know that. And I don't have to tell you, do I, what's going to happen if you should happen to slip and say something...inappropriate to your attorney?"

Margaret Ann slumped against the back of the seat. Part of her wanted so desperately to be done with this nightmare that she almost didn't care how it ended anymore.

"You don't have to remind me, Larry," she said. "I've heard you threaten to kill me a million times."

"Is there some doubt in your mind that I would?"

"Not a bit. I appreciate your problem that killing someone isn't as easy as people might think. Dead bodies to get rid of, sudden disappearances to explain. All that bother. And now, of course, everybody's watching. But I'm sure someday you'll find a way to do it without too much risk. Someday soon, I imagine."

"You've left me without much choice, haven't you? I'm glad we understand each other, sweetheart. Now, look at me and listen to this."

Something in his voice compelled her to obey, and she rolled her head toward him and opened her eyes.

"If you shoot off your mouth to Lericos, you can add him to your list of people I'm planning to get rid of."

Pausing, Silver tilted his head and frowned slightly. "That bothers you, doesn't it? I figured you were staying with him because of the little mess I left at your apartment. But maybe not, huh? Maybe you've got something going with him. I can't figure out how you'd have managed it, but don't go getting ideas about him saving you or any rot like that. I promise you, getting rid of Lericos wouldn't take two seconds' thought. Nobody would even notice when he suddenly disappeared again. So you tell him anything, Marge, and he's dead. You hear?"

When she only went on staring at him, he reached across the seat to grab her upper arm. "Answer me!" he demanded, shaking her.

"I—I hear," she whispered. "I haven't told him. And I'm not going to."

Silver's eyes skimmed her features warily before he let her go. "I want the kid back."

"No."

"You want Lericos dead?"

"I won't tell you where Jimmy is."

"Yes, you will, Marge. And you'll tell Lericos you want another attorney. You get him off this case, or I swear to God, I'll make you sorry you were ever born."

He already had. But she could be even sorrier. As long as there were people she cared about, he could hurt her. She had more or less grown accustomed to being afraid for Jimmy. But the new outrage and anxiety that filled her at the thought of Peter being harmed was shocking and every bit as intense as any she had ever felt. It was as though he were a part of herself; she had to protect him.

Not, however, by giving Jimmy back to Larry.

"Let's have it, Marge. Where's the kid?"

When his demand was met with only silence, he started to slide across the seat, his hand out to grab her. She cringed as he growled, "Listen, you bitch, I've had about—"

Silver broke off and Margaret Ann screamed when the car took a sudden sharp turn into the curb. They came to a jarring halt, and Margaret Ann had to grab the back of the front seat to keep from flying forward. The impact knocked the wind out of her, and it was a moment before she could look around to see what was going on.

"Get out," Silver snapped. "And remember, this was a friendly ride."

For the first time, she realized there were sirens blaring. They were at a right angle to the curb at the corner of Cathedral and Saratoga streets; it was a jammed, oddly angled intersection, and drivers were going crazy trying to get their vehicles out of the way of the three police cars that had screeched in to block off all turns. The entire scene was a visual madhouse, with flashing blue lights, red, green and yellow traffic signals, and the glaring white beams of several dozen vehicles.

"Get out!" Silver repeated, and reached across her to throw open the door.

He practically pushed her onto the street, and she was sure he would have taken off if he could have. But five police officers were walking toward the car, hands on their guns. Margaret Ann stood on the sidewalk, confused and frightened, watching them approach and wondering if the police, for some reason Larry had cooked up, had come to arrest her.

From up Cathedral Street she heard a familiar voice shouting her name, and her bewildered gaze caught Peter dodging toward her through the cars, his 'Vette abandoned in the stopped traffic. Her impulse was to run to him, but she couldn't. She wanted to believe she was safe because he was there, but she wasn't. She was faint with relief at seeing him, but she wished he would turn around and leave before Larry saw him, too. Torn in a dozen directions, she knew in another minute she would be hysterical.

Then the police were there, Larry and his driver were out of the car, and horns were honking as people tried to work their way through the mess.

Peter was breathless as he grabbed her shoulders and gasped, "Are you all right?"

She waved her hands helplessly, looked from the police to Larry, then glanced up at Peter. She didn't know what to say, or who to say it to. So she hugged herself with folded arms, closed her eyes and nodded, yes, she was fine. He squeezed her shoulders briefly, then strode away to confront her abductor over the hood of the big white car. His furious voice carried over the general chaos.

"Silver, what the hell is this?"

"Well, Pete Lericos! Say, it's good to see you. I was glad to hear that business got cleared up for you back—"

"Stow it. I want to know, right now, what you think you were doing hauling my client off at gunpoint."

"Gunpoint!"

"I saw it. I saw your driver force her into this car with a gun in her ribs. Officer, have you searched these men and the car?"

"Yes, sir. No weapon's been found, but—"

"Marge, did you see a gun?"

"This man is harassing my client, and—"

"Marge! Turn around here! The police want to know if you saw a gun!"

"You leave her alone, Silver. You tell her once more what to do, and I'll—"

"Wait." She had to stop this. "Wait, Peter. It's—Don't."

Margaret Ann felt nausea rising inside her, but she made her feet move the few steps to the curb where Peter was standing. His head jerked around, and his gaze shot down to meet hers as she touched him lightly on the arm.

"Please," she whispered. "Take me home."

His eyes widened, and he started to say something, but Larry spoke first.

"Is there something wrong, Lericos, with having a friendly talk with my ex-wife?"

Peter's eyes flashed back to Silver. "You're not going to get out of this one," he growled. "You just cooked your ass, and you know it."

"I don't know what you're talking about," said Larry, his tone exasperated. "Officer, I think this man is making a rather bad mistake. Marge, tell him. *Tell* him, Marge."

"I warned you, Silver—"

"Peter, please, let's go."

"Miss, we'd need probable cause to arrest these men."

"Was I harassing you, Marge?"

"Did you hear me, miss? Were you forced or threatened in any way to get into Mr. Silver's car?"

Somewhere in the middle of it all, she passed the limit of her endurance. Something died inside her, something precious that Peter had given her. A grain of hope that there was still goodness in the world—and that she might share in it. But there was no goodness in what she had to do, no truth, no honor. Only the lonely satisfaction that, in betraying Peter's faith, she might protect him from something worse than any emotional pain she could inflict.

"No. No, Officer. I—I didn't see a gun. I wasn't . . . forced into the car."

"There. You see, Lericos? I told you, everything's fine."

"Miss, are you sure?"

"Yes. I'm sure. We were . . . only talking. It's fine."

It wasn't fine. If, by some miracle, she lived to be very, very old, Margaret Ann knew she would never forget the look on Peter's face.

She didn't understand why he hadn't left her standing on the street. She didn't know why she was sitting in his car, riding toward his house. But the words running through her mind finally burst out of her in a choked sob.

"I'm s-sorry. I'm—I'm . . . so sorry!

"Don't apologize to me, Margaret Ann. It's not me you're hurting. It's yourself."

But she had hurt him. She heard the pain in his voice.

"Peter, you've g-got to believe me," she cried, only half-coherent. "Arresting Larry would . . . You can't fight him. You just c-can't! He'll—"

"He'll what? Kill you?" Peter gave her a pitiless glance. "The game's up, Margaret Ann. And I'm going to tell you just one thing. If he does kill you, it will be your own fault."

"No, I— Oh, Lord, Peter, you don't understand! And I can't explain it! You've got to—"

"You *can* explain it," he shot back. "What have you got on him? What do you know about him that he's so damned desperate to keep anybody else from finding out?"

"Nothing! Don't you see, that's . . . Oh, God, *please* . . ."

"What is it? Something personal? He's gay?"

"No!"

"Some business deal he's involved in? Something that could put him in jail?"

"There's nothing!"

"Bull. There's something. And we both know it. But you've made up your mind that before you'll say anything, you'll go to jail *for* him. And you know what?" He uttered a harsh laugh. "It's not going to seem a whole lot different. *This* is jail, Margaret Ann. You're in it. You've given up your personal liberty, your freedom of speech and the right to make any choices about your life. You've turned yourself over, body and soul, to a man who wants to destroy you. He's terrorized you into thinking he's omnipotent. And until you realize the only power he's got is *what you give him*—" Peter shook his head "—lady, you're lost. I can't help you. Nobody can."

Chapter Thirteen

When they arrived back at Peter's house, Margaret Ann ran to her room. Peter watched her fly up the stairs, then shut himself in the study and called Nicholas. Nick was disturbed by what had happened but had no immediate solutions to offer. At midnight, having spent another hour sitting at his desk staring into space, Peter went to bed. But fantasies of Margaret Ann standing on a street corner, trembling with fear and begging him to take her home, kept him awake. As did fantasies of Margaret Ann sitting in a cell block for the next twenty or thirty years—and Margaret Ann lying dead on the ground.

He knew what had transpired in the car between her and Silver. Threats and more threats. Terror piled on terror. He had been livid with her for caving in under the pressure—and even angrier at himself for not realizing sooner how deadly the situation was. Now, though, he was sorry for having taken out his fury on her; she was only trying to survive.

But, Lord, it had hurt that her terror of Silver was greater than her trust in him—trust, when it came to Margaret Ann, being equated in his mind with love. And that was stupid of him, really, because trust and love were *not* the same thing. Besides, he'd spent the evening destroying what trust he had so painstakingly built between them, hadn't he? And as for love—well, they had never even talked about it.

Did she love him? He had only the way she looked at him, the tone of her voice and one precious memory of her clinging to him in passion to go by. She had never spoken the words. Nor had he, although he had thought his presence ought to speak pretty well for itself. The uncertainty of her future was a harsh reality, and to talk of love or commitment seemed...what? Inappropriate? Premature?

Frightening. That was closer to the truth. What if he told Margaret Ann that he loved her—and then had to watch her carry his heart off to prison with her? But would that be worse than if he didn't tell her? What if the unthinkable happened—Silver managed to kill her—and he had to live the rest of his life never having declared his love or his intentions?

One thing was certain. He wasn't going to stop loving her, no matter what he thought of the way she was handling Silver, no matter how it came out in the end. And his own fears about how he would live without her seemed petty and small beside what she was struggling with.

At 4:00 a.m., when he heard her creep down the stairs, he pulled on a pair of cutoffs and followed. The noise she was making led him to the kitchen.

What he found made him want to laugh and cry all at once. He stood in the doorway, surveying the chaos. Cake pans, empty cream-cheese wrappers and graham crackers made up the bulk of the mess, with Margaret Ann in the middle of it. Dressed in blue baby-doll pajamas, with her hair piled on top of her head in a knot of curls, she had the electric mixer whirring away in one hand and a rubber spatula in the other. As he watched, she ducked to wipe tears away on her shoulder.

"Maggie, what are you doing?"

His gentle bewildered question brought her head up, but she only glanced at him before burying her attention once more in the mixing bowl.

"Baking cheesecake," she answered. "Wanna make something of it?"

He shook his head. "No."

A minute later, he spoke again. "Can I help?"

"That depends."

"On what?"

"Can you do it without opening your mouth?"

"I don't know."

"The only topic I'm willing to discuss is cheesecake. If you think you can handle that, put those graham crackers between two sheets of wax paper and start rolling."

"Are you going to give me the sacred family recipe?"

"I'll will it to you."

"That's not funny, Margaret Ann."

"Just roll, Charlie."

At four o'clock Saturday afternoon, they pulled into Peter's parents' driveway with three magnificent Flo's cheesecakes tucked in the trunk of the Corvette—one with blueberry topping, one with curls of semi-sweet chocolate and one plain. Neither of them had gotten any sleep, and they hadn't spoken more than a half dozen words in twelve hours.

Margaret Ann felt as if she were going to a wake, not a party, and she didn't know how she was going to get through the evening. A sidelong glance at Peter made her wonder if the guest of honor would do much better; he looked awful. Which made it all the more startling when, the instant they got out of the car, Peter's face split into an enormous grin and he let out a shout that made her jump.

She had time to get out of the way—barely—before a rowdy passel of children streaked past her shouting, "He's here! Uncle Peter's here! He's here!" Margaret Ann counted seven of them, and they bombarded Peter with exuberant kisses and excited chatter as he somehow hugged them all at once. When the pandemonium had settled down a bit, Peter winked at her over the head of the smallest child, whom he had tucked in one arm.

"Nick's and Maria's kids," he said, as though an explanation were required. And he reeled off their names.

His sister, Maria, and her husband, Thad, accounted for Anthony, Sophia and Catherine. Nicholas and his wife, Sandy, had four, the youngest being Michael at age seven, then Helen and Angela, and finally a lanky, dark-haired youth of about fourteen, who, in looks, could have been Peter's own son.

"And this is my godson, Alex," Peter told her. There was pride in his voice and in the approving once-over he gave the oldest member of the Lericos clan's third generation.

Alex scuffed the toe of his high-top on the driveway and tried to look unaffected, but the look crumpled into one of pure adoration when Peter hooked him around the neck and pulled him to him, holding Alex's head against his shoulder as he kissed the boy's forehead and spoke a few quiet words close to his ear. Alex nodded and looked up at Peter, his bright eyes, brimming with tears, matching his uncle's.

"Okay, everybody, listen up." Peter clapped his hands once, then made an elegant gesture across the top of the car. "This is my friend Margaret Ann. And she's made dessert for dinner tonight. There are three *cheesecakes* in the back here, and you're going to have to help carry them in."

Margaret Ann had her doubts, but she helped Peter supervise the process, unloading the cheesecakes one by one into the hands of three of the children.

They were following the parade up the walk toward the white Cape Cod house when a tall woman with waist-length black hair came out on the porch. Peter threw his arms wide, and she was in them in seconds. Margaret Ann knew this had to be his sister, Maria, and she nearly cried along with the two of them, watching the reunion.

Such joy! Such uninhibited expressions of love. The love flowed out of everyone in Peter's family as easily as rain fell out of the sky. Effortlessly and without a care about whether it would ever be returned. She had known that kind of love with her parents and her aunt, and she had known it with Jimmy. But in each case it had been taken from her, and suddenly she was filled with a dreadful bleak sadness as she realized in a way she had not before that she was facing the rest of her life without any love at all.

The sadness, though, was nothing compared to the appalling regret that Jimmy would never know the acceptance and unashamed affection she was witnessing between Peter and his sister. At least, not from her or in a family they made together.

Margaret Ann fought stoically to put her feelings aside, though. This was Peter's day. She couldn't let her unhappiness cast a shadow on him or his family. Besides, she was here with him now. And she might never have the chance to be with him again, to enjoy his presence, to share his family. And so, for a little while, she allowed herself to pretend it could go on this way forever.

Dinner was a great success, with fourteen of the Lericos tribe, plus Margaret Ann, packed around the long, food-laden table. Everyone talked at once, making actual conversation impossible, and Margaret Ann found herself drawn into the boisterous celebration. By the time the children had been shooed outside to play and the adults were groaning about how they might never move again and that they couldn't believe they had eaten three pieces of cheesecake, she was able to look across the table at Peter and smile.

He grinned back at her. "Just think. All those nights I wasted lying awake doing nothing, I could have been baking cheesecake."

She chuckled. "Oh, really? Where? On the hot plate in the Kenworth?"

"Hey! You making fun of my truck, woman?"

"Not the truck—the idea of you cooking anything more complicated than canned stew."

"Ha!" Tilting his chair back on two legs, Peter folded his arms across his chest. "Well, let me tell you what I'm going to start making, now that I've got an *oven*. I'm going to take two cups of cream cheese and beat it till it's gooey, dump in three-quarters of a cup of sugar, two tablespoons of lemon juice—"

"Why, you sneak!"

"—two tablespoons of flour, half a teaspoon of salt and two teaspoons of vanilla—"

"I can't believe it!"

"—and beat them all together. Then I beat six egg whites and a quarter cup of sugar until they stand up in little peaks, then fold them—"

"You rotten creep, you memorized it!"

Peter looked at his father. "Listen to her, will you? She makes fun of my cooking, then gets mad when I stay up all night trying to improve myself. I tell you . . ."

"Will you two cut it out? It's too hot to expend the energy it takes to listen to you." Nick scraped the last smear of blueberry topping off his place with his finger and stuck it in his mouth. "Lord, that was delicious. Is there any left?"

"Not a slice," his wife, Sandy, answered.

Mrs. Lericos beamed at Margaret Ann from her chair at the foot of the table. "Such a lot of work you went to!"

"No more than you did," Margaret Ann replied. "The meal was delicious. And it was a pleasure to contribute. Besides—" she lifted her chin "—I did have assistance."

"Speaking of assistance." Sandy cast a woeful look through the kitchen doorway at the counter full of dishes. "Come on, Maria, we better get started or it'll be midnight when we're finished."

"I'll help," said Peter, bringing several vehement protests down upon his head.

In the end, Sandy and Maria agreed to do dishes. Mr. Lericos joined Alex in front of the TV to check on the Orioles game, and Mrs. Lericos, who had cooked the enormous dinner, was sent off to relax on the couch. Margaret Ann was about to offer to help in the kitchen, when the two youngest children, Anthony and Michael, came running into the house, calling for Peter to build Legos with them.

"Leave Uncle Peter alone," Maria reproached the young ones. "He played with you for an hour before din-

ner, and he's not ready to play again right now." She gave
Peter a doubtful look. "Are you?"

Margaret Ann could see he was about to say sure, he'd
play with them, but it was clear he was exhausted.

"What sets do you have?" she asked, capturing the
children's attention.

"Well," Tony drawled, "I've got two space stations,
and Mike's got the castle set."

"The giant one? That's my favorite. I've made it doz-
ens of times."

The children's eyes grew round. "Really?"

She nodded. "I can do space stations, too."

"Tony's got the motorized set."

"Gosh, that's great!"

Tony shrugged. "Yeah, but I don't know how to work
it, and neither does Mike." He looked at her hesitantly.

She grinned. "I do."

"Gee. Do you think you could . . ."

"Come on. I'll show you." Margaret Ann smiled at Peter's grateful look, then, rising from her chair, cast a
questioning glance at Maria.

"Go on." Maria laughed. "Anybody willing to keep
them busy is exempt from housework."

Margaret Ann went off to build Legos, which left Nicholas and Peter alone at the table.

For several minutes Peter observed the scene unfolding
on the living room floor. Through the arched doorway, he
watched Margaret Ann plop down, cross her legs and pick
up a Lego motor to show Anthony and Michael how it
worked. The gauzy flowered thing she was wearing had a
ruffle around the hem, and it floated around her in a way
that made her look feminine and infinitely desirable; when
the dress got in the way of her play, she tucked it carelessly into the space her crossed legs made. Her face was

animated. Happy. Laughing at something one of the children had said, she lifted a hand in an absent gesture to tuck her hair behind her ears.

Peter smiled, remembering the first time he had seen that mass of shining red curls. Remembering how soft and warm she had felt that morning when he had awakened with her in his arms. Remembering the moment when he had looked into her eyes and known he was falling in love with her....

"What am I going to do, Nick?"

The despair in his voice drew a sigh from his brother. "I suppose that depends on whether you're talking personally or professionally."

Peter snorted in self-derision. "I thought they could be the same thing. But she won't allow it."

"You mean Silver won't allow it."

Peter tore his eyes away from Margaret Ann and gave his brother a baffled look. "Are you saying she's powerless against him?"

"No. I'm saying she *thinks* she is." Nick took a sip of his coffee, then frowned. "You know, you're expecting an awful lot of her. Too much, maybe."

A burst of childish laughter drew Peter's attention, and he looked to see Margaret Ann demonstrating the first successful run of Michael's motorized Lego space walker, much to the children's delight. Was it true? Had he endowed her with superhuman qualities she had no hope of living up to?

"Maybe," he conceded. "But I would have sworn she wasn't so afraid of anything that it would immobilize her."

Nick snorted softly. "That's how blackmail works, isn't it? You terrorize some perfectly reasonable human being into being scared to move—to *breathe*—for fear something ungodly is going to happen. And she's been living with it how long? Maybe since she was eighteen? All things considered, I'd say she's doing damned well."

Peter acknowledged his brother's statement with an affirmative grunt as he thought of all Margaret Ann had accomplished in spite of Silver's attempts to beat her down. She was such a funny mixture of wide-eyed innocent, down-to-earth practicalist and world-weary cynic. So young in many ways, so old in others. What Nick had said was true: she could have been fighting Silver for what amounted to her entire adult life. And it seemed nothing short of miraculous that she was as clear thinking, as utterly sane, as she was. He knew, if she would only give herself the chance, it wouldn't be long before she had put this whole ugly business behind her. Margaret Ann Miller was, by nature, a survivor.

His fear was born of the knowledge that even a survivor had limits as to what she or he could endure.

"Think about it," Nick said. "Just try to imagine what it must have taken for her to steal that child and run. And even under all the pressure, she's obviously found someone who'll keep him for her." Quietly, he added, "And she found you. She's a remarkable woman, Peter. I don't think you're underestimating her. I just think she's at the end of her rope."

"She got caught." Peter's voice was a quiet rumble. "She poured everything she had into that one desperate effort to get away. If she'd made it, I think she would have put together a good life for herself and Jimmy. But she lost. Jimmy's safe, but, as far as she's concerned, it's over."

The scene was changing in the living room. The children were on their own now, engrossed in their new construction. Peter saw his mother, who had been sitting on the couch behind Margaret Ann, say something that made

Margaret Ann's face cloud over. Then his mother spoke again, and Margaret Ann glanced at her, a blush on her cheeks and a hesitant smile on her lips.

His jaw clenched and he spoke in a thick whisper. "But it *can't* be over, Nick. I want to marry her."

When Nick didn't respond, Peter turned to find his brother's troubled gaze searching his features.

"That's going to be a little difficult, isn't it?" Nick murmured.

Peter closed his eyes, and, throwing his head back, he drew a ragged breath. "I thought my being here would make a difference to her. I thought . . . God, I don't know what I thought. I hoped she'd see me and fall in my arms, I'd take care of this little problem she's got with Silver, and that would be that. But here I am, and she's not falling. And she's doing everything she can to prevent me taking care of Silver."

His fist hit the table squarely. "Dammit! It seems she's committed to going to jail or sitting around waiting for Silver to kill her. And frankly, if the idea of never seeing her son again isn't enough to shake her out of it, I don't think there's a chance in hell that *I'll* make any difference."

"Maybe the boy's not enough."

Nick's comment seemed absurd, and the look Peter gave him said as much.

"Well, now, wait a minute." Nick leaned forward, his arms forming a loose circle on the white damask tablecloth. "Look at how long she's been carrying the burden of protecting him. Sure she loves Jimmy, but if you were she, and you saw a way to get out from under the anxiety, wouldn't you grab it?"

"Not if it meant rotting in prison."

"That's not fair, Peter," Nick shot back. "You spent two years at Hagerstown. Her three days doesn't begin to compare. It's still a fiction to her. An ugly place where maybe nothing good is going to happen, but maybe nothing horrible is going to happen, either. A place where she might be safe, and her son *will* be safe because she's there, and she won't have to worry about either of them anymore."

It made sense. Peter had to admit that. But where did that leave him? "What am I supposed to do?" he asked. "Throw her back in and let her sit for a while? Or maybe give her a guided tour of the DOC's women's facility?"

Nick shrugged. "That might work, if you can make her more terrified of prison than she is of anything Silver might do."

Fight terror with terror. The very idea made him cringe, and his gaze slid almost unwillingly to Margaret Ann as he considered it. No, after the scene in his bedroom the previous night, he had no stomach for anything even remotely like it.

"I can't do it," he said. "I want to love her, not terrorize her."

"If things keep going the way they did on that street corner last night—" Nick shook his head "—you won't have a chance to do either."

"There must be a way. A way to make her believe the fight's not over. A way to make her want to…to sweep up the ashes and make the bird fly again."

"The phoenix?"

"Mmm." Peter's eyes glittered as they narrowed, focusing sharply on the object of both his deepest affection and his greatest frustration. "Now, what sort of challenge do you offer a woman who's already lived through hell?"

* * *

Margaret Ann was pleased with her space walker and with Tony and Mike's reaction. She grinned, watching the two of them crawl after the multilegged robotic gizmo, intent upon the details of its construction and equally intent upon producing authentic sound effects to go with it. Sitting back on her heels, she leaned an elbow on the couch and tossed a smile over her shoulder at Mrs. Lericos, who sat watching.

The older woman chuckled indulgently at the antics of her grandchildren, but when she shifted her gaze to Margaret Ann, her expression became somber. "You must miss your little boy terribly."

The soft-spoken words caught Margaret Ann off guard; suddenly her eyes lost their sparkle, and her chest grew tight.

"I know what it is, dear, to miss a child. To wonder whether you'll ever see him again."

Margaret Ann's gaze rose to meet the dark brown eyes that were regarding her with such deep sympathy.

"My heart aches for you," Mrs. Lericos said quietly. Then a smile formed on her lips. "This is a horrible time for you, Margaret Ann, and there's nothing I can say that would make it better. But I think you'll know what I mean when I tell you how grateful I am to you for bringing *my* son home to me."

Her cheeks flushed, Margaret Ann said, "I'm very glad for all of you. It's wonderful seeing your family together this way." And as she thought about the serious man she had met a month ago, whose flashes of humor had been sharp and vibrant but too infrequent, she added, "It's wonderful seeing Peter so happy. So full of life. But *I* didn't bring him home."

Mrs. Lericos arched an eyebrow. "Now, Margaret Ann, if you didn't, tell me who—or what—did."

Margaret Ann shrugged. She felt awkward and unsure of what to say, yet the sympathy offered a moment ago by the older woman—genuine sympathy, not a meaningless pat on the hand—demanded a certain honesty. Besides, it was impossible to resist the chance to cut through her loneliness and isolation.

"Peter was ready to come home," she said. "I only gave him a reason to do what he's wanted to do all along." Her eyes closed briefly as she added, "Mrs. Lericos, he's given me so much. He's the most generous, caring person I've ever known. He's helped me at a time when I didn't think anyone would, and in ways that—" She broke off, shaking her head. "Well, I just don't think there are many people on earth who even would have considered helping me, much less had Peter's understanding of what I've been going through. I'm the one who should be grateful."

Mrs. Lericos smiled as she looked toward her eldest child. "My son is a good man. A strong man," she said. "I'm proud of him. I'm proud of all my children for how they've stood by one another, even when it caused them great sorrow. I remember how Nicholas looked when he'd come back from visiting Peter at that place. But he went regularly, and so did Maria and her husband." She waved a hand, grimacing. "I'm a coward. Peter knew it and told me from the start he didn't want me to come. But I wrote, and I talked to him on the phone. Such heartache! I can't tell you what it was like. But we never let him forget we loved him."

Margaret Ann's gaze swept the room, took in the children playing, Mr. Lericos and Alex watching TV, Peter and Nick wrapped up in conversation in the dining room, and the two women washing dishes together and laughing in the kitchen. If any one of them had been hurt or in trouble, the rest would have rallied to do whatever could be done to support the afflicted one.

It had been years, but she suddenly felt a terrible urge to cry for her mother. To cry for *somebody*.

"Margaret Ann."

It cost her a great deal to give Mrs. Lericos a brittle smile, and the pretense crumbled instantly as the older woman continued.

"I watch the news, and I read the papers. I know what's being said about you. But my son is no fool, and neither am I. I see you here, in my home, eating dinner with my family, making jokes with Peter and playing with my grandchildren. And I think, how can anybody have taken this woman's child from her? What idiots they are being! How can they make this tragic mistake!" She shook her head, her face anguished. "Oh, but people *do* make mistakes. Terrible ones. Mistakes like the one Peter made, marrying that selfish, scheming woman who didn't love him. Mistakes like the people made who sent him to prison."

Mistakes like I made, trusting Larry Silver. The thought ran through Margaret Ann's mind, along with the usual self-blame. Suddenly, though, something was different. The notion of other people making mistakes, too, made her seem a little less culpable. People like Alyce Lericos and Larry Silver didn't make mistakes; they perpetrated calculated acts on their victims. Mistakes—genuine mistakes—were honest and without guile. And if Peter could forgive the jury that had sent him to prison, recognizing that their verdict had been only an honest mistake, perhaps she could forgive herself for falling prey to a charming, handsome man at a time when she had been young and vulnerable. After all, she was by no means the only one Larry Silver had conned, and it occurred to her to wonder why she had always felt *her* honest mistake was somehow worse than those made by the people who voted for him.

"I think you must be a very strong woman."

Margaret Ann glanced briefly at Peter's mother before lowering her gaze. "I don't feel strong, Mrs. Lericos, but I appreciate your saying it. Maybe it'll help me feel it."

Mrs. Lericos reached out to pat Margaret Ann's hand. Then, her frown deepening, she gestured toward Peter. "I don't know how my son will live with himself if he can't find a way to return your boy to you. And if they lock you up the way they did him... Ach!" She shuddered, her eyes closing. "I don't know. I think he'll go crazy."

"Oh, no! Please don't say that." Margaret Ann scooted around to face the older woman. "I know how important it is to Peter to win my case. I know how compelled he's felt to help me because... well, because I remind him of himself, in a way." At the other woman's puzzled expression, Margaret Ann explained, "Somebody who's being victimized—I guess that's the best way to put it. And I know it will upset him if... if I lose. But, really—" she smiled with as much reassurance as she could muster "—now that he's gotten over the hump, so to speak, about being back in Baltimore, I don't think anything that happens to me could take him away from you again."

Mrs. Lericos's puzzled look became one of confusion, then, slowly, of amazed disbelief. "Did Peter tell you that's why he's here? Because he'd like to—to get revenge?"

"No." Margaret Ann shook her head. "No, of course not. He didn't tell me anything, except that he wanted to be my lawyer."

Mrs. Lericos's lips formed a silent O. As she glanced from Margaret Ann to her son, a worried frown appeared on her brow, and she spoke as though to herself. "It's sad to believe he's changed so much. He didn't used to hide what he was thinking so well. He's been away too long from the people who love him. He's been alone too long."

A moment later, her dark eyes focused sharply on Margaret Ann. "I think you should take a long, hard look at my son," she said.

Puzzled, Margaret Ann frowned. But as though it were an order, her gaze slid nervously toward the man about whom she felt so many things she was trying to deny. When she found him watching her, his eyes glinting gold beneath a dark scowl, she tried to look away but couldn't. Her lips parted slightly, her cheeks staining red, as Mrs. Lericos's words fell upon her.

"Ask yourself this, Margaret Ann. If Peter's so happy here in this city, with his family that loves him so much, why has it taken him a year to come home? My son is a strong man. But I think something has made him stronger. And I'm not talking about the muscles he's gotten from lifting boxes and driving a truck."

Chapter Fourteen

It was late when Peter and Margaret Ann arrived home, and both of them were ready to collapse. Yet Margaret Ann knew there was something she had to tell Peter before the day ended, before it got any harder. She followed him into the kitchen and stood wringing her hands as he dumped the empty cake plates into the sink.

"I'm beat," he said, turning. "I'm going to head on up—"

"Peter, I think—I think, tomorrow, it would be a good idea if I went back to my apartment."

In the silence that met her announcement, Margaret Ann's eyes flickered over the dirty dishes in the sink, the cut flowers on the table, everything in sight, except Peter's face.

"Your place is still a mess," he said.

"Yes, well, I'll have to clean it up sometime."

"You don't have to leave."

"Thank you, but there doesn't seem to be any reason—"

"Am I being fired?"

"Well, there really isn't any point in your—"

"I *am* being fired."

"Actually..."

"Yes or no."

"Yes."

There was another flash of silence. Then, turning away, Margaret Ann mumbled, "I'm sorry. It isn't you, it's—"

"It's your decision."

"Please try to understand. I appreciate what you've attempted to do. But, well, like you said, nobody can help me. And I don't want you to get... to get hurt trying, so—"

"Did Silver threaten to kill me if you talked?"

"I am *not* going to talk about Larry!" The harshness of her own voice startled her, but with an emphatic shake of her head she insisted, "I'm not going to discuss it anymore. Last night was awful, and I can't stand to go through that again. I know you don't understand, but I can't talk to anyone. And there's just no point in your being involved in something that's bound to... to end badly."

Margaret Ann forced herself to turn and look at Peter, her eyes searching the unrevealing planes of his face as she said, "I am sorry. I'd give anything to be able to help you win this case. I know how important it is to you, and I—"

"Do you?"

She stared at him for a moment, then, with a shrug, she turned and moved toward the table. Leaning against it, her fingers gripping the edge, she shrugged again. "Sure. I mean, I don't blame you. If I were you, I'd jump at the chance."

"What chance?"

"Come on, Peter, you're always the one telling me to stop avoiding the issue. The chance to right the wrong. The chance to let this city know they blew it and that you're not going to stand by and let them do it again. I don't know exactly how you think of it, but it boils down to some affinity you feel with me as a victim of circumstance and . . . and someone else's treachery."

She made an impatient uncomfortable gesture, but her tone was less harsh as she added, "Your faith in my innocence has been very important to me. I'll never be able to tell you how important. But we both know there are things I'm not innocent of, and I don't want to see you get hurt in any way because of me."

In her mind's eye, Margaret Ann envisioned Peter's lethal amber gaze searing holes in her back. She was totally unprepared for his astonished whisper.

"Is this actually what you think? That I'm using you?"

"It's okay. Really." She whirled to face him, forcing a smile. "It's not surprising or—"

"You *do!* You think that's what this is all about! That I've got defending you wrapped up in my mind with—" his hand searched the air "—with vindicating myself in the eyes of the justice system and the whole damned city of Baltimore!"

"Peter, there's nothing wrong with it. I understand perfectly why you—"

But her words were cut off when, with a thundered oath that made her wince, he erupted. Swearing, slamming around the kitchen, gesturing to the heavens and hollering things that made no sense to her at all, Peter launched into a tirade that lasted long enough to make her wish she had never opened her mouth. But she had been determined not to sneak off again without telling him.

At last he seemed to run out of steam. Banging his hands flat on one of the kitchen cabinets and leaving them there, Peter heaved one great sigh and swore a final time.

"Idiot," he said flatly and to no one in particular. "I'm an absolute idiot. I should have known your suspicious little mind would cook up some cockamamy story like this. The one time in my life I don't spell it out in spades, and look what happens."

Margaret Ann frowned in confusion. An instant later, though, when he turned to face her, her eyes filled with wonder. It was all there—all the warmth, the tenderness she'd been longing for. His eyes were on fire with it, and his face, that harsh mask she had thought so unrevealing, was transformed into the most breathtaking sight she had ever seen.

He sighed again, a tired, heavy sound. "Before this goes any further, Margaret Ann, I think I'd better make one thing very clear."

Slowly he crossed the room to stand in front of her. His eyes roamed her features, finally coming back to fasten on her eyes as he laced his fingers through her hair and bracketed her face with his hands. "Maggie," he said, "the only reason I'm here is because I love you."

"You..."

He nodded solemnly. "I love you so much it makes me shake inside. I love you so much that, when Nick told me you'd been arrested, I didn't care how bitter I felt or how hard it was going to be to face people. The only thing I cared about was you." His voice was thick and strained as he added, "I can't make you fight for yourself, but I'll never stop fighting for you. Because I don't know what I'll do if I have to spend the rest of my life without you."

Tears brimmed in her eyes, and she blinked them away to see him clearly. "Then all that about wanting to be my lawyer..."

"What I *wanted* was to get you out of this god-awful mess so you could spend the rest of your life with me. I should have told you. Just like I should have told you who I was when we met. But I'm scared, Maggie." His hands tightened on the back of her neck, shaking her gently. "Can you understand that? I'm scared of making a mistake with you. I'm scared of frightening you, of making demands you can't handle. I'm scared you don't love me the way I love you. But you do, don't you?"

When her chin dropped forward, he placed a gentle finger under it and coaxed her to lift her gaze to his once more.

"I'm not wrong, am I?" he asked. "You do love me."

With a tiny sound, she grabbed one of his hands and clasped it against her racing heart. Then she closed her eyes and nodded.

Peter's eyes drifted closed, too, and he shuddered as the tension drained out of him. Pulling her to him until her forehead rested against his chest, he brushed the top of her hair with a kiss, murmuring, "And it scares you to death."

She nodded again, her sobs muffled against his shirtfront. "It was so hard to leave you. But I was afraid if I didn't, I'd lose the last control I have over my life. And I was afraid for you and for Jimmy and...and of what would happen if I really trusted you. Oh, Lord, Peter, I thought I'd never see you again! And...and then, there you were—but it *wasn't* you! I was never so happy to see anybody in my life, but... Oh, it'll never work! It'll just never work!"

"It will if you want it to."

She uttered a bitter laugh. "What I want never makes any difference. You're not like that, I know. You decide about something, and you do it. But I keep wanting things I can't have."

"You can have me." And his hand, still clasped in hers against her breast, spread open to cover her heart.

"Please, don't!" She flung her head back, squeezing her eyes closed against the reminder of a time when, indeed, she had gotten exactly what she had wanted. "Please, don't talk like that," she whispered. "Don't *do* that."

"Why not?"

"Because it makes me..." Her words trailed off when his hand crept slowly across her breast.

"Makes you what?"

"You know."

"Tell me."

She rolled her head to the side, shivering when his mouth made contact with the skin below her ear. "I can't."

"Try."

"It's...Peter, it's not fair."

No, there was nothing fair about the hot, languid kisses he was placing on her neck and shoulder. Her fingers dug into his biceps, clinging, and the panted words she spoke were filled with yearning, yet she was rigid in his arms.

"You want something I can't give you. You want a home and a family. You want a wife who will be there with you when you're both old and gray, watching your grandchildren grow up. You want a future. And, dear Lord in heaven, it makes me die to have to say it, but I haven't got one to give you."

His mouth wended its way across her cheek and onto hers. "You do if you want one. If you let yourself believe it."

"I thought about it all day yesterday when we were out together," she confessed, her lips quivering under his kisses. "And this evening, watching you with the children, laughing with you at the dinner table. But—" she turned her head aside "—it's only pretend."

"No, baby, it's not. It's as real as this." His hand brought her back to him, and he kissed her fully, hungrily, drawing her taste and her scent into him and giving her his until they were both gasping. Raggedly, he told her, "This is no fantasy, Maggie. It's as real as our making love was. Do you remember that? Do you remember how real it was?"

For an answer, she melted into him with a wrenching moan, her small, supple body turning liquid in his arms.

His hands moved over her back, her hips, his strong fingers sinking into her bottom as he pulled her tight against his loins. "You feel that, Maggie? That's what remembering does to me. Being inside you was like finding the other half of my soul. I want to be there again. I want to feel us loving each other until we go off like skyrockets. Until we can't breathe or move or even speak, and we don't care, because just being there, holding each other, is enough. Lord, Maggie, don't you want that, too?"

She gasped, her body arching when his arms went around her and he lifted her against him, lifted her high, until his face was buried between her breasts. His mouth went searching and found her nipple, wetting the thin pieces of fabric and lace as he drew on her.

"Peter!" His name was both a sob of pleasure and a cry for help as she clutched his shoulders. "Peter, I'm scared. He'll find a way to ruin it. I know he will!"

With his lips and teeth tugging at the elastic neckline of her dress, he kissed his way to the other breast, saying, "He might try. But he's not that powerful. No man is. Take a chance, Maggie. Take a chance that you and I together are stronger than he is. That there's a future out there for us, a wonderful future. Tomorrow after tomorrow full of love and hope and plans we make together."

He let her slide slowly down the hard frame of his body, kissing his way over her flower-scented skin as he urged,

"Imagine it, Maggie. A life with a family that loves you. A family that loves Jimmy and will give him something he's never had. Something Jane can't give him, something even you can't give him by yourself. Oh, Maggie—" His voice broke as he nuzzled into the curls that fell around her ear. "Imagine our children. Imagine the beautiful, strong babies you and I could make. Can you see them, Maggie? Do you want them?"

"Oh, Peter," she moaned, her body curling into him. "They'd be perfect, wouldn't they? And we'd love them so much. Peter, it's true! Dear heaven, it's true! I want your babies, and I want my Jimmy back again, and I want you to help me raise him. I want it all!"

His face was level with hers when their eyes met.

"It's yours," he breathed. "I'm yours. Please, Maggie. Be mine."

Her breath caught. His heart pounded against her breast. For the space of a few infinitely fragile seconds, the world stood absolutely still. Then, slowly with a quivering delicacy that tore a hoarse sound from somewhere deep inside him, her fingertips trembled across his face, across the silky hair falling on his forehead, across the warm, smooth skin of his cheek, the beard-roughened line of his jaw, feeling the strength, learning the wisdom, wondering at the adoration she found there.

Yes. Her lips formed the word silently. Then, suddenly, her eyes widened as though the heavens had opened up and cast a beam of precious golden light before her, where there had been no light at all.

In the next instant, the word burst from her.

"Yes!" And she threw her arms around his neck and gave to him what she had never given to any man. Her heart. Her soul. Her every hope and dream. "Yes! Oh, yes, I'm yours! I want your babies and a home with you and to grow old and gray and happy with you. I love you. Oh, Peter, I love you, I love you. I love you so much."

She imparted her gifts in a shower of kisses. Kisses strewn everywhere across his face, kisses that tasted salty tears clinging to his eyelashes. Kisses that became one kiss. One eager joining of lips and racing hearts. A luscious mating of wet hungry mouths, filled with tiny gasps and sounds of pleasure. A feverish kiss that soon turned steamy, grew slower, deeper, until it became a hot throbbing longing, pulsing through their heated bodies.

"I love you, I love you," she was still whispering when his mouth parted from hers.

"Lord Almighty." He took a couple of shallow breaths. "Maggie, I think I'd have died if you hadn't said it."

"I'll never stop saying it. Being scared has stopped me for the last time. And if you think I'm going to forget, just remind me that the most marvelous thing that ever happened to me happened because I wanted it enough not to care how scared I was."

"What was that?"

"Making love with you."

He kissed her again until her bones turned to jelly and she had to pull away to gasp for air. "Peter, I have to tell you, as much as I like your kitchen table, I think I'd like your bed better."

"Are you saying it's time to go upstairs?"

"If you keep doing what you're doing, we've got about ten seconds before it's too late."

He chuckled, a rich happy sound. "Let's save the kitchen table for some other time," he said, carrying her, just as she was, slanted full-length against him, up the stairs.

Margaret Ann wilted, her head falling on his shoulder. "I've never felt so...so..."

"Seduced?" he supplied, turning his head to give her neck a gentle bite. "So now we're even."

"I didn't—"

"You did. I loved it. You were shameless."

"No, *you're* shameless. But I'm going to learn to be."

"Oh, you are, are you?" His eyes were a sultry gold as he lowered her to stand beside his bed and, without a pause, whisked off her dress. Then, with his fingertips trailing over her, he murmured, "Lord, Maggie, you wear the prettiest things. Pretty lace...oh, and such pretty breasts."

"See? That's exactly what I mean," she told him, her fingers trembling as they worked their way down the buttons of his shirt. "Starting right now, I'm going to learn to say wonderful, shameless things like the ones you say to me that make me go all mushy."

"Are they going to make me go mushy, too?"

"If they do, I'm going to be very disappointed."

His laughter was husky and carnal, and his mouth was hot against her belly as he peeled off the last scrap of lace covering her. "Baby, I swear, there isn't a chance either of us is going to be disappointed."

With her cheeks turning rosy under his bold regard, Margaret Ann pushed the shirt off his shoulders. Then she sighed as her hands and gaze began wandering over him. "You can't imagine how many times I sat beside you in the truck, watching you drive with your shirt off, looking at the way these muscles, right here, move under your skin, and wondering what you looked like with all your clothes off."

He kicked his slacks and briefs aside. "Oh, really?"

"Mmm." Her hand crept slowly down the flat, muscled plane of his belly. "I'd think about that first night I climbed into the truck and you only had your shorts on.

They were dark blue—and tight. And I had the hardest time not looking at this.... No, definitely not mushy."

"Margaret Ann." His breath sucked in, then rushed out in a whisper. "I love you."

"Oh, Peter, I love you, too. And that's why I want to do all these wonderful things to you." She fell with him onto the bed, rolling instantly to brace herself over him. "I've wanted to touch you for so long," she breathed. "Those nights you held me, all the times I wanted just to put my hand here, on your chest, and feel your heart beating. Or put it here, on your thigh, when you'd have your leg up against mine." Burrowing her lips through the silky hair on his chest to taste the warm, man-scented skin, she murmured, "You don't know how many times I've wanted to kiss you here ... and here..."

"Maggie..."

"—and here."

"Ah, God, Maggie ... Oh, baby..."

"And this. I've wanted to do this." In a single graceful motion, she knelt over him. "I've never...done...this before. Oh, my. Oh, Lord, Peter..."

With his hands gripping her hips, he arched into her, gasping. "Maggie...Maggie, look at me." And when her eyes were bound with his by an intimacy so acute it was nearly unbearable, he spoke in a ragged whisper. "This is forever. You know that."

"I know," she whispered back. "You meant it forever the last time, didn't you?"

"Yes."

"I knew no man could make love the way you did and not mean it forever. I'm sorry I hurt you. I'm sorry for every moment of doubt I've caused you. But I *do* love you, Peter, and I've never meant anything more in my entire life than this, what we're doing right now. I love you, I love you, I love you...."

And as their bodies moved together, she continued to say it, the words ringing clear and true from her heart. They were breaking away from all the lies and the ugliness and the horror. They were a declaration of war. An act of triumph. A cry of hope. And they both knew it.

She made the act of love itself her solemn vow, telling him with her hands and her lips, each breathless sound she made, each impassioned movement of her body that took him deeper into her, that she was his and his alone. It was he who cried out first, and she who clasped him to her breast as his pleasure took her with him into that place where the only thing either of them knew was sensation entwined in love.

And when it was over, they slept. The sound dreamless sleep of lovers who know their love will never be betrayed.

It was an hour before dawn when Peter awoke, his sleep disturbed by the uncanny awareness that Margaret Ann was awake. She was utterly still, lying curled at his side with her head on his shoulder, but the arm she had flung across him had a certain tension in it. Half-asleep, he reached up to stroke the tension away.

"I saw Larry Silver and another man commit a murder."

For an instant he thought he was dreaming. But then the words hit home, jolting him instantly into full awareness. She was trembling, and his arms tightened around her as he urged, "Go on, Maggie. I'm listening."

Her face turned into his shoulder, and her arm had a death grip around his ribs. He thought for a moment that she wasn't going to be able to continue, but then she began in a quavering, nearly incoherent whisper. He had to strain to hear the words.

"I came home early. My evening class was canceled. I went up to Jimmy's room, but he wasn't there. I went downstairs to look for him, and I heard men's voices in Larry's study. The door was half-open. I knocked once—at the same time the gun went off. Larry didn't do it. It was the other man, his friend. I expected Larry to yell. Call the police. Something. But he made some remark I don't remember—he laughed, I think—and I realized he wasn't going to do anything. That he wasn't surprised or upset. I started to back away, but Larry saw me in the doorway before I turned and ran."

She was shaking so hard, Peter could feel it all the way to his bones, and her body was slowly curling up into a tight, freezing knot. Rolling to his side, he pulled her up beside him until their foreheads touched on the pillow. Then, taking the fists she had clenched against her chest, he drew her arms around his back, saying, "Hold on, baby," as he wrapped his own arms around her slender form. Pressing the solid, warm length of his body against hers, he spoke in a tone imbued with tenderness and love. "It was the night he raped you, wasn't it?"

Her fingers dug into his back as she nodded. "I should have left the house, gone for help, but I was in shock, I guess. Frantic. Not thinking very well. I was throwing things into a suitcase when he came into my room. I told him I was leaving. He took my suitcase and dumped it on the floor. Then he . . . attacked me." She shuddered. "Peter, he . . . he did horrible things . . . and he wouldn't stop. And he kept saying the only reason I was alive was because he was allowing it. He could kill me if he wanted to, that maybe he would. I was sure he would. But he didn't, and he was very careful not to bruise my face or . . . or leave marks that would look suspicious to anyone else. When it was over, he said if I told anyone what had happened that night—any of it—I'd never see Jimmy again. He'd sent him to one of his friend's houses to spend the night. Maybe the murder was planned, and he wanted Jimmy out of the way."

"How did you get to the hospital?"

"He took me. But first he gave me a shot of something. I was too much of a mess to have any idea what he was doing, but when I tried to use the hospital records in the divorce trial, I found out he'd given me heroin."

"He framed you."

"Yes. He'd told them at the hospital that I'd come staggering into the house, falling over everything, until I finally fell down the stairs. Then, in court, he 'admitted' that he knew I'd been with my lover—someone he gave a detailed description of but who was conveniently never found. Peter, I never had a lover! Even if Larry hadn't known where I was every minute of the day and I could have hidden something like that, I wouldn't have. And I'll never, ever forget sitting in that courtroom, listening to him twist and mangle the truth until everybody was looking at me like I was some kind of...of..."

"Margaret Ann, I love you. And we're going to get through this. I swear it."

She started crying then but pulled herself together quickly to give him a little nod. "I-I'm okay."

He kissed the tears off her cheek. "What you are is phenomenal. Now, tell me, you waited to leave him because you were afraid? Afraid he'd find you and hurt you again?"

She laughed bitterly. "I waited because it was a while before I was physically capable of doing anything, then because I didn't have access to any money. My name wasn't on any of Larry's accounts. But mostly I waited because I didn't know where Jimmy was."

"He'd hidden him?"

"He kept him away for a month—sent him off on a vacation with his friend's family—just so I'd know he meant business, he said. I begged him to let me have a divorce. I told him I wouldn't tell anyone anything. I just wanted to get out of his life. But he told me if I ever tried to divorce him, I'd regret it. I didn't doubt that was true, but I had to get out. Jimmy came home happy and suntanned, and by then I'd sold my mother's cake recipe, so I had some money, and I'd gotten a part-time teaching position for the fall. I waited until I thought Larry was sure of me. Then I left to go to class one morning, but instead I went and hired a lawyer. Once a lawyer was in the picture, Larry knew he had to lay low for a while. I picked Jimmy up from school, and we went to live in the apartment I'd rented the week before."

"But he got Jimmy back."

"Yes. In court, no less. And as long as Jimmy was with him, he knew I'd never do or say anything against him."

"But now he doesn't have Jimmy, and his only recourse is—"

"To kill me. I've been expecting it. The only thing holding him back, I think, is that he doesn't know where Jimmy is."

She was warmer now, relaxed against him, and her voice, rather than being choked with terror, was almost normal. Moving his head on the pillow to look at her, Peter frowned slightly.

"If you were dead, why would Silver care where Jimmy is?"

"Because I think he's afraid Jimmy saw him with drugs."

"The time he canceled your visit?"

"Yes." She nodded. "I can't be sure. Jimmy wasn't very clear about what happened. On the way to Jane's, he told me he'd knocked on his father's door, but Larry didn't answer. So he walked in. Larry was sitting behind his desk, folding little pieces of paper and using them to push this 'white stuff' around.''

''Cocaine.''

''That's what I assumed.''

Margaret Ann levered up on a elbow to look down at him as she spoke quickly. ''Peter, I've known for years that Larry was involved in things that weren't legal. That's why he married me. I overheard a conversation he had with a man about a kickback payment. He knew I hadn't really understood what I'd heard, and I don't think it worried him at first. But when I told him I was pregnant and refused to have an abortion, he must have started worrying. He was getting ready to run for city council, and it wouldn't do to have me pop up with an illegitimate child *and* a story about his shady activities. So he gave me all that love-and-devotion garbage I told you before, and he told me how good I was for him. How I was so honest, and I'd be a model for him.''

She sighed, rolling her eyes at her own gullibility. ''I bought the whole line. I even felt flattered, like maybe I was doing a good thing, helping this committed public servant stay on the straight and narrow.''

Peter reached up to tuck a curl behind her ear. ''Yeah, well, we all have our moments. Remind me to tell you about how I got kicked out of college for filling the president's office, floor to ceiling with black balloons in a war-on-poverty protest.''

The look she gave him was priceless. ''And they actually took you back?''

His grin turned into a chuckle. ''I cleaned up the mess. Which translates to, I grew up and discovered ways to prove a point that didn't make the wrong people furious. But it sounds like growing up for you must have been one hell of a disillusionment.''

She grimaced. "In slow degrees. For a long time, until Jimmy was a couple of years old, things were okay. I wasn't happy, but I wasn't miserable. Larry spent a lot of time making me over into his image of the wife he needed to further his political career. He was all for my going to school, although he wanted me to take business courses. He made all the decisions. Hired the decorator for the house, picked out my clothes, signed me up for every charity function that came down the pike, chose my friends. Everything. I didn't realize that he was deliberately isolating me from everyone and everything I'd known. In public, he was the perfect husband and father. At home, he ignored Jimmy and insulted me constantly."

She looked away, hesitating, before adding, "I thought it must be my fault he was so dissatisfied with me, with our marriage. I was only nineteen when he said he was bored with me. He had other women, he said, who were far more interesting. He moved me into another bedroom, and we never slept together after that."

"Thank God for small favors," Peter grumbled. "I take it you got my message."

"What message?"

"The one that says any man who wouldn't want you in his bed is out of his mind."

She smiled a little. "Ditto that from me to you."

He smiled back. And the look they exchanged said all that ever would need to be said to heal the scars past lovers had left on them.

Peter sighed. "So there you were, playing the princess in public and Cinderella at home. When did the blackmail start?"

"The day I listened to the messages on our recorder and heard a man talking to Larry about warehouse space to store drugs."

Peter's eyebrows shot upward. "Oh, really? How interesting. Go on."

It had become a story, now, something she could talk about as though it had happened to someone else. Margaret Ann sat up and scooted around to face him, crossing her legs and tucking the sheet across her lap. Peter smiled to himself at her small concession to modesty and elbowed his way up to lean on the pillows piled against the headboard. Listening to the bizarre horrifying events she was relating made him feel as if he were on another planet or in the twilight zone. But he let his eyes roam over the very real, womanly curves before him, and it helped keep things in perspective.

"Larry still runs a small brokerage," she said.

"Yes, I know."

"Well, he's been using it as a front for organized-crime activities."

Peter wasn't surprised, but his voice was disbelieving as he asked, "And did he usually use your home phone recorder as a message service for this, uh, business?"

"No. No, of course not." Margaret Ann shook her head. "The machine hadn't turned off when he picked up the phone, and he didn't realize it. The whole conversation was there."

"I see. And how did he know you'd heard it?"

She sighed. "You're going to think I'm very stupid."

"You're not stupid. You were very young, and you're not exactly ancient yet. You're also a lousy liar, Margaret Ann. I take it you told him yourself you'd heard the message."

"Yes. I made this righteous speech about how he'd promised me he'd be honest. And how he either had to stop what he was doing and get help for his problem, or I was going to turn him over to the authorities. Needless to say, he laughed at me. I didn't have proof, he said. The tape wouldn't be admissable evidence against him. I didn't care. I was going to tell them anyway. And I was leaving him, too. He laughed again. I could never leave him, and I couldn't tell anyone what he was doing, unless I wanted to go to jail. He said I'd be charged with obstruction of justice, because I'd known for years about the kickbacks he'd taken and hadn't said a word about them."

Peter snorted. "Protecting, encouraging and abetting, it's called. And he might have been right. Except that I don't think there's a court in the country that would have upheld the charge, given your age and the circumstances at the time it happened."

"Well, I didn't know that. I was terrified."

"He was counting on it."

"After that, he barely tried to hide all the things he was doing. The man he'd been talking to on the tape started coming to the house regularly. He was awful! So polite and deferential. Always said nice things about Jimmy and talked about his wife and children. Oh, but Peter, he was so cold! He terrified me." She hugged herself, shivering, as she finished, "It didn't really surprise me to see him holding a gun and that man lying there, on my carpet, quite obviously dead."

"What was his name? The man with the gun."

She shook her head. "I don't know his whole name. All I ever heard Larry call him was Vinny."

"Vinny!" Peter shot forward to grab her shoulders. "Are you sure?"

She looked at him, startled. "Positive."

It took Peter less than half a minute to race down the stairs, find the newpaper he'd left lying on his desk yesterday morning and run back up to the bedroom. Margaret Ann was sitting on the side of the bed, and she gave him a baffled look when he landed beside her, shoving the newspaper into her hands.

He took a second to reach for the lamp, then demanded, "Is this the man?" And his fingers stabbed at the picture on the front page of the local section.

Margaret Ann blinked, squinting against the sudden light. Peter waited impatiently while she focused on the page.

"Yes," she said. "But who—"

"You know that beyond a shadow of a doubt? You'd be willing to swear you saw *this* man, in your home, shoot another man dead?"

"Yes. But, Peter, who is—"

With a shout that was pure victory, Peter flung the paper aside, surged off the bed and scooped Margaret Ann into an enormous hug. "Baby, you just won the lottery! My brother is going to love you forever." And he kissed her soundly before dumping her back onto the rumpled sheets to begin snatching his clothes off the floor. "Go pack your suitcase, Maggie. We've got to get rolling if we're going to get to Nick's, then out to the Kenworth before daylight. It'll take some fast shuffling to get away from Silver's thugs without him knowing you've left town. I hope you've still got that god-awful hat."

Margaret Ann didn't move. "Where am I going?"

"To Jane's." He buttoned his shirt, aiming a look at her that was in dead earnest. "Things are about to get very nasty, and until it all goes down, I want you out of the way in case something leaks and the wrong person gets wind of what's happening."

"You mean Larry," she concluded.

"Him and a few other characters who are making billions of dollars trafficking drugs through Baltimore." Peter slammed the closet door closed, coming to stand beside her as he pulled on a pair of jeans.

Gesturing with a nod toward the paper that had fallen to the floor, he explained, "Len Vincent—Vinny, as most

people know him—is a big man in one of the largest organized-crime families on the East Coast, and he deals
mostly in drugs. Nick works with the strike force in the
attorney general's office that investigates local organized-
crime activities. About a month ago, they arrested Vinny.
He's out on bail, and Nick's afraid they won't be able to
make the charges stick because of some technical foul-ups.
But this could turn it around entirely. An eyewitness to a
murder is pretty damaging. Damaging enough that it
might make Vinny dance."

"Dance?"

"Talk. Turn State's evidence. Vinny's lawyers can cut a
deal with Nick. It's not the best of all possible worlds, but
Vinny could get immunity on the murder charge if he
agreed to testify against his boss. *And* against Larry Silver."

She looked up at him with open-mouthed astonishment
as he sat down beside her. "Peter, do you mean this man,
this . . . this *criminal*, could put Larry in jail?"

"That's the general idea."

Peter couldn't help the thrill it gave him to see her eyes
widen even further as she realized the possibilities. Power
was, indeed, a truly awesome thing.

Her voice was filled with breathless wonder as she asked,
"Do you think it will work?"

"Yes, I think it will work," he replied, but his look sobered abruptly as he took her hand, his eyes searching
hers.

"I think it will work," he repeated. "But, Margaret
Ann, we both know that things that ought to work sometimes don't. And if anything should go wrong—" He
broke off, then went on with a grim certainty. "You're
going to Jane's. And you'll stay there until I come for you.
Don't make phone calls. Don't go anywhere. Your where-

abouts—and Jimmy's—is between you and me. No one else. And it will stay that way. Do you understand?''

She nodded, her eyes fastened on his. And with that simple gesture, Peter felt the burden shift from her shoulders to his. There would be no argument, no hedging. She would let him take her to Jane's. And in doing so she was placing not only her own life but also her son's life in his hands.

''I don't know how long it'll be before this gets cleared up,'' he continued, ''but I'm not going to take the chance of calling you. The people we're dealing with have ways of knowing things that would make you wonder if it's safe to brush your teeth. So you'll just have to sit tight and wait for me to come get you.''

''Peter, Larry did threaten to kill you,'' she whispered, ''You'll be—''

''I'll be careful. And I think the likelihood of anybody getting killed is very slim. Really. Trust me.''

''I do.''

He kissed her once, very thoroughly. Then, with a wink, he smiled. ''Come on, Maggie mine. Let's go get Nick out of bed and make his day.''

Chapter Fifteen

Mommy, when's that man, Peter, coming back?''

"I don't know, Jimmy. He has some important business to take care of first. It might be quite a while."

Margaret Ann smiled at her son as he hung over the top rail of the pasture fence, his eyes fixed on the bay mare inside the enclosure, who was placidly swishing flies with her tail. He had asked the same question with increasing frequency during the past ten days, and each time her answer had been the same. Obviously, he was no more satisfied with it than she was.

Folding her arms along the rail, Margaret Ann leaned her chin on her hands. "You like him, huh?"

"Yeah. Is that truck he brought you in really his?"

"It sure is. It's got a refrigerator and a bed and lots of gauges and dials, like in an airplane, and all sorts of other neat stuff."

"He said he'd take me for a ride in it." Jimmy's blond curls glinted red gold in the sun as he turned to give her a skeptical look with eyes as blue as her own. "Do you think he meant it?"

"Absolutely."

When Jimmy swung a leg up to straddle the fence, Margaret Ann bit her tongue against telling him to get down. The cast he wore—which was, by now, rather scruffy looking—served as too vivid a reminder of how fragile life was. It was hard not to be overprotective, although the truth was he was more than capable of sitting on a fence or, as he had demonstrated earlier, of climbing Jane's big apple tree.

Margaret Ann turned to lean her back against the fence, her eyes automatically checking the long gravel road that led from the main road to the yard before coming to rest on the rambling frame house that sat in the grove of trees to their right; the house was a couple of hundred yards away—well within running distance. Jane and Mark were at the store, and there was no movement anywhere. Not even a breeze stirred. It was only midmorning, but Margaret Ann's cotton halter top clung damply to her skin, and the short cutoffs she was wearing felt like too much.

"You like him, too, don't you?"

They were still talking about Peter, it seemed. Her eyes lost their focus on the house as she answered. "I like him a lot."

"He kissed you when he said goodbye."

"Mmm. I kissed him back, too."

"Does that mean you're going to marry him?"

"I want to. Would you mind?"

He thought about it for what seemed to her a very long time. "He says he's got these kids who are his nieces and nephews."

"That's right." Margaret Ann scaled the fence to sit next to her son. He was busy tracing splinters in the top rail and didn't look up to notice how closely she was watching his reactions. "Peter's brother, Nick, and his sister, Maria, are both married, and their children are Peter's nieces and nephews. There are seven of them—I've met them. In fact, I built space stations with Tony and Mike when I went to dinner at Peter's parents' house."

Jimmy picked at an especially long splinter, pulling it off the rail. "He's got a mother and father?"

"Uh-huh. They're very nice."

"If you married him, would they be my grandparents?"

"They'd be your stepgrandparents, but that's just as good." *Please,* she prayed, *don't let me be building his hopes about something that isn't going to happen.*

It had been the longest ten days of her life. The furtive early-morning trip to Nick's house, waiting while the two brothers got someone from the state's attorney's office to meet them on a Sunday morning to take her statement, sneaking out a back door with Peter and riding away in Nick's car, while Nick drove off in Peter's—it all could have happened a year ago. Peter had spirited her to Jane's in the Kenworth, which no one outside his family and Jane knew he owned, and after that— Well, the joy of seeing Jimmy had been tremendous, but the worry had set in too quickly. And it was getting worse by the hour.

Where was Peter? Her faith in him was unswerving, but it would have been naiveté of the worst sort to believe nothing could go wrong. They were dealing with criminals, real criminals, not street-corner thugs. The possible scenarios for tragedy that ran through her mind would have done credit to the bloodiest 1930s' gangster movie ever made. Peter and Nick and the state's attorney had been, oh, so reassuring that no one would get hurt. But

Nick and the other man had been quick to agree with Peter that she should be out of the picture or, at least, under some kind of protection. It didn't help to know that, if something dreadful happened—which, to her could only mean harm befalling Peter—no one knew where she was to tell her. Her only source of information was the news. And so Jane kept her company in front of the television each night, after the boys were asleep, for the eleven o'clock newscast.

She had finally told Jane everything, from beginning to end. All the things that had been too painful and terrifying to speak of before. Her friend had been horrified for her, completely supportive, and even more determined to keep their pact. Being pragmatic, Jane continually reminded her that Peter was not, by any means, attempting to do anything single-handedly. He had a great deal of help. He had Nicholas. And he had the drug enforcement unit of the state's attorney's office and the Baltimore police department. It was all being very carefully planned. Nobody was going to get hurt.

But *she* had been hurt. And Larry *did* own a gun. And she had seen Vinny shoot a man to death.

The waiting was dreadful. Margaret Ann's thoughts were wandering over all the things Larry and his criminal friends might be doing at that very moment, when Jimmy spoke again. And his innocent hesitant question sent a shiver of dread racing up her spine.

"Am I going back to live with Daddy?"

"No."

The word came out too harshly, and Margaret Ann cleared her throat, as though to say her tone was not intentional. It was the first time he had mentioned his father, and she was genuinely relieved he had finally broached the subject. She was determined to keep her own feelings to herself.

"No, you're not," she said in a voice approaching normal.

A minute later, Jimmy asked, "Will I see him again?"

"Sweetheart, I'm not sure. Maybe not. Your father is... He's got some bad troubles, and I don't know how they're going to work out." She studied him a moment, then asked quietly. "Would it upset you very much if you didn't see him again?"

His skinny shoulders lifted in a loose-jointed shrug. "I don't know. Would it be all right if— I mean, is it wrong if I don't miss him?"

"Oh, Jimmy." Her arm went around his shoulders. "If that's the way you feel, it's not wrong."

His voice was muffled against her arm. "I missed you."

"I know. And I've missed you, too."

"Mark misses his father. But he died."

"Yes. It's very sad when somebody you love dies."

"I'm glad I'm not going back to Daddy. Mom—" He pushed away to look at her. "If...if you get married to Peter..."

"Yes?"

"Would he be my father?"

Margaret Ann took a deep breath and let it out slowly. "Well, a lot of people grow up with someone who isn't really their mother or father but who feels more like one than the real one did. Peter would be your stepfather, the man you'd grow up living with. He'd do things with you— take you to ball games and things like that. And he'd help me take care of you. And you'd have to listen to him, like you do me."

Jimmy lowered his gaze back to the fence. "Would I have to love him like I love you?"

"You never *have* to love somebody, Jimmy. Love doesn't work that way."

"You mean he wouldn't have to love me, either?"

"Oh, sweetheart, he wouldn't have to, but I know he'd want to." There was a lump in her throat, but Margaret Ann made herself smile as she ruffled his curls, saying, "Don't you worry about it. When the time comes, the two of you will work it out."

"When's it going to be time?"

"I don't know." *Maybe never?*

"Maybe right now?"

"Well, no—"

Before she could finish her sentence, Jimmy was off the fence and racing away. She started to call after him, but when she looked down the road and saw the cause of his excitement, she let out a cry, jumped off the fence and ran after him.

The Kenworth rumbled to a halt in the shade of the big side yard. The engine died, the air brakes hissed, and the cab door bounced open all at once. Peter was hardly out of the cab before Margaret Ann was in his arms and he was holding her, kissing her, wiping the tears from her face, telling her over and over how much he loved her.

"Oh, Peter... oh, you're here!"

"Yes, baby. I'm right here."

"And you're not hurt or... Oh, I was so afraid. So afraid something would happen to you. I had nightmares all week. I'd try to scream for help but couldn't, and I'd—"

"It's all right, Maggie. Now, hang in there a second. Let me—" He broke off but continued to hold her as he spoke over the top of her head. "Hi, Jimmy. How's it going?"

"Why's she crying?"

The wariness in her son's voice made Margaret Ann cry harder, and she gratefully let Peter handle it.

"She's happy," he said.

"Oh. Yeah. She's been hugging me and stuff, too," came the commiserating reply. "Are you going to take me for a ride?"

Beneath her ear Peter's chest shook with suppressed laughter. "That's what I'm here for. You want to climb in and take a look around?"

"Really?"

"Really." And he somehow managed to put a hand under Jimmy's backside and give him a push up into the cab without entirely relinquishing his hold on her.

Margaret Ann swiped at her cheeks and called, "Jimmy, be careful! Don't touch—"

"It's all right, Maggie." Peter drew her away from the cab. "The keys are in my pocket, and the brakes are set. There's nothing in there he can hurt himself with."

She groaned. "I just can't seem to stop worrying about him."

"Gets to be a bad habit, worry does."

"But the truck—" Stopping halfway back alongside the trailer, Margaret Ann swung around to face him and grabbed his arms. "Why did you come in the truck? Why are you dressed like this?" Her eyes made a quick scan of his faded jeans and sleeveless T-shirt before coming back to lock with his. "Are we running away again?"

"Shame on you, Margaret Ann. A lawyer doesn't run from the law. Only pretty, freckle-faced Latin teachers do things like that."

"Peter, I'm afraid to ask."

The teasing sparkle in his eyes mellowed, leaving only tenderness as he said quietly, "It's over, Maggie. Larry Silver is never going to hurt you again."

"What—what happened?" she whispered.

"What happened was that you blew the top off of one enormous can of worms. It'll take months to sort it all out, but Vinny's lawyers and Nick worked out a deal, and a lot of people's heads are probably going to roll before it's over. The main thing is, though, that Vinny gave them enough evidence to get Silver on a first-degree murder charge and both federal and state charges of conspiring to use and distribute drugs.''

Her eyes widened.

"The court issued an arrest warrant," he continued, "but, unfortunately, Silver found out—don't know how yet. He hopped a plane to Buenos Aires."

"South America?"

Peter nodded. "It looks that way. Anyway, he's gone. And if he ever tries to set foot in this country again, the Feds will pick him up so fast it'll make him think he's hit a time warp. If Vinny's family doesn't get to him first."

Margaret Ann frowned. "'Vinny's family'? Why?"

"Because they know they can't trust him. And because of what he did to you." Peter's hands squeezed her shoulders. "Don't misunderstand me, Margaret Ann. Len Vincent is a murderous bastard who has no conscience whatsoever. But he knows something that Larry Silver will never know—the importance of loyalty. In Vinny's rather bizarre moral code, family and marriage are sacred. And a man isn't a man who has to win his wife's loyalty by raping and beating her within an inch of her life."

Peter's look softened, became mildly amused as he added, "Vinny sends his regrets that you had to put up with a slime-ball like Silver and wishes you every happiness for the future. Which means, if Vinny gets a chance at him, Silver is dead, and he knows it. You're safe, Maggie. Really and truly safe."

"Oh, Peter. I can't—" A short bewildered laugh bubbled out of her. "I can't believe it! I mean, it has to be true, because you wouldn't say it if it weren't, but—" She shook her head.

He gave her a crooked grin. "Kind of blows you away, huh?"

"Well, yes, I guess it does. It might take a while to sink in."

"I'll give you a couple of minutes."

Her gaze snapped to his. "What about the charges against me?"

"Dropped. Without Silver there to testify, and with the charges against him being what they are, no one was interested in prosecuting you. You're a free woman, Margaret Ann. Free to go anywhere you want, do anything you want."

"Free to get married?"

The question fell from her lips in a hopeful rush, and, as though he had caught it, Peter drew a quick breath.

"If that's what you really want to do," he answered, his eyes searching hers.

He couldn't be serious, Margaret Ann thought, but she listened in amazement as he explained.

"I know what it's like to have your life taken out of your own hands, and how disorienting it is when, all of a sudden, it's given back to you. You've been living under Silver's threats for a long time. I'd understand if you wanted a chance to...well, to experience your freedom for a while."

He was so determined, she thought, so committed to doing the right thing, but the low shaky quality of his voice was heartbreaking.

"Is that what you've been doing this past year?" she made herself ask. "Experiencing your freedom?"

Peter gave her a sad smile. "I've been lonely as hell. And you know it."

"So have I. For seven years. Except for Jimmy, I haven't had anybody. And as much as I love him, he's a child. What I need is a partner and a friend. And a lover."

Her eyes turned hazy blue as her hand lifted to rest against his cheek. "I love you," she said. "And being able to look into your eyes and say it *is* freedom to me. I don't want to wait, Peter. I need your love—now."

He caught her hand and buried his lips in the palm of it. "You know it's yours, Maggie. And the only chains you'll ever feel from it are these—" his arms encircled her "—when I hold you."

"Chains?" She wrinkled her nose, poking a finger into his rock-hard biceps. "These things? These aren't chains. They're wings. Phoenix wings."

"Phoenix wings! Margaret Ann, sometimes you say the silliest—"

"Beautiful, strong phoenix wings." She planted a line of kisses down the inside of his upper arm. "I think I might be growing some myself."

"Hmm." His hands began roaming her back and hips. "I'll have to check this out."

Shivering at the feel of his hard body pressing against her, she sighed. "Unfortunately, that will have to wait until later. Peter, it's been awful waiting for you—in more ways than one."

"Tell me about it," he growled near her ear. "I waited three days to change the sheets on my bed because they smelled like you."

Her moan was lost as she buried her face against him. "Are you trying to torture me?"

"No, I'm getting you ready for our honeymoon."

"Honeymoon.... Oh, that does sound lovely."

"You remember that cabin I told you about in Oregon?"

"Your friend Paul's."

"I called him. He says we can have it for as long as we want. It's on the Rogue River—rustic, but not primitive—and it's got two bedrooms."

He smelled warm, and she could feel his heart beating where her lips were pressed against the base of his throat. "I like it already," she murmured.

"You'll love it, Maggie. It's a beautiful place. We've got three weeks before school starts, and I thought it would be a good chance for Jimmy and me to get to know each other. And for you and me to have some peace together."

" 'Peace.' What a blessed word."

"Isn't it, though. Anyway, I'm selling the rig to Paul. So we'll ride out in it, then fly back."

Margaret Ann leaned back in Peter's arms to give him a quick grin. "All of which will delight a certain six-year-old no end."

"That thought did cross my mind."

He returned her grin with a slow smile, and she sighed happily. By the time they got to Oregon, her son would be as much in love with Peter as she was. And she didn't doubt for a minute that the feeling would be mutual on the part of the man who would be, in spirit if not in fact, her son's father.

The humor left her face as she whispered, "He's ready, Peter. He needs you."

Peter nodded. "I won't let him down, Maggie. Or you. We'll get him through this."

"I know we will," she replied. Then, as she lifted a finger to brush away the lock of hair on his forehead, her expression became wistful. "And someday, when he's older," she mused, "I'm going to tell him—and all our other children—a story about how one dark night, long, long ago, this marvelous bird, with beautiful black-and-silver wings and eyes the color of sunshine, rose up from the ashes to save this frightened—"

"To save his love." Peter's fingertips touched her lips. "Because he knew the love they could make together would be strong enough to survive anything they'd ever have to face. And it will be, Maggie. I swear it."

His certainty rang true in her heart, and she wrapped her arms around the man whose love had given her the power to soar.

* * * * *

Silhouette Special Edition

COMING NEXT MONTH

Silhouette Special Edition

presents

★ LOVE AND GLORY ★

from
Lindsay McKenna

Introducing a gripping new series celebrating our men—and women—in uniform. Meet the Trayherns, a military family as proud and colorful as the American flag, a family fighting the shadow of dishonor, a family determined to triumph—with
LOVE AND GLORY!

June: **A QUESTION OF HONOR** (SE #529) leads the fast-paced excitement. When Coast Guard officer Noah Trayhern offers Kit Anderson a safe house, he unwittingly endangers his own guarded emotions.

July: **NO SURRENDER** (SE #535) Navy pilot Alyssa Trayhern's assignment with arrogant jet jockey Clay Cantrell threatens her career—and her heart—with a crash landing!

August: **RETURN OF A HERO** (SE #541) Strike up the band to welcome home a man whose top-secret reappearance will make headline news . . . with a delicate, daring woman by his side.

Three courageous siblings—
three consecutive months of

★ LOVE AND GLORY ★

Premiering in **June**, only in
Silhouette Special Edition.